Sexy Surprises Volume 5: 24 Scandalous Sex Stories

Giselle Renarde

Published by Giselle Renarde, 2023.

Table of Contents

Sexy Surprises
Volume 5

24 Scandalous Sex Stories
Giselle Renarde

As Seen Through Windows

Every morning when I wake up, I open the curtains over my bed... and then I let out a big sigh and fall back into my pillows. That's my morning routine. Doesn't matter what the weather's like. Could be raining, sunny, sleeting, snowing. I sigh every morning because I don't want to get up.

There are a lot of days when I call in sick even though I'm not physically ill. I don't do anything fun on those days off. I just stay in bed, under a few cosy layers of blankets.

Sometimes I sit up and watch the day go by. I live in a condo complex, and when I look out my bedroom window, I see a lot of other bedroom windows. Living room windows, too, but the bedrooms are more interesting.

There's a courtyard between my building and the next, so if I look straight down I see the tops of a few young trees. I wonder if I'll live here long enough to see them grow all the way up to my floor and obscure my view of the building across the way.

On the one hand, it would be nice to look outside and see leaves, hear birds, all that. On the other hand, I'd never see Dirk and Shola ever again.

Dirk and Shola probably aren't their real names. "Dirk" just seems appropriate for the big black man over there because he looks like he's got a good sense of humour, and Dirk is a funny name. I call the woman Shola because her long waves of auburn hair remind me of a woman I used to work with whose name was also Shola. I have no idea what their real names are. Those are just the ones I bestowed upon them one day while I watched them fuck.

And now I've revealed *way* too much about myself.

Yes, I'm the kind of girl who enjoys spying. It's not like I'll go out of my way to do it, but if I happen to glance out the window and the shadows across our buildings fall so there's no glare, and if I happen to spot through those glare-less windows a couple going at it? Well, I'm not going to look away.

But, really, who would?

I don't think Dirk and Shola live together. From what I've observed, the condo is hers and he only comes for the odd visit, always during the day. Shola never closes the blinds (in fact, I don't think she has any blinds) so I often watch her in the evenings.

At night, when our condo units are all illuminated from within, it's much easier to see what people are up to. I sit in the dark sometimes, just watching her. It's not that she's doing anything particularly interesting, but it sort of feels like having company.

Like having a friend.

In a sense, I spend my evenings with Shola. I very rarely go out, and neither does she. If I had to guess, I'd say she works from home, something involving her computer. She doesn't get out of bed until mid-morning, or later, but once she's up, she's on that laptop morning, noon, and night.

She gets her bowl of cereal, sits on the couch, and balances her laptop on her knees while she eats. I've even seen her take that thing into the bathroom. She must be a really hard worker. Although, I suspect she spends some time on YouTube, because I often see her laughing the way I do when I'm watching crazy cat clips.

I also think she spends a bit of time on porn sites, because... well, first of all, she never really gets dressed. Shola usually wears something slinky around the house, like a silk negligee, or even something more adventurous like a corset. Maybe it helps her concentrate to be so bound up. She has one corset-type outfit that's a lovely shade of purple, with lace up the front and matching panties. Usually, she'll wear stockings too, since the corset has garters hanging off the bottom. It never takes her long to get "dressed," but she always ends up looking very well put together.

The reason I think she sometimes watches porn is that I'll often see her set down her laptop on the coffee table. She'll stand up and slide off her panties, then sit back down and straddle the computer, just open her legs to it.

The first few times I saw her do that, I wished I had a better view.

That's why I bought myself a good pair of binoculars.

She starts slow, rubbing her naked mound in smooth, sweeping circles. If I'm in the right mood, I'll even join in. Shola is a beautiful woman, and watching her touch herself always sparks a forgotten arousal in me.

I watch her work her clit with her fingertips, round and round. Her pussy is so wet it glistens. Mine isn't quite there, but I work at it, holding the binoculars with one hand, flicking my clit with the other.

I don't get off—I haven't had an orgasm since I was in my twenties—but that's not really the point. I love watching Shola dance her fingers around her pussy, slapping her clit every so often and gasping in response.

She has a drawer full of toys. Sometimes she'll turn on one of her vibrators, press it to her clit, and come pretty much right away. Her face contorts beautifully as she comes. I almost think I can hear her across the courtyard, even though both our windows are closed and she's rather far away.

Other times, she'll place a dildo on the couch and straddle it. She works her clit while she lowers herself down on the thing. She takes her time because the fake cock is massive.

Shola must be incredibly wet to take on a dildo that size in one smooth motion.

I'd love to touch her pussy one day. I bet it would feel soft and welcoming, and so moist her juice would drip all the way down my arm. Something tells me she'd be tight, too, but that wouldn't stop me wanting to shove my whole fist inside of her.

She's beautiful, and so is her cunt.

I sigh as I watch her ride that big dildo. She works her clit while she's bouncing, and I watch her pussy devour the thing. It's purple, just like her corset. She rides it like a cock, like a man.

She rides it the same way she rides Dirk, when he's around.

But I've noticed that Shola always folds her laptop down when Dirk is on his way up. If I'm home watching, like I am today, and I see her answer the phone, I can tell right away if it's him ringing up from down in the lobby. He doesn't have a key of his own, apparently—another sure sign that the two don't live together.

I know it's him because I see the way she looks around. She always glances at her computer first, and she usually closes it before she does

4

anything else. After that, she tidies dishes, mail, whatever's lying around. That's about all she gets around to before he knocks.

Shola stands behind the door while she opens it. I would assume that's because she doesn't want any neighbours who happen to be passing by in the hallway to see her so scantily clad. Every time I see her do that, I feel a little guilty in the pit of my stomach. *I'm* a neighbour and *I'm* watching her live and eat and work and get off—on her own and with Dirk. Would Shola be embarrassed if she knew? She probably would be, and I feel bad about that.

But not bad enough to stop watching.

When Shola closes the door, Dirk looks her up and down. I see his lips moving, and I imagine he's saying, "Mmm-mmm, you look fine!" That's what I would say if I were him.

Shola smiles and pulls him into the bedroom. He kicks off his shoes en route. He's dressed in a security uniform, as always, and it suddenly occurs to me that he might be the guard for Shola's building. That makes perfect sense! It's just after noon. He probably comes up on his lunch hour for a bit of afternoon delight, then goes back to work after.

I wonder if he's married. I don't see a ring on his finger, but you never know. Maybe after work he heads home to his wife and kids. Maybe Shola is just his bit on the side.

That would explain why he never stays the night.

I wonder how they met. I wonder how this thing started between them.

One of life's great mysteries, I suppose.

She pushed him down on the bed and he lets her. She unbuttons his shirt, then unzips his pants. She does all the work, getting him undressed. I've seen Dirk naked many, many times, but I always get antsy at this stage. I want Shola to move faster, show me what's underneath those familiar layers of clothing.

His skin is dark, like polished wood. She licks his chest and I see him groan. I feel it in me.

I wonder if she'll ride him today. Usually, that's what she does. I think Dirk likes it when someone else is in charge. If they were performing solely for my viewing pleasure, I'd rather see him take her from behind, pound that firm cock into her juicy cunt over and over, then pull out and spray thick ropes of cum all up her back. That would be my preference.

But I'm not calling the shots. They are.

Dirk says something, and Shola laughs, nods, rifles through her underwear drawer. She holds up two silk scarves, and he bounces his feet against the mattress. She looks around like she's not sure, and then sheepishly digs something out of her closet.

When she gets near enough to the window, I can see that it's a length of rope.

Dirk grins from ear to ear, nodding, making some joke, I imagine, like, "Oh you just happen to have one of those, huh?"

Shola ties up his wrists first, then secures his feet to the bed frame. She pulls tight and he jerks back, like he's surprised that she knows what she's doing. I can see his mind reeling.

Next, Shola uses the silk scarves to secure Dirk's wrists to the headboard. When he's totally strung up, he looks like an X on her bed. She gazes at him inquisitively, one hand on her hip, the other supporting her chin in mid-air. Shola's mind is reeling too. She's wondering what she should do.

Dirk says something, and the tension between them is broken. Shola climbs into bed and sets herself between his spread feet. His cock sticks straight up in the air, but she doesn't grab for it. Instead, she licks him. She starts at his ankle, and he watches while she works her way up past his knee. She bites his thigh and he grins. Then she looks up at him and they share a moment.

I watch as it all plays out.

He must think she's about to suck his cock. That's what I would be thinking if I were him. But Shola starts over on his other ankle, licking a smooth trail up to his thigh. When she gets close to his dick, she stops. She bypasses his erection, and licks his belly, working her way up to his nipples. I watch her flicking them with her velvety pink tongue, one and then the other.

She sucks and he smiles.

After his nipples, she veers toward his neck and nibbles there, working her way up to his full lips. Just as she's about to kiss him, though, she pulls away and smirks. They converse back and forth, both chuckling, and then Shola straddles Dirk's face by manoeuvring her calves underneath his shoulders.

6

Shola's thigh blocks my view of her mound and his mouth, but it's crystal clear what's happening. She's hovering over him. He's licking her clit. Long, slow strokes, I bet.

That's the one thing I miss about partnered sex: the sensation of someone else's tongue on my pussy. There's nothing else in the world that can replicate that sensation. I know they make little sex toys and vibrator attachments that look like tongues, but how could that possibly feel the same as warm, wet flesh on flesh?

I bet Dirk enjoys eating pussy. I bet he loves the taste of Shola's cunt. If I had to guess, I'd say she tastes musky and sweet and tangy and a little sour.

Imagine if I could sneak in to her apartment right now. You know what I'd do? First off, I'd put on one of her corsets and a pair of her panties. They'd be too small on me, of course, but that's half the appeal. I'd feel the elastic of her thong digging into my belly and my thighs, hugging my pussy and rubbing against my asshole. Her corset would suck in my gut and bring my boobs jutting forward. I'd barely be able to breathe, but that just might bring me closer to orgasm. If I could only use half my lung capacity, I would come or I'd pass out trying.

If Shola were riding Dirk's face like she is right now, I would climb in behind her. I'd straddle Dirk's big body, but I'd press my front against Shola's back. I'd feel the sizzle of her skin where my boobs were bare. I'd rub up against her until they burst out the front of the corset. My nipples would harden against her back.

I don't think I'd "do" anything, like fuck Dirk or demand satisfaction. I think I'd just reach around Shola's body and play with her tits while Dirk licked her pussy. We'd bring her to orgasm together.

If Dirk wasn't around and I was alone with Shola, that would be a different story. I would love to feel her tongue on my clit. There's something about her that makes me think she'd be great at eating pussy.

I would sit on her couch and open my legs. She'd kneel between them and hold my thighs apart. The sight of that pretty face diving at my mound would probably reawaken my capacity for orgasm, and the sensation of her warm tongue would surely put me over the edge. I can't imagine being with her and not coming.

But it doesn't bother me to see Shola with Dirk. After all, we're only close in fantasyland. In real life, she wouldn't know me from a hole in the ground.

Anyway, I like watching her receive pleasure, whether it's from herself, from porn, or from good old Dirk. He seems to do a pretty good job of getting her off.

I wish I could see his tongue as he licks her, but her reaction says it all. Her eyes roll in her head, and she leans back so far her long hair dances against Dirk's erection. She turns her head like she's trying to reach it. She sticks out her tongue, but she can't quite get there, can't quite lick him.

When Shola pulls herself to standing, then awkwardly steps away from Dirk, I catch sight of his face. Tremors run through me. His chin and cheeks are glistening with Shola's pussy juice. I can't tell you how I envy him. He licks his lips and I lick mine, hoping to taste my favourite girl. All I taste is cherry chapstick, but I know what Dirk's got on his tongue. He's got Shola.

She turns full around with her legs spread on either side of his wide chest. Bowing down on top of him, she grabs his cock with both hands and shoves her pussy in his face. They're sixty-nining with her on top.

I bet Dirk would love to take that great ass of Shola's in his hands and squeeze, but she's secured him too firmly to the bedposts. He isn't going anywhere.

Pumping his big cock in her two hands, Shola licks Dirk's cockhead. I can feel his reaction, even across the courtyard. I almost can't imagine what it would be like to have a dick, but I try. Whenever I'm watching Shola devour Dirk's erections, I always think how it would feel to drive it down someone's throat, or lie back like Dirk and let Shola go to town on me. The warmth of her mouth must make him crazy.

Dirk's moving more, now, than he was before. His feet and his hands are rattling the bed. I bet he's grunting and slurping as he works Shola's clit. I bet he's holding back, as well. He probably wants to come already, after all the build-up.

Shola pulls away from his mouth again. She crawls down the bed without looking back, and collapses on his dick. I gaze from the junction of their bodies to the expression on Shola's face. Her eyes are clenched shut. I bet it hurts. He's so big.

She can't really move in that position, so she turns around until she's straddling him but facing him too. When their gazes meet, they both smile. They say something and laugh. It's adorable.

Then Shola sets her palms down on his chest and starts riding him slowly. I bet she's brushing her clit against his pelvis. Her pussy's probably pulpy and throbbing after feeling the wrath of Dirk's tongue.

I wish she would take off her corset now. I want to see her breasts swinging while she fucks him, but it's not up to me. Would Dirk like to see her tits, I wonder? Not that he could touch them. His hands are still bound over his head.

Shola works hard and fast. I watch her bum jiggle as she rides him. She's amazing, this woman. The pleasure she's giving Dirk is right there on his face. He doesn't hide a thing.

I can only imagine how tight her pussy must be, and how it might feel when she hugs his cock with it.

She picks up speed and Dirk throws his head side to side. He's coming. I can see it not only in his face, but in the way his body writhes and hops. He's coming, and so is she. She stops moving and straightens up, rubbing her clit with her whole hand, up and down, frenzied motions. They're coming together. You always hear that people don't do that in real life, but Shola and Dirk do. All the time.

Once she's untied him, they lie together on the bed and talk. I wish I could hear what they were saying. Maybe I should learn to read lips. Or maybe, if I knew, I wouldn't like them so much anymore. Who knows? Maybe they're horrible people.

But I don't think so. I watch them so often that they've nestled in close to my heart. I wouldn't want to ruin the affection we share by actually meeting them. Better to stay by my window, watching. That way, they'll always be my friends.

I Watched Her Wash a Cucumber

I never would have believed it was possible if I hadn't seen it with my own eyes—and then experienced it for myself.

When I stepped out of the end stall in the washroom at work, Nazrene from Accounting was cradling a field cucumber in both hands, holding it under the faucet. The building had installed those fussy automatic sinks that never turned on when you wanted. While she tried to get the water running over her cucumber, the liquid soap dispenser spewed all over the wrist of her suit jacket. She swore under her breath, shaking it off.

"You're making a salad for lunch?" I asked.

The moment that question was out of my mouth, I realized how strange it was that she was washing produce in the bathroom. There was a sink in the kitchen, after all.

"Hmm?" Nazrene got the water running, and rubbed the cucumber between her hands.

I stepped up to the sink next to hers, watching and wondering why she'd opted for such an unwieldy cucumber. When she caught me staring, she scowled.

Flustered, I stammered, "I haven't had one of those guys since I was a kid. The skins are tough, don't you find? I only buy the English ones now."

"Ahh." Nazrene held the field cucumber in one hand while she rubbed off the sharp little nodules with her fingers. She didn't even look up at me.

"So, I'll see you in the lunchroom?" I said, hoping to spark some reaction.

I waited for a response, but with none forthcoming I pushed the door open with my elbow and left.

Nazrene never showed up in the lunchroom that day.

She wasn't a weird girl, but she was quiet and nobody at the office knew much about her. I'd always found her pretty, in a conservative buttoned-down way, but beyond her looks I didn't think about Nazrene at all.

Not until that day I watched her wash a cucumber.

What could she have done with it? It couldn't be what I'd convinced myself it was. Images kept flashing through my mind of Nazrene taking that giant cucumber into a bathroom stall, hiking up her skirt, throwing down her panties, and fucking herself silly. Is that really what she'd done?

You know what they say: the most obvious answer is usually the right one.

About a week later, I stepped out of the washroom stall to once again find Nazrene at the sink. Just like before, she had a field cucumber between her palms and she was rubbing it under running water.

I watched her wash it, mesmerized by the motion of her golden brown skin against the cucumber's deep green flesh. Her rings glided up and down her wet fingers as she rubbed the thick, long vegetable. My knees went so weak I had to lean my hip against the sink to keep from keeling over.

"Will I see you in the lunchroom?" I asked. My voice was a whisper. I could barely hear myself, so I wasn't surprised when Nazrene didn't answer.

When I left the bathroom, she was all I could think about.

The third time this happened, I was bold enough to ask, "What's with the cucumber?"

She looked up at me, looked straight into my eyes, and said, "I'm going to the roof."

"The roof?" I wondered if that was any kind of answer to my question. "Isn't it locked? I didn't know we could get up there."

"The lock's broken. I'm going up." She tugged a few paper towels from the dispenser and dried off her cucumber.

I couldn't stop staring at the thing. I couldn't figure out what was going on, if she was inviting me up, if she was actually going to eat that thing, or if she would do what I kept picturing.

"Can I come too?" I asked.

Nazrene shrugged, and that was good enough. My lunch was in the fridge, but I could forego a meal if it meant discovering the fate of that big cucumber.

Following Nazrene up six flights of stairs, I watched as she pushed the roof door open with her hip and stepped out into the gleaming sunlight. Shading my eyes, I walked out after her.

To my surprise, there was a garden on the roof with a few small trees and hardy rushes. I walked past them, away from door, and meandered along a path to the soft little flowers that grew close to the ground. I couldn't resist bending to stroke their downy petals.

"Pretty, aren't they?" Nazrene smiled when I looked up at her. She eased her long body down into the patch, cucumber in hand.

Though I had my suspicions, I asked, "What do you do up here?"

She never stopped smiling. In fact, she beamed so intensely I started to back away a bit. It wasn't until she raised the cucumber to her lips and kissed the end of it, grinning like the devil, that I halted. What could I do? I just stared at her, my jaw slack.

Nazrene raised her eyebrow—only one, not the other—and I knew it was an invitation. Maybe it was the heat of the sun or the altitude, or even just the softness of the flowers under my bare knees, but I wanted her. I wanted everything she wanted, and maybe even more.

Leaning back on one elbow, Nazrene opened her legs, drawing her business-length skirt up past her hips. I gasped when I saw that she wasn't wearing any underwear. Her pubic hair was black but very trim, and I couldn't take my eyes off the glimmer of juice coating her pussy lips. I watched in amazement as they opened to reveal the perfect pink glistening inside her labia.

Right away, there was a thick pulse between my legs. It beat so forcefully I would have touched myself if Nazrene hadn't been there staring at me.

I didn't think I could speak, but the words tumbled out of my mouth hot as lava: "Put it in."

Nazrene tilted her head, smirking. Then she extended the cucumber in my direction and said, "You do it."

I grabbed the thing from her. There was a part of me that wanted to ram it up her snatch just to see how she'd react, but I knew she'd put her trust in me. I knew she had faith. So I was gentle. I took it slow.

I'll never forget the way Nazrene's pussy lips glistened as I traced the domed end of that cucumber around them in sweeping circles. Every time I got to the top, I nudged her clit a few times and she opened her legs even wider, bucking her hips off the ground. Tossing her head back, she hummed her approval like a song, and the sound of her voice like that, full of longing and desire, turned me on more than I ever could have imagined.

My palm was sweating so much it was hard to keep a firm hold on the cucumber. It was just so massive I didn't know if it would really fit inside her. I had to pull the big vegetable away just to get one more look at that tight little hole. Her slit was deep pink bordering on red, and that wet flesh seemed to be grasping for the pleasure I'd taken away.

"Put it in. Put it in!"

Nazrene's voice was thin, and it cracked when she begged. The sound made my pussy clench, just like hers was doing as I watched, and I ached to spread those engorged lips. I wanted to use my fingers, or even my fist. I wanted to drill inside her with my body.

"Put it in," she repeated, again and again, like a mantra. Her eyes were closed now, her head tossed back, lips slightly parted. Her long black hair swept the groundcover, shimmering in the brilliant sunshine. "Please."

I couldn't resist any longer. Pressing the tip of the cucumber flush to her slit, I pushed with enough force to make her yelp.

"Sorry!" I cried. "Did I hurt you? I'm so sorry!"

She raised her hips and her head simultaneously, glaring at me for a good beat before offering an impish smile.

"Keep going," she said, and I did, twisting the cucumber as I went. Every time I turned the thing one way or the other, Nazrene writhed along with it. Her breasts rose up in the air and, God, they were gorgeous—so full and round. I could smell the tang of her cunt overlaying the aroma of garden flowers as I forced the cucumber inside her, watching her pussy open to a big O.

How could something so tight accommodate something so big? It seemed impossible. I'd never been penetrated by anything so huge, and I didn't want to be. Big cocks scared the hell out of me, and this cucumber had a greater girth than any flesh-and-blood man in existence.

Even so, I felt strangely empowered as I held that thing in my hand. Jamming it into Nazrene's beautiful cunt, I felt like a superhero.

Not roughly, mind. The last thing I wanted to do was hurt her. Nazrene had opened herself up to me in the most intimate way imaginable. She'd stretched my boundaries, and all I wanted to do was fill her with pleasure. For me, I knew that would involve more than just ramming a cucumber in my pussy. For me, it would take some clit stimulation.

I wondered if Nazrene was anything like me. I wondered if she'd like what I liked, but I didn't wonder for long.

Leaning forward, I breathed in the musk of Nazrene's cunt. Now that my fingernails had pierced the cucumber's flesh, I could smell its freshness so much that I was salivating wildly as I plunged my face against her crotch.

With her pussy lips spread wide, all I could do was plant myself above her clit and lick that tender bud. The cucumber was filling her now—I could tell by the resistance her cunt muscles exerted as I pressed forward—so I used the lust she'd inspired to lick her like crazy. I don't think my tongue had ever flicked so fast. Nazrene went wild, hollering as she dug her hands into the groundcover, sending up earthy scents of soil and grass.

She looked like a totally different person this way. Around the office, Nazrene was so buttoned down, so put together. Now she was a wild woman, crying out, "More, yes my lovely, more!"

I gave her what I could, licking her little clit like crazy, hoping that was enough. Her screams caught somewhere between exultation and torment. How could I leave her hanging?

And then her hand was in my hair, twisting it into a rope, pulling, yanking, hurting me. I didn't care. Her insistence only made me work harder, and the better I did, the more I gave, the more her pussy clenched around the cucumber, making it jerk in my hand.

Bucking her hips, she fucked the massive vegetable, grinding her clit against my tongue, getting off on both at once. The cucumber whacked my chin, but what could I do? Nazrene wasn't saying words—only screaming, crying, yelling out nonsense syllables while she thrust her hips.

Her excitement made my heart race, and I licked her as fast as my tongue would let me. My jaw ached, but I couldn't stop. I wouldn't quit until she told me to.

And that came soon enough. Nazrene bucked high up off the ground, teeth clenched, squealing through them, fists balled in my hair. I tried to move the cucumber in her cunt, but she was just too tight. No matter how much I licked her clit she didn't loosen up.

"No!" she cried, which was the opposite of what I was used to hearing in bed. "No more! Too much, no more."

I looked up at her, and her eyes were wide as dinner plates, like her orgasm had put her in shock.

"Careful," she warned as I pulled the cucumber from her pussy.

She smelled so good, like salad and musk. I wanted to eat her in every way possible.

Nazrene held that pose, leaning back in the bed of flowers as I held her cucumber. She watched me like I'd watched her when she was washing it—with an expression of sheer intrigue.

And then she said, "Lick it, my lovely."

God, the way she looked at me when she said those words... how could I refuse? I'd somehow managed to ignore my own arousal while I got Nazrene off, but now that she was spent and sore I wanted my turn. If I licked her cucumber, would she lick my pussy? I certainly hoped so.

I hadn't gotten the full taste of my beautiful co-worker's cunt just by flicking her clit with my tongue. When I took a long, languorous lick of the vegetable, the taste of Nazrene hit me full on. It had a sweetness to it, as well as the brightness from the cucumber's spritz, but it was the dense musky aroma of pussy that really stuck in my throat. I turned the thick vegetable in my hand, lapping up every trace of pussy juice.

By the time I'd finished, the cucumber shone with saliva and my throat was thick with the taste of Nazrene.

"Your turn," she said with a sly grin.

I smiled. "You want to eat my pussy?"

"No." She gave me a curious look and then glanced at her beloved cucumber. "I want to fuck it with that."

My stomach knotted as I looked between Nazrene and the giant cucumber. "What? No way."

She nodded slowly and then snatched the cucumber away from me. "Yes!"

"No," I said, though I'm sure she could tell I was fidgeting to hike my short skirt up and over my hips.

"On your knees," she instructed, like her word was final. "I'm going to fuck you from behind."

I just sat there staring for what felt like forever. My heart pounded so hard I felt it in my cunt. I couldn't think of any reason to resist her... or the cucumber.

Pulling my slick panties down to my knees, I bent over so my ass was in the air and my forehead touched the soft groundcover. I could feel my whole body cringing as I waited for Nazrene to make her move.

She pushed up my skirt to get it out of the way, and then rubbed my ass cheeks with her palm. When I thought about her staring at my asshole, I felt so humiliated my brain started to buzz. This was all so... weird!

And then suddenly—smack!—she slapped my slick pussy lips with that big green monster. I rolled my head enough that I could watch from underneath while she smacked me again. Boy, it made me shiver when the cucumber drew a gossamer strand of nectar from my snatch. In the bright sunlight, my pussy juice actually shimmered.

"Fuck me," I groaned, though the idea of that huge vegetable filling my pussy still made my stomach clench. "But go slow. Don't hurt me."

She said nothing as the cucumber's rounded tip met my slit. I thought it would be cold, but it wasn't. Being inside Nazrene's pussy must have softened it up, because when she started pushing it into me it didn't feel quite as huge as I thought it would. Not that it wasn't gigantic, but I really thought it would hurt.

"Play with yourself," Nazrene instructed. "Touch your clit, my lovely."

My bud was so engorged I actually gasped when I touched it. I couldn't keep still. I arched off the ground.

"Stay," Nazrene commanded, pressing down on my lower back. Her hand was so hot I wouldn't have been surprised if it left a brand on my flesh.

I could feel the cucumber pulsing in my cunt, opening me wide, and I tried not to think of what Nazrene's pussy had looked like when I'd forced that same veggie into it. I couldn't imagine being stretched that wide. I couldn't believe it was happening to me.

Rubbing my clit, I said, "More! Give me more!"

My pussy was unbelievably sensitive: my lips were thick and my clit throbbed, begging for release. Nazrene put more pressure on the cucumber and I felt its smooth curves opening me wider. My fingers whacked the monster as I scoured my bud, lifting one shoulder and crushing my cheek into the soft ground. I wished I could open my blouse to feel the soft flowers and grasses caressing my naked nipples, but my breasts were pressing down too hard. Anyway, I was too turned on to be coordinated.

That's when Nazrene started twisting the cucumber inside my cunt, just like I'd done to her. It entered me deeply, and it felt so foreign, so unusual, so unabashedly huge that I wasn't sure how I could handle its girth.

"Come for me," Nazrene chanted as she turned the cucumber. "Come, my lovely."

She juiced me like an orange, and it felt so oddly wonderful that I knew I'd find my orgasm if I just kept stroking.

I was right.

Shocks erupted through my belly, streaming down to my tits, exploding like fireworks. I lost all control at that point. Without fear or reservation, I bucked back. Nazrene held steady, driving the mammoth cucumber into my pussy as my orgasm took over.

Up on the rooftop, I grunted like an animal, like I wasn't human anymore. "Awww yeah, fuck yeah fuck yeah fuck yeah!"

My voice was gravel. I didn't recognize it, except that it resonated in my chest like a canon blast. When I squeezed my eyes shut, galaxies exploded against the darkness of my lids. My skin was on fire, and that fire blazed through me until the only sensation left was the stretch and pull of a massive cucumber lodged in my snatch.

I lost track of time until Nazrene carefully slid the monster out of me. My pussy ached for it, but I knew I couldn't bear any more. I'd be feeling my distension for a week.

Nazrene stretched out beside me and licked my pussy juice from the cucumber's dark green skin. It was quite a spectacle, and my clit started pounding again as I watched her. I was just about to touch it when she said, "Back to work. We're late already."

A deep flush consumed me when I saw the grass stains across the front of my blouse. How was I going to explain that away around the office? My heart started thumping again, and my knees went so weak I didn't think I'd be able to stand, until Nazrene helped me to my feet.

Before edging into the dark stairwell, Nazrene shielded her eyes from the sun and asked, "Would you do it again?"

My pussy was swollen and sore, I had grass stains on my boobs, and my panties were soaked. Any sensible woman would say no, but the word stuck in my throat and before I knew it I'd said, "Any time."

On our way downstairs, I asked Nazrene, "What are you going to do with that cucumber?"

She held it tight and said, "Slice it up, add some tomatoes, red onion, Greek dressing—makes a nice salad. I'll bring some for lunch tomorrow, if you'll share it with me."

What could I say? "Yes, please."

My mouth was watering already.

Melonhead

J ai's hand just didn't do the trick anymore.

It came as no surprise—he'd been using the damn thing for as long as he could remember. At home, he had all kinds of substitutes, everything from studded sleeves to a fake ass. It was a lot to hide when his parents came to visit.

Good of his mother to dogsit while he was off on one of his business jaunts, but there was a reason he'd bought a toy box with a solid padlock. His mother had to be the nosiest person on the planet, and the thought of her presence in his home always sent a shiver down his spine.

Adjusting his laptop bag on his shoulder, Jai inched forward in line. It seemed like half the industry was checking into this hotel all at once. The guy in front of him was wearing ocean-cool cologne, and the scent filled Jai with a warmth he forced himself to resist.

He always got antsy after the hurry-up-and-wait of air travel, the web of "random" security checks his brown body always seemed to get caught in. If he wasn't so sure his baggage would get rummaged through forty times along the way, he might even bring a toy or two along for the ride. Damned if he didn't need release at the end of the day.

That's why he'd stopped at a little fruit market en route.

Jai never left home without a plan.

"Bienvenue chez l'Hôtel des Reines."

The pretty Asian girl behind the desk smiled expectantly, which made Jai more nervous than it should have. Realistically, he could have responded in French, but he'd visited Montreal enough to realize most hospitality workers spoke English too.

"I booked a room online. The name's Jaipala Balasubramanium."

He fully expected this, girl whose gold nametag read *Yuja*, to stare blankly at him for about ten seconds, and then ask, "Spell that for me?"

She didn't.

Pronouncing each syllable back to herself, she typed his name into her computer and nodded. "We had to switch you from a double queen to a king room. Hope that's okay."

Switch rooms? Was that okay? Before Jai's brain could fully mull over the question, his mouth was asking, "Does it have a microwave?"

"I'm sorry," Yuja said. "It doesn't. Do you need one?"

"Definitely!"

The urgency in his answer just slipped out. Jai didn't even know where it came from. He was usually so patient with blips like this, and he knew from experience you caught more flies with honey. Now he got the wide-eyed reaction he'd expected when he'd given his name, but he felt like crap for speaking to the girl so bluntly.

"I'm sorry...Yuja. That's a nice name, by the way." Jai's face felt hot, though the girl's demeanour hadn't changed, except that the tip of her tongue now protruded from the corner of her mouth.

She was probably biting her tongue to keep from answering back. He'd have deserved it, whatever she had in mind to say.

"Sorry," Jai said. "I just...I need a room with a microwave. Is there another one available?"

Her attention shifted to the computer, and she gazed intently at the screen while she tapped at the keyboard. Finally, she shook her head without looking up at him. "I'm sorry."

"Nothing?" Jai held the paper bag from the market tight in his hand, resting the fruit against his side.

Yuja shook her head.

What could he say now? Why was it so important? What kind of a reprobate was he?

He leaned across the desk, although its marble expanse kept him far from the girl on the other side. "Listen, I really need a microwave in my room. I know it doesn't seem like a big deal, but it is. It's..." In the moment, it seemed like a brilliant manoeuvre: "It's a medical thing! I need to heat up my...medication!"

He didn't intend to meet the girl's gaze straight on, but when he did he saw concern in her eyes. That broke his heart a little bit.

"Well," she said. "I'm sure there's some way we can accommodate you. Maybe the kitchen staff could heat it up, and I could get a porter to bring it to your room. Would that work?"

"I...don't...think so..."

Would it? Jai tried to envision the look on this girl's face when he rolled a cantaloupe across her desk. No, that was crazy. She'd know exactly what he planned to do with it. Wouldn't she? Did girls know about stuff like that? Did they realize guys could take any ordinary household object and make it fuckable?

"It's the least I can offer you, Mr. Balasubramanium." His name tumbled from her lips easy as Smith or Wong or Gagnon, and that put him uncommonly at ease. "If it's a medical issue, we'll make whatever accommodations are necessary."

Her business jargon only increased the distance between them. He pulled her closer in by saying, "Please, call me Jai."

Was that too forward? He didn't want to give the impression he was coming on to her or anything. He just wanted to get his melon microwaved.

A hint of a smile broke across Yuja's pink lips. "If you leave your medication with me, I'll make sure..."

"It's handled discretely?" Jai interrupted.

Maybe if he asked her to keep it in the bag...maybe that wouldn't be so bad? She'd never know for sure what was in there.

Yuja raised a brow, and then seemed to catch herself. Lowering it quickly, she bit her lip and gazed at her computer screen. "Of course, discretion...of course..."

Jai's heart thumped against his ribs. His cock threw itself at his fly like it was begging for escape.

How could he deny himself the pleasure he'd looked forward to throughout the "routine" searches and airport screenings? The woman beside him on the plane spent the whole trip shooting him suspicious looks, those glances that asked, "Why are you *really* here?" and "What have you got hiding under that suit? Is your shoe really a bomb?"

All he could do to soothe his building irritation was close his eyes and imagine how good it would feel when he checked into his hotel and stuck a melon in the microwave.

"Please..." Jai's voice retreating to a whisper as he passed the paper bag, folded over and over and over at the top, across the marble expanse of Yuja's desk. "...don't open the bag, okay? It's just... really... personal... medication?"

"Of course."

When Yuja's tiny fingers grasped the paper bag, every muscle in Jai's body tensed. He clung to the sack, feeling suddenly sheepish and perverted. He was being ridiculous, wasn't he, insisting like this?

Swallowing hard, Jai pulled back on the bag. "On second thought, don't worry about it."

"It's no trouble at all," Yuja insisted. "Really. It's not a problem."

She tugged on the paper bag so hard Jai got scared it might tear. He let go without warning. Poor Yuja stumbled back, clinging to the bag that looked like it contained a bowling ball.

Jai could see the headlines now: *Hotel worker falls on her keister, drops sack, cantaloupe goes rolling, everybody points and laughs.*

After that most public of disgraces, he'd lose his job, his parents would disown him, his own dog would shun him, and ultimately he would end up living over a heating grate and begging for quarters.

Luckily, that's not what happened. Yuja recovered her footing like a gymnast and offered a beseeching smile. "Wow—heavy."

Jai traced his finger across the veins of the marble desk. "Yeah...heavy..."

She didn't ask, and he didn't say anything more about the bag, except how long to heat it and to please, please not look inside.

For some reason, he trusted this girl. If he didn't, he'd never have handed over the cantaloupe. She just seemed so... professional.

Forty-seven minutes later, Jai was pacing the industrial carpet in his hotel room.

It shouldn't take this long. Why was it taking so long?

Maybe they'd microwaved it for too many minutes.

Maybe his melon had exploded!

A knock at the door sent Jai hurdling across the expanse, his heart thudding like crazy as he grabbed the door handle. He kept telling his hand to open it, open up, especially when the knocking continued, but the muscles in his arm froze up.

"Mr. Balasubramanium? Jai? Its Yuja from the front desk."

Now his arm sprang to life, tearing the door wide open like it had a mind of its own.

Jai nearly jumped out of his socks when he caught sight of the cantaloupe huddled inside a white hotel towel in Yuja's arms. He nearly passed out when he realized she wasn't alone. There was another girl with her, a white girl with hair so red it looked like she'd dyed it with beet juice.

They both wore hotel uniforms: navy skirts that rested just below their knees, matching jackets, white blouses and silky red neck scarves.

"You... you... you opened the bag!" Jai stumbled backward, catching himself on the mahogany writing desk.

The redhead caught the door before it could slam shut, and Yuja waltzed right in. "I know I said I wouldn't..." She held the melon flush to her belly. "...but the kitchen staff wouldn't microwave something without knowing what it was. I assured you discretion, and I kept my word, Mr. Balasubramanium."

"Jai..." he said off-handedly.

"So I told the kitchen I'd do it myself on my dinner break. They said that was okay as long as I made sure it wasn't, like..." Yuja looked down at the towel ball, like she was ashamed by what she was saying. "...like, a bomb or whatever."

Real original. Just like the airports!

The straight-faced redhead stepped inside the room, letting the door close softly behind her.

In his hazy bafflement, Jai asked, "Who are you?" He shook his head, ashamed to have asked such a forward question. "I'm sorry, that was rude. But seriously, who *are* you?"

"Nikola," the girl said, shrugging one shoulder and tilting her head.

"Okay..."

Jai looked to Yuja, who'd perched herself against the bathroom door, but it seemed to take a moment before she realized his focus had shifted to her.

"Oh, sorry," Yuja said. "Nikola and I take our breaks together. She just didn't want me coming up to a man's room all by myself... carrying a melon..."

23

The redhead cracked a smile, which quickly bled into hysterical laugher. When she'd calmed down she said, "Sorry—Dirty Dancing..."

This was a nightmare: Jai ready and waiting in a hotel room, his cantaloupe ready and waiting in the arms of a hotel worker, and these two girls staring at him like he was... like he was what? He glanced back and forth between the pair, trying to decipher those matching gazes.

Judgemental?

No.

Apprehensive?

No.

Curious?

Maybe...

Whatever the look, Jai just wanted to get rid of them and get down to business while his melon was still warm.

"Thank you both." He pulled out his wallet and handed them tips, which they glowered at. "I appreciate everything. Really."

Yuja didn't hand over the melon, and Nikola seemed to be inching toward the bed.

"Do you mind if we sit?" Nikola asked. Her accent was powerfully Quebecoise, twangy and obtuse. "My feet are killing me."

"Yeah, same here." Yuja climbed clumsily onto the king-size bed, clutching the swaddled melon to her breast. "Oh, that's better."

The girls looked up at him expectantly. What did they want, a live sex show? Who did they think he was?

"So... thanks..." he repeated, inching toward the door. "You can just leave the... towel... on the... bed."

Still, they didn't budge.

"Oh," Yuja finally said, perking up noticeably. "We thought this might help."

Unravelling the towel, she revealed their work to him. Obviously, they knew exactly what a microwaved cantaloupe was used for, because they'd gone ahead and cut a hole in it for him—perfect size, by the looks of it.

But that was the least of his embarrassment.

All around the hole, they'd spread lipstick—the same dark red shade Nikola was wearing—and they'd drawn a button nose with two little dots for nostrils, plus eyes with huge curly lashes.

Nikola's grin seemed almost canine. "Looks good, hein?"

Jai collapsed into the bulky chair by the window and let his head fall helplessly back. Luckily, he'd closed the curtains first thing.

"I've never been so embarrassed in my life!"

His heart seemed to have fallen out of his chest and rolled under that big bed. He couldn't feel anything anymore. This was all unreal, like a hellish dream.

Yuja crawled across the bed on two knees and one hand—the other was clutching the cantaloupe to her chest—but suddenly squealed, "Oh!" Jumping off the king, she said, "This melon is hot! Don't burn yourself."

Nikola's dark eyes gleamed as Yuja extended the melon to him, face-first. He looked down at its titillating expression and felt his erection pummel his pants. When he didn't take the thing from Yuja, she set it between his knees and smiled proudly.

"She's ready for you," Nikola said. "Just look at those lips. She'd be licking them if she had a tongue."

Jai just wanted to crawl under a rock and die, but his cock was insistent.

"She needs a name," Yuja suggested, resting against the corner of the bed. "How about..." She paused, cocking her head sideways and lifting an eyebrow towards Jai. "Melonhead?"

Jai laughed despite himself. The warmth emanating from the cantaloupe was crawling up his legs now, relaxing his muscles. He looked back and forth between the girls. "Is there any way I'm going to get a little privacy for this?"

They shook their heads in unison.

"You... what, you want to watch me?"

Both heads nodded in the affirmative.

It seemed... bizarre. Why would any woman want to see something so lewd? So unusual? So perverse?

But, hell, who was he to judge? He was about to fuck a cantaloupe.

Abandoning every ounce of pride, Jai scooped the melon up with one hand. With the other hand, he unzipped, unbuttoned, unbuckled. Before letting his bottoms tumble to the floor, he looked to the girls on the bed. "You're not going to get me arrested after this, I hope."

Nikola tilted her beet-red head. "Arrested?"

"Saying I subjected you to this strange, lascivious torment?"

They both chuckled like Jai was the crazy one.

Yuja said, "Go on, before your melon gets cold."

Jai sighed, knowing what a stupid idea this was, but dropping his pants anyway. His cock sprang up, solid and aching, aiming itself at the melon's lipsticked mouth. "This is nuts."

"Those are nuts." Yuja pointed while Nikola crawled toward her to get a better look.

Jai tried to ignore their gleaming eyes. "Oh! Baby oil. It's in the bathroom."

He tried to waddle in that direction, but, with his pants around his ankles, he didn't get anywhere fast.

"I'll find it," Yuja offered, running to grab it and handing it off to him with that same eager smile plastered across her face.

Jai thanked her and squirted the clear lube around that warm melon hole.

This had to be a dream. None of it could really be happening, so what difference did it make what he did?

"You ready?" he asked the girls.

They squealed, clapping their hands like children at a magic show. This wasn't at all how Jai had envisioned his evening playing out, but it was still better than getting interrogated at the airport.

Wrapped in its hotel towel, the melon looked like a woman fresh from the shower, her wet hair bundled in a heap on her head. This was the first time Jai had ever looked down at a cantaloupe and seen a woman's face. The image was jarring, but no more so than being stared at by two female observers. Strange, how differently this whole scene would have played out had they been hot young guys. Jai could only dream...

Squinting until the face became a blur, Jai guided his waning erection to the cantaloupe mouth. The second his sensitive cockhead met that warm, wet flesh, his hard-on was back full-force. A moan escaped his lips, tortured, longing...

God, he'd been waiting so long for this moment.

Shutting his eyes completely, Jai gripped Melonhead with both hands and eased his cock slowly inside. Fuck, that hole was tight, tight, tight. Tight like a virgin ass, yet far more yielding. The orange flesh made way for his dick as he gave a few slow thrusts inside that beautiful warmth.

It was perfect—not too hot, not too cold. Like Goldilocks' breakfast, this melon was just right.

Jai issued a couple more shallow shoves before plunging his dick in deep. "Oh, fuck..."

Nothing in the world could compare to the sensation of warm, squishy seeds and gooey innards housed in sticky fruit flesh. His cock strained damn hard, and his thighs along with it. He couldn't do this standing.

Turning toward the chair, Jai rested his knees against the edge of the seat cushion. He gripped Melonhead with both hands. This position relieved the tension in his legs, and, if he thought he was hard before, well, this cantaloupe was in for the surprise of its life.

He rammed its mouth hole, driving his dick straight in, burying it to the root in warm, gushy wetness. Damn, he'd looked forward to this. So much so that he didn't even care if two strange girls were watching him every step of the way.

Tossing his tie over his shoulder—he hadn't taken the time to remove his shirt, undershirt, or suit jacket—he caught a glimpse of the girls on the bed. Jai's breath caught in his throat when he realized Nikola was hovering close behind Yuja.

Very close.

So close her clothed breasts must have been pressing against Yuja's clothed back.

Jai gulped, turning his attention back to his melon. Its eyes seemed to grow wider as his erection surged inside of it.

If that poor cantaloupe had been a real person, it would be gagging by now. A human could only deepthroat a dick for so long before choking. Maybe a melon was better all around. Certainly Jai had never been the type to pick up some stranger in each new city. How awkward would it be to watch a stranger suck his cock? No, melons were better. Melons didn't judge.

Slurp, shlerp, squelch.

The cantaloupe was getting vocal now, making all kinds of wet, slobbering noises. Jai loved this part. The fact that Melonhead could generate these rude, crude, sucking sounds around his fat dick made it almost seem real.

And then there were other sounds, too: *ooh, mmm, ahh!*

Jai looked over his shoulder to find Yuja's eyes closed in ecstasy as Nikola kissed her neck. Yuja was holding her blue uniform skirt up above her waist and Nikola's hand disappeared under the elastic of the girl's prim white panties.

His surprise bordered on shock.

This wasn't at all what he'd expected of these two. There was something strangely and unexpectedly arousing in the sight of two girls teasing and pleasing one another. They'd watched him with his cantaloupe and become aroused. Now he turned fully around and fell back into the chair, holding Melonhead between his thighs, and watching them. They'd come full circle.

Setting both feet on the ottoman near his chair, Jai pumped slowly into the cantaloupe. He let his cock swirl inside the melon, sensing every soft seed, every warm nook inside that shell. The suction built every time he pushed the thing up, away from his body, and then back down on him.

Melonhead drooled liquids down the base of his shaft. Crystal lubricant combined with peachy cantaloupe juice to bead in his pubic hair. The image was nearly as hot as watching the outline of Nikola's hand cupping Yuja's pussy underneath white cotton panties. Every time she rubbed, those panties rode up at the sides.

When he caught a glimpse of Yuja's black pubic hair, he found the sight strangely unsettling, like it was something he had no right to see.

Melonhead was eager for cum, sucking hard, building pressure, making everything tight despite the wetness. All that was missing was the prickle of stubble. Nothing else made him come as fast as the brush of a beard against his thighs. The very idea made his balls clench, and he wished he could hold the cantaloupe with only one hand so he could cup his nuts with the other.

God, his thighs were shaking, like he was having a seizure from the waist down. He was ready to pump this melon full of jizz, and all it took to get there was the sight of Nikola's hand sneaking underneath Yuja's blouse to squeeze her little breasts.

Jai couldn't hold back any longer. As Yuja turned her head to greet Nikola with a kiss, he exploded inside the cantaloupe.

That melon drained him, siphoning hot cream from his dick, devouring every last drop, its lipstick smudged, its eyes seeming hazy and shy after everything it had done. He pulled it from his cock, spilling the juices of their shared arousal across his thigh.

The girls seemed to emerge from a dream as Jai held the spent cantaloupe with both hands, looking for the garbage can.

Slowly, like sea life undulating on the ocean floor, Nikola pulled one hand from Yuja's top and the other from Yuja's panties. Her fingers sparkled with wetness. When she licked them, the sight made Jai's spent cock twitch.

"We can dispose of Melonhead for you," Yuja said. She squirmed a little as she let her skirt fall back down below her knees.

"Oh." Jai gazed at his blissful melon, feeling a little sad to say goodbye. "Yeah, thank you."

Nikola hopped down from the bed, inching toward the door. "We're already late getting back."

"Oh shit! We are?" Yuja grabbed the melon and wrapped it roughly in the hotel towel that had fallen to the floor. Before racing to the door, she looked into Jai's eyes and said, "I hope you enjoy your stay."

He stammered some combination of "I will" and "I have" as Nikola and Yuja began their exit. Before they were all the way out the door, he found his voice enough to say, "Hey, thanks. That was pretty awesome, right?"

They both nodded, huddled together in the doorway, probably wanting to leave about as much as Jai wanted to see them to go.

For the first time, a slight blush appeared on Yuja's cheeks. Her glassy lipstick had spread to Nikola's lips, and that detail summoned to mind the image of the two girls kissing.

"We get off at eleven," Yuja said, exchanging smiles with Nikola. "And we know a great all-night fruit market."

Jai's spent cock twitched again.

Baby Got Bach:
The Rockstar, His Boyfriend and Me

I'D NEVER SEEN JAMIESON Lynch in concert. He was kind of an ethereal hipster geek, but he played skeevy little clubs that made me cringe. I just waited until somebody uploaded footage to YouTube, then I'd perv over his performance all night long.

But there was another side to Jamieson Lynch. Apart from being a barely-recognized indie rocker, he was also a world-renowned classical pianist. He had kind of a Jekyll and Hyde thing going on, musically. His hipster fans didn't participate much in the institution of the symphony, and his classical followers had no interest in his "popular" stuff.

Me? I liked both.

I worked as an usher at the concert hall, so when they announced Jamieson Lynch was going to tackle the Goldberg Variations, I pretty much flipped out. It was a big deal, and not just to me. Any time a pianist took on the Goldbergs, critics came out in droves. Some people thought the Goldberg Variations should have been retired after Glen Gould died, the same way star players' numbers were retired in sports.

They needed someone to greet Jamieson as he came offstage, and escort him to a little meet-and-greet with VIP patrons. Obviously, I volunteered.

Before my shift began, our music director, Pawell, brought me backstage to meet the guy I'd had a mad crush on for a solid three years. My stomach flipped, flopped, and fell into my shoes.

When Pawell knocked at the dressing room door, Jamieson ripped it open. "He's not coming!"

"Who?" Pawell asked, looking pretty darn shocked.

Jamieson's corn-blonde hair rose in a wave. It reminded me of a tsunami in a Japanese woodcut. His red eyes blazed, somewhere between madness and despair. "Daniel's not coming. He said he wouldn't, and he's not. He's just *not*!"

Pawell's jaw fell. "Daniel is your... man-friend?"

"Boyfriend!" Jamieson spat. "Child! Juvenile fucking piss-ant who can't set one little argument aside to watch the guy he's supposed to love play the Goldbergs."

"I'm so sorry to hear that." Pawell stepped inside. "I want you to meet Julia, but perhaps now is not the best time."

I felt like a deer caught in the headlights of a Mack truck.

"Mr. Lynch," I said. "I'll be escorting you to the meet-and-greet, so don't be shocked when I grab you after the show, okay?"

Jamieson fell back on the white leather couch in his dressing room. I couldn't be sure if he'd heard me, but in that moment all I could do was stand and stare. He lifted one fine Italian shoe onto the coffee table, so his legs in pin-striped pants fell open, just for me. My gaze shot straight between them, looking for cock, locking onto the outline of his shaft under that fine fabric.

What was it about gay men that could drive a girl wild?

"Excuse us, will you, Julia?" Pawell stepped past me and closed the door.

I stood outside, but with all the commotion backstage I couldn't hear a thing. Maybe Pawell was calming Jamieson down by... no, my imagination ran wild, but real life didn't work that way.

As I rushed off to my usual job seating patrons, my mind wandered back to Jamieson Lynch's dick. I pictured myself falling between his legs and tracing my cheek across the soft cashmere of his trousers.

Sometimes I wondered if I had some kind of sexual affliction, because the only guys who appealed to me were extremely effeminate. I wondered, often, if I was a lesbian in hiding, but tits and clits kind of scared me. I wanted these guys who flicked their hair and spoke with a lisp. I wanted to tear off their clothes and worship their cocks.

When the concert began, I took a spare seat in my section. There was a short modern opus, and then a sorrowful Vaughan Williams before Jamieson took the stage. It was extremely unusual for a solo pianist to perform during one of our concerts. The rest of the orchestra cleared off, and obviously he didn't need a conductor, so it was just him. All alone on stage.

As he tapped out those first few notes—the ones transcribed on Glen Gould's gravestone—you could hear a pin drop. It was riveting. I escaped into the music, lost in melody, until Jamieson's quirky syncopations gave me a jolt.

Whispers and grumbles rippled through the audience.

"What the hell does he think he's doing?"

"Don't mess with Bach."

"He's no Gould."

"I can't wait to blog about this train wreck."

My stomach plunged. I wanted to shush them all, but I couldn't tell where the voices were coming from. It's not like patrons were shouting their disapproval, just quietly clicking their tongues and whispering their displeasure.

What assholes! They'd come convinced Jamieson would fail, and they were only proving themselves right. Why couldn't they be open to his interpretation? If they'd shut their faces for five seconds and really listen, they'd hear how beautifully Jamieson played.

I couldn't take it. Storming from my section, I raced backstage and listened to the rest of the Variations from there. No rest from the barbs! Orchestra members were standing around, whispering. Even the men in black, whose job was to move chairs, complained that the Goldbergs were too ambitious for such a young pianist. Like Jamieson was a prodigy or something! He was almost thirty, for fuck's sake!

When his performance met mild applause, Jamieson stormed offstage. I caught hold of his arm, and sparks exploded like fireworks. Just touching his jacket brought me closer to coming than the last time I'd had sex.

"Wonderful performance, Mr. Lynch. I thoroughly enjoyed your take on the Goldbergs." I pulled him toward the lobby entrance, but his will was stronger. He dragged me toward his dressing room. "No, you've got your meet and greet, remember?"

"I remember." He opened the door, and I followed him inside, still clinging to his arm. "I'm not going out there. They hated me."

When he closed the door, the dressing room felt insular and quiet. The world around us had fallen away.

"But, see, they came here to hate you." I hoped that would make him feel better. "They were never going to like your version, except the people who have to suck up to you."

"Like you."

"No!" I still hadn't let go of his arm, and we stood much closer than strangers normally would. "I honestly thought you were amazing. Me? I love your indie music, and I could really hear how you brought that sound back to Bach."

"You got that?" He cocked his head and looked down at me. He was so tall I had to arch back to look him in the eye. "I mean, that's what I was going for. I'm glad somebody picked up on it. Daniel said it was a terrible idea. He said there wasn't enough of a cross-over audience for anyone at the symphony to understand what I was getting at."

"He's right," I said. "Is that what you fought about?"

Jamieson nodded. "He said he couldn't sit there while all those catty dicks badmouthed me."

"Well, that's understandable," I said. "I couldn't, either."

His expression fell. It was probably stupid of me to acknowledge that other patrons were talking down his performance. It just slipped out.

"It pissed me off because he wasn't supporting me," Jamieson said. "He should have just been here. He should have come, no matter what."

The heat coming off Jamieson's body made me weak, and I pulled away even though I wanted to push closer. When my back met the door, I squeaked, "I'm sorry. What can I do to make things better?"

Jamieson shrugged. "What can anyone do?"

Reaching for the door handle, I said, "It's my job to get you to this meet-and-greet. Please? I'm sure people will be nice. And, honestly, you were amazing... if that means anything coming from a nobody like me."

His sullen lips curled at the edges until it almost looked like he was smiling. He leaned forward. Surely he was just reaching for the door. But no... he came closer to me, closer to my face, until those pouting pink lips were just a whisper away. This couldn't be happening! Jamieson Lynch was gay. He had a boyfriend.

But it was happening—in slow motion, no less. He was... he was kissing me!

Okay, so not on the lips. Just a sweet little peck on the forehead. No sexual innuendo. Just a gesture. But his intention didn't matter. My knees turned to jelly and my eyes rolled back in my head. I had to bite my lip to keep from moaning. So stupid.

And then he asked, "What's your name, again?"

My heart slumped, and for a second I couldn't remember. But I recovered and told him, "Julia. My name's Julia."

He'd forgotten already? I guess I shouldn't have been surprised.

"Well, Julia, I don't want to get you in trouble with your boss. Let's do this meet-and-greet, shall we?" He threw his long arm around my shoulder and shuffled me away from the door. "Let's do it hardcore!"

I was right, of course. People were nice to him, in that phony upper-crust way symphony-goers always were. But Jamieson didn't seem confident until a grubby hipster stepped out of the crowd. His eyes lit up, and he ran to the guy, crying, "Daniel!"

My heart skipped. That's how happy I was for Jamieson. The love of his life had appeared. He was so overjoyed. It was a beautiful moment to behold.

"Did you come?" Jamieson asked, wrapping his arms around the guy like he was hugging a giant teddy bear. "Did you hear it? Were you there, in the audience?"

"Yeah," Daniel said. "I changed my mind at the last minute." Daniel clutched Jamieson to his wrinkled plaid shirt. "I couldn't not come. I mean, honestly. It would have killed you."

"It very nearly did." Jamieson turned around like he had to share his enthusiasm with someone, and I just happened to be in the right place at the right time. "Julia, this is Daniel! Meet Daniel! Daniel, this is Julia. She works here."

We shook hands, and I felt star-struck all over again. Daniel wasn't famous, but he was Jamieson's guy. That made him special.

The meet-and-greet crowd was dispersing, so I asked Jamieson if he'd like me to show him back to his dressing room. The concert hall was a bit of a labyrinth, especially backstage. When he said yes, I figured I was just there to lead the way. But when we arrived, he invited me to join him and Daniel for champagne.

"Oh, I don't want to intrude." I felt my cheeks bristling. I was giddy and hot. "Unless you really want me to."

"Sure!" Jamieson hooked his arm around my shoulder and pulled me inside. "I like you, Jules. I don't know what it is."

"Yeah, I like her too," Daniel said.

They both looked at me, and I got a weird tingle. I wasn't sure what they were thinking.

I opened the champagne and poured three glasses while the guys talked on the couch. Daniel loved Jamieson's performance, of course. He didn't mention the audience whispers. He didn't say, "I told you so."

What a great guy.

We sat around chatting like old friends. I perched cross-legged on the coffee table, praying its legs wouldn't shatter under my weight. My head spun out of control. This had to be a dream. I was in Jamieson Lynch's dressing room, talking about music with him and his boyfriend. How could I believe it? This was the daydream I kept coming back to while I passed out programs to faceless concertgoers. It would totally freak him out if he knew how often I fantasized about him.

I don't know why I told him that...

The boys weren't shy. Daniel laughed and clapped his hands. Jamieson leaned forward and asked, "What do you fantasize about?"

My heart fluttered. "Oh, I don't know."

"Sure you do." Daniel leaned forward, too.

A pack of wolves, those guys.

They were enjoying this.

I shrugged. "Just... the usual, I guess. You know. I don't know."

"One man's usual is another man's fetish," Daniel said.

"And vice versa." Jamieson shot Daniel a knowing glance. "Tell us about your usual."

I laughed because I was nervous. I took another swig of champagne. "I don't know. I'm such a dummy. Like, I can never seem to have a crush on just your run-of-the-mill straight guy."

"So you're saying you have a crush on me?" Jamieson asked.

35

"I... I..."

He moved his ass right to the edge of the couch, until his knees touched mine.

More booze. Please!

"It's okay," Daniel said. "I won't be mad."

They felt so close to me, like ghosts. I closed my eyes, and they felt even closer. I was sweating when I said, "I think about you and I just feel giddy. I want to do things."

"What things?" Jamieson prodded.

Even with my eyes closed, I could see Jamieson's glowing smile egging me on.

"Naughty things," I admitted.

"Like what?" Daniel asked. "It's okay. You can tell us. I bet it's nothing we haven't heard before."

My eyes fluttered. "Really?"

"Oh yeah." Jamieson crossed his legs. "Girls hit on us all the time."

"What, you mean they can't tell that you're gay?"

Daniel threw his head back and laughed. "They hit on us *because* we're gay."

Jamieson nodded meaningfully. "We're a hot fucking commodity, Jules."

"No more excuses." Daniel reached forward and grabbed my thigh. "Tell us what you'd do if you got Jamieson alone in a room. Naked."

"Oh my god." I pressed my palms against my eye sockets so hard I saw starbursts against a background of black. "It's not here."

"What's not here?" Jamieson asked.

"My fantasy." I looked up for a second, then buried my face back in my hands. "Oh, you guys, this is so stupid. Are you sure you want to hear it?"

They both said, "Yes!"

I kept my hands over my eyes, but I forced myself to confess my sinful thoughts. "It's on the stage. I always imagine you onstage here. It's right after a performance, and all the audience has left. Everyone's gone but you and me."

"Too bad," Jamieson cooed. "I thought you were going to say you want to do me in front of a big crowd."

I laughed so hard I almost cried. "No! No way. I'm not like that. I can hardly talk about this stuff in front of two people."

36

"Go on," Daniel said, encouraging me with a squeeze to my knee. "Say it. Get it all out."

My breath rattled in my chest. I pushed my palms harder into my eyes. "Everyone's gone, and I come up on stage and I... it's really stupid."

"Say it" Daniel encouraged.

"Oh..." I could hardly breathe. "Okay, well... I come up to you while you're sitting at the piano. You're playing something amazing that you wrote. It's really dense and sensual, lots of ethereal layers. You're so good at that."

"Thanks," Jamieson said, barely a whisper.

"I come up behind you, trying to be super-quiet, but you stop playing all at once. You just sit there while I stare at the back of your head."

When I stopped talking, Jamieson asked, "What next?"

"It's so stupid." I waited for them to say something, but they didn't. "Okay, I plunge my hands into your hair and I... I don't know... I fondle it, I guess."

"You fondle his hair?" Daniel asked—not judgemental, more fascinated. "Just, like, run your hands through it?"

"Yeah, and I smell it." I pressed my palms harder against my eyes, until they hurt.

"What does it smell like?" Daniel asked.

"I don't know." Then I laughed, because I remembered. "It smells like root beer. Oh my gosh, I'm so weird, because my fantasy is that I plunge my face into your hair and just inhale, and toss my head around, and your hair is so soft and just... I'm crazy, aren't I?"

"No." Daniel grabbed my wrists and pulled them away from my face. When I opened my eyes, Jamieson was kneeling on the floor in front of the coffee table, at the perfect height for me to stick my face in his hair.

"Go for it," he said.

"Really?"

"If that's your fantasy."

I dug my fingers into the soft wave of his hair without really thinking. It smelled more like cream soda than root beer. "Well, that's not the whole fantasy, because after I'm done smelling you, I trace my hands down your front, and then across your sides. I find your pockets and plunge my hands inside. I find your..."

37

"Cock," Daniel said.

"Yeah." I swallowed hard. "I find it and it's hard, and I rub it with my fingers, but you say *harder*. You want more. So I wrap my fist around your hard..."

"Cock," said Jamieson."

"Yeah, and again you say harder, so I really strangle it this time. It's still inside your pants, and I'm grasping it basically with the inside of your pocket, but I can feel it like we're skin to skin. You're incredibly hot, like steel or something, but every time I trace my fist up your shaft, I feel the flesh moving over that hardness. And when I get to the tip, my god, it's like a hot little mushroom."

"Yeah?" Daniel asked.

"Yeah," I said, though I was still mostly talking to Jamieson. "I squeeze it and you moan. I can't believe this is really happening. You don't even know who I am. You never asked. It's like it doesn't matter, as long as you get off."

"And do I get off?" Jamieson asked.

I gulped. His hair smelled so damn good. I let the strands play across my cheeks, tickling my lips, my ears, and everything in between. Sweet and lovely, a miniature wheat field in front of my face. I opened my mouth and let his hair land gently on my tongue. I sucked it.

"Does he get off?" Daniel asked.

"Of course." I chewed on Jamieson's hair. It tasted like candy. So good. My reality was like a fantasy. It must have been the champagne.

"Well?" Daniel sat on couch in front of Jamieson. "How do you get him there, in this fantasy of yours?"

I can't believe I'm telling them all this. I can't believe I'm sucking Jamieson Lynch's hair!

"It takes something special," I said. "I've got one hand wrapped around his..."

"Cock," the guys both piped up.

"Yeah, and the other one kind of rides his thigh. I feel around until I've got hold of his..."

"Balls?" Daniel asks.

"Yeah, and when I squeeze them he sort of yelps. I think he's gonna come right then, but he doesn't. I know I've got to do more, something a little extra, and my mouth knows what."

"Oooh," Jamieson cooed.

"No," I said. "Not that. It's my teeth, I guess. They know. My lips trace down his neck, right to the place where it meets his starched collar. I throw myself at him, throw my face into just that spot on his neck, and I sink my teeth into his flesh."

"Like a vampire!" Daniel said, laughing.

"Not that hard," I told them. "I don't draw blood or anything. Just bite him in the neck while I'm throttling his..."

"Cock."

"Yeah, and squeezing his..."

"Balls."

"Yeah, and that's what does it. He unzips fast, just in time, and shoots cum all over the piano. Those black and white keys are covered in hot cream. It gets on that gleaming, black, expensive grand piano. There's something I really love about that image of debasing something so valuable."

"Yeah, for sure," Daniel said.

I set my hands on Jamieson's shoulders and placed my cheek against the back of his head. I still had some of his hair in my mouth. I was still sucking it.

"Is that everything?" Daniel asked. "You don't dream of getting fucked by a fag? You don't want a gay guy to eat your pussy?"

"I don't know," I admitted. "It's hard to explain."

"Hey, be nice," Jamieson said. "The girl's got a fantasy. That's really personal. It's not easy to share. You're pretty brave, there, Jules."

"Thanks." I sighed contently, like I'd really just experienced the things I'd always envisioned.

"Well, I've got a fantasy of my own, Julia." Daniel unzipped his pants and opened up his wrinkled plaid shirt.

My heart pounded as I watched his erection rise from his fly like a cobra from a fakir's basket. I gulped and asked, "What's your fantasy?"

He smirked, exposing his gleaming canines. "I'd like you to watch while Jamieson sucks my..."

While Jamieson lunged at his boyfriend's hardness, I jumped at the chance to say, "Cock."

At It Again

"They're at it again," Max told Pauline. "Showing up the old folks." "I don't think they're doing it to make a point," Pauline replied. "I think they're just horny. Anyway, we're not old folks."

"Compared to them, we are." Max gestured out the window. "You know why those two make love with the curtains open? They're stickin' it to us!"

Pauline tsked. "Nobody's sticking it to anyone."

"*He*'s stickin' it to *her*. Look! There's the stick!"

These neighbouring houses were incredibly close together. Couldn't be five feet between the two. Never was a problem until those sorority sisters moved in next door. What kind of people don't close the drapes when they're making love?

Staring at the young couple next door, Pauline said, "Anything she can do, I can do better."

Max didn't catch his wife's drift.

"If you think they're sticking it to us," Pauline explained, "we'll stick it right back."

He wasn't too sure what she was plotting until later that evening, after the young man had departed and the woman sat alone at the desk by the window, tapping at her computer.

Pauline came out of the bathroom wearing a sheer black negligee. Max had seen it before, and he knew what it meant. He was already in bed, having closed the blinds before undressing.

His wife made a show of sauntering toward the window, pulling down on the blind, and releasing.

"What are you doing?" Max hissed. "Our light's still on. The girl's right there. She'll see—"

"Precisely," Pauline said, raising an eyebrow. "You want in, yes or no?"

Max looked, with alarm, out the window. His gaze met that of the young woman who loved showing off her naked body in the throes of wild lust. Why not give her a taste of her own medicine? Show her the old folks could still get it on?

Casting off the covers, Max strode naked across the bedroom. He kissed his beautiful wife. Was the exhibitionist next door getting a good eyeful? Could she handle the sight of two lovers in their sixties, who knew precisely what felt good?

When Max kissed Pauline's neck, she nipped at his cheek, catching his silver beard in her teeth and tugging gently. She grabbed his bare ass as he slid his hand down the sheer fabric of her negligee.

"You look gorgeous tonight," he said.

She offered a throaty chuckle. "You look gorgeous every night, and you don't even have to try!"

He didn't contradict her, though her assessment was wildly incorrect. *Trying*, for him, meant hitting the gym every day, without fail. Trying meant trimming his facial hair so it wouldn't get in the way when they kissed. He didn't wear makeup or lingerie for her, the way she did for him, but that didn't mean he wasn't trying.

When his knees buckled, he tempted her to bed. Was the girl next door watching? Would she eye their every move?

Pauline said, "You have no idea how attracted I am to you."

He knew why she made a point of saying such things: same reason he went out of his way to assure her that he found her incredibly alluring. She didn't often get wet for him and he didn't always get hard for her. Age was to blame. They discussed the matter often enough. It helped to remind one another the attraction was still there, even if the response was hard to come by.

Tonight, they got lucky. He was already at half-mast by the time Pauline started stroking him. When she climbed down his body to put him in her mouth, Max very nearly snuck a peek out the window. No, he decided. He didn't want to know whether they were being watched.

He focused on his loving wife, certain his attention would pay off in spades.

Often, they made love with the lights off. It wasn't deliberate—they ended up in seduction mode once they were already in bed. Watching his wife devour his dick was a treat, and he couldn't get enough. All the same, it wouldn't be fair to make her do all the work—or let her have all the fun, depending how you looked at it—so he slid his finger along her shoulder and whispered, "How about a sixty-nine?"

Pauline climbed eagerly onto his face. The world grew a tad darker, thanks to the negligee. Max found his wife's clitoris easily, and offered soft licks to start. Pauline wasn't having it. She ground her lower lips against his tongue, going for what she wanted, no signs of waiting for him to catch up.

Her arousal increased his. With her mouth wrapped fully around his shaft, her lusty words were muffled, but he could always interpret her level of arousal by the frequency of her shrieks. At first, they got higher in pitch. Then, they went low. That was stage one of her orgasm process.

Max never felt as though he were doing any work, when his wife rode his face. She knew what she wanted. She knew how to get there. She used his tongue as a toy, and he didn't mind one bit.

Her intensity boosted his.

She sucked with fervour at his solemn erection, wrapping both hands around his shaft as she pressed her breasts against his belly. Shame they weren't naked. He loved to feel her skin against his. But the negligee felt nice, too. He knew how lucky he was. He got the sense his friends' wives wouldn't ride their faces in front of the girl next door.

"Your beard feels so good!" Pauline growled as she stroked herself firmly against his tongue. "So good, Max! So good!"

Sometimes it seemed as though Pauline's orgasms went on forever. She rode them like waves, one to the next. Max was really rather jealous of that. He wouldn't mind trying out an ongoing orgasm.

But he couldn't begrudge his wife her extended pleasure when she brought him the kind of climax he sought. He felt it on the horizon, in his spine, travelling closer. Pauline's ongoing cries sped the sensation along, until it gripped him by the balls, clutching and twisting most enthrallingly—or was Pauline doing that? Hard to tell what was happening.

The thrill of orgasm took hold, forcing him to thrust his hips unwittingly, and fill his wife's throat with the froth of his pleasure. Sexual delight went on and on, explosion after blissful explosion, to the point where he felt that perhaps he was riding his wife's lustful wave. Perhaps they were riding together.

Pauline didn't move from his face, even after they'd taken their time panting and moaning, assuring one another that no other orgasm had ever felt so intense. She rested upon him, her juices and his saliva mingling in his beard.

Max resisted the urge to turn his head, to gaze beyond his wife's bare thigh.

The girl next door—was she sitting at her window? Had she been watching all this time? Did she like what she saw?

Perhaps it was better not to know.

Home Again, Home Again

When I got to my ground-floor apartment, I found company waiting. A young couple, maybe early twenties, sat outside my front door. They looked familiar, but I couldn't exactly place them.

The girl had that fresh, clean yoga look about her, wearing one of those long white peasant skirts and a light blue tank top.

At her side was a young man with lovely tan skin and black hair. He'd taken off his coat, and had it curled up in his arms.

I searched my memory banks for their names, but it wasn't happening. I drew a total blank.

"Hi Lexi." The young woman stood up from the floor, leaving a backpack, stylish parka, and fleece sweater on the ground where she'd been sitting. She flipped her long brown ponytail behind her shoulder. "I'm not sure if you remember us. I'm Natalie, Ramona's sister. This is my fiancée Elio. Remember? We met at Ramona's *Rocky Horror* party?"

"Oh yeah, of course."

I did remember them now. This was the adorably shy couple that hovered about, listening to other people's conversations. Pretty young Natalie seemed nothing like my friend Ramona. I mean, Ramona was pretty out there, and this sister of hers seemed so dime-a-dozen.

Okay, so now that I knew who they were, what were they doing waiting outside my apartment?

"Ramona gave us your address if that's what you're wondering," Natalie said. That was just one of the many things I was wondering about, but it was a start. "I hope you don't mind."

"Not at all," I said in the most hospitable tone I could muster.

Man, I was tired, but I had to invite them in, right? Miss Manners and all that. Did I have to cook them dinner? I really wasn't in the mood for entertaining.

"Wow!" Elio exclaimed as I opened the door. "Your place is so chic. I wasn't expecting it to be so... decorated."

What's that supposed to mean?

"Do you guys want a drink or anything?"

Elio looked to Natalie.

"No thanks," she said.

Would it be rude to grab myself a beer if they weren't drinking anything? I poured myself a glass of orange juice instead.

"So, you two must have some romantic plans for the evening," I said as we took a seat in the living room. They weren't like me, these two. They were conventional. A dozen red roses, heart-shaped box of chocolates, obligatory missionary. *Blah!* I could never live like Natalie and Elio.

"Sort of," Elio said. Natalie shot him a daggered stare. "I brought breakfast in bed to her dorm room this morning."

"Fast food," she said dismissively.

Trouble in paradise?

I smirked behind my juice glass. "That's really sweet." The boy's efforts deserved applause. He was pretty adorable.

Natalie cut to the chase. "You must be wondering why we would just show up like this when we barely even know you. It's because..." She looked over at her boyfriend. "Elio?"

Apparently this was a tag-team couple.

"It's because we were listening to you talk at that party and you seemed really..." He paused.

"Open-minded," Natalie filled in the gap. "We figured if we asked you, you might not be too judgmental."

The young couple exchanged glances. They seemed to be mouthing, 'You ask. No, you ask.'

Finally, Elio asked, "Would you videotape us?"

I nearly did an orange juice spit-take. "Videotape you? Doing what?"

This was such a sweet, shy couple. They couldn't possibly be asking what I thought they were asking.

Natalie lifted a camcorder out of the mauve and dark purple backpack she'd brought into my apartment. "We tried to do it ourselves, but we ended up filming the wall and then the ceiling, and then the third time the whole thing was just a blurry shot of Elio's butt. We can't seem to get it right on our own. We just need someone to hold the camera and keep it on us."

"And maybe get some close-up shots?" Elio added.

"You mean you want me to film you having sex?" I tried very hard to make it sound like I was only clarifying, not to criticizing.

The pair giggled and nodded in unison. *Do they do everything in unison?*

Kind of crazy that they'd ask some random person, but I liked the idea of spying on this pair through a camera lens. At the same time, I was about to drop dead from hunger and exhaustion. All I really wanted to do was fall into bed and crash.

"This is our Valentine's Day gift to each other," Natalie explained. "We're making our own porn. That way neither of us has to feel like we're being unfaithful if we watch it. Good idea, right?"

"But you don't know me," I found myself objecting. "Wouldn't you be more comfortable doing this with a friend, or at least somebody you've met more than once?"

"No," they replied in unison.

Natalie continued, "That's exactly why we're asking you. We couldn't have sex in front of someone we knew, but we don't know you so we wouldn't mind. Plus, we know how open-minded you are, so you wouldn't laugh at us."

Elio chimed in, "And you wouldn't get turned on because you're...."

Natalie stomped on Elio's foot to keep him from saying anything too stupid.

"A lesbian?" I asked flatly.

Why did everybody think that? Was it my clothes, my hair, or my toolbox? Maybe I was just giving off lesbian vibes after my close encounter with Sunita. But does giving another woman lip service automatically make you a lesbian? And what did that have to do with getting turned on by another couple? Either way, I was too tired to argue.

"Please will you do it? We really want to see what we look like," Natalie pleaded.

Wondering what shy activities two little bunnies might get up to in bed, I agreed to help them out. *Am I insane?* Perhaps. But we all knew that.

When I asked for directions back to their house, where I assumed we would be doing the filming, they stammered, "Oh, well we're both university students..."

"And we both have roommates at our dorms, so...."

"No privacy."

"Plus, your apartment is beautiful!" Elio continued. "It makes our rooms look like a dump. Could we do it here?"

I couldn't help but shudder at the thought of two strangers having sex in my bed. On the other hand, Elio was giggle-provokingly cute, the very image of a Latin Lover. The impressive muscles bulging out from under his T-shirt had me clawing to know if he might have a package to match. Natalie, for her part, had that incredible college-girl cleavage and perky nipples calling attention to themselves from under her camisole. Hey, it might be sort of kinky to watch this pair get it on in my bed.

"Okay, but you two are buying me new sheets afterwards," I said with a generous smile.

Escorting Natalie and Elio into the boudoir, I rushed to remove the duvet from my bed. It was a real hassle to wash. While Elio showed me how to use their camera, Natalie got to work lighting the mountain of candles she'd brought along. Stretching out in the cushy chair at the corner of my bedroom, I pressed record and sat back to watch the cute-ass kids in action.

They started out by facing one another at the edge of the bed. Latin Lover brushed College Girl's cheek as she ran her fingers over his lips. Holding her head in his hands, he kissed her softly three times. One, two, three, and they seemed to have forgotten I was there.

I followed with the camera as Elio pecked his girlfriend's shoulder, sending a multitude of kisses down her arm. *How sweet!* As he laid her down on the bed, pulling her top up a bit to kiss her belly, Natalie gasped. She wriggled out of the cami under which she wore no bra. Her breasts were firm and young. Those erect pink nipples were Elio's to kiss and caress.

"My Valentine," he cooed.

"I want to see you strip," Natalie replied. Her voice sounded different, not quite as nice as before.

As Elio stood up, I zoomed out to capture him removing his T-shirt. His chest, strong and muscular, did not disappoint. When the gorgeous guy removed his jeans and his underwear, I got a great shot of his well-developed butt muscles. When he turned his handsome ass around again, I nearly fainted!

"Now eat me, you dirty little whore!" Natalie commanded.

I just about dropped the camera. *What did she just say?*

Elio began removing Natalie's long skirt, but she slapped his hands. "Did I tell you to take off my skirt?"

"No ma'am," Elio replied, meek as a saint.

Kneeling on the floor beside the bed, he crawled under Natalie's skirt. All I could film was a tent in the shape of Elio's head between her legs.

"How do I...?"

"Just shift my thong to one side, bitch. Jeeze, this isn't brain surgery!"

Elio must have done as he was told, because I could hear him sucking and lapping his girlfriend's juices. He was a noisy boy down there.

Suddenly, Natalie slid off the bed. "You lick like a dog, Elly. Do you know what I do to noisy little dogs like you?" Little Miss Domme slipped out of her frilly white skirt and cotton underwear.

"Yes, m'am!" Elio responded, a little too happily for Natalie's taste.

She slapped him on the ass and scolded, "Get on all fours, you little bitch!"

From her purple backpack, Natalie pulled out a strap-on harness complete with a short but thick curved dildo. Never in a million years would I have expected *this* from *them*. I filmed Natalie as she slipped into the harness and lubed up the fake cock. Kneeling behind Elio on the bed, she snarled, "Are you ready for your punishment, dog?"

"Yes ma'am."

Before I shifted the camera's focus from Elio's face to his muscular ass, I caught an anticipatory smile developing across his lips. When Natalie directed the dildo into Elio's hole, the poor baby winced and let out and "*ohhh*" sound.

Natalie took her time entering his ass, and I caught every moment on tape. His tight little hole opened up as she forced her fake cock inside of him. Did Natalie wax Elio's crack? He had almost no hair there. I had to wonder.

49

"You like that, do you Elly?" Natalie brought the dildo all the way out and then thrust it right back into his asshole, unforgivingly this time.

"I love it," Elio responded as Natalie thrust the fake cock into him.

"You love it *what*?" Natalie barked, scratching her nails down Elio's back, and then digging them into the sides of his butt.

"I love it, *ma'am*!"

I panned the camera out a little, scanning Natalie's pert body. Her bouncing breasts mesmerized me, and judging from the contorted smile on her face that the harness must have been stimulating her clit every time she thrust. The harder she ploughed into Elio, the larger her smile grew, and the louder Elio moaned.

"Please, have mercy on me!" he cried.

As I focused the camera on the begging cock between Elio's legs, I wondered precisely when this cute couple was going to ask me to join in.

"Very well," said Natalie to her sub. "You've been a good dog today, Elly. Now I want to see you flat on your back."

Natalie removed the strap-on and squirted a little lube into her hand. When she rubbed his cock, her firm grasp made it jump and grow. "Tell me what you want, bitch," she growled at her puppy boy.

"I want you to fuck me, ma'am." He shrieked as Natalie bent forward to bite his big shaft.

"Very well," she replied, licking her lips.

When Elio met the hardness requirements demanded by Natalie's discerning taste, she climbed on top and sank down on him. The couple moaned in unison as his big cock entered her glistening pussy. I got a great close-up of that.

"Arms!" Natalie commanded, bouncing on his prick.

Elio took the instruction, raising his hands up over his head. Leaning forward, the college Domme grabbed his wrists. She pinned him down on the bed, thrusting wildly, grinding against her man. I had to move to the side of the bed to get a good shot of the action. They'd probably wonder why so much of this video featured Natalie's tits, but I loved the way they bounced and bobbed, their perfect pink nipples hard as pebbles.

When the two started grunting and moaning, I panned out to get their pleasure-riddled faces in the shot. Natalie straddled her boy, burying his cock in her cunt. Her pretty pussy sat flush to his pelvis, her glistening lips splayed while she rubbed her clit against his dark pubic hair. Her enjoyment was clear in the way her lips contorted and her eyes squeezed shut, deep lines settling into her brow. She grinded and bucked against him, and I could only imagine how tightly her pussy was squeezing that big cock.

I wanted to lick her. I wished she would ask me.

Elio didn't last long, but neither of them seemed to need much time fucking, given the build-up. The couple came explosively and, not surprisingly, in unison.

While Elio whimpered and whined like a puppy dog, Natalie cried, "That's right, little bitch. You fill my tight little pussy with cum. Give me so much hot jizz it floods my cunt and comes dripping down my thighs. You give it to me, bitch."

"Yes, ma'am." He nodded, gazing worshipfully into her eyes.

I caught their orgasmic expressions on film.

Letting go of his wrists, Natalie fell forward onto Elio's strong chest. He wrapped his muscular arms around his fiancée. After a long while, the pair kissed and smiled and sighed, saying, "I love you" and "I love you more" and "You're my pretty Valentine." All those saccharine statements people made when they were head over heels in love.

Suddenly, I felt like I was intruding on a private moment. Everything else seemed like a show, but these kisses and *I love you*s belonged to the young couple. This was their Valentine to each other. It didn't involve me.

Setting the camcorder on my night table, I left the serene pair in my bed, closed the bedroom door behind me, and wandered into the kitchen. I could have devoured a steak in three seconds flat, but I didn't feel like cooking. A box of crackers would have to do. I put water on for tea and searched the fridge for cheese.

As I waited for the kettle to boil, I wondered how many couples existed in the world versus how many *happy* couples existed. How many of the people out in fancy restaurants tonight were overpaying for a meal with someone they barely liked out of pure desperation? It seemed to me the well-adjusted couples were the ones like Elio and Natalie. They didn't need to give each other jewellery and dinners. They knew how to make meaningful gifts with their own two bodies. I liked that.

The kettle rolled to a boil and shut itself off. I yawned as I poured. If I weren't so goddamn exhausted, would I have found my Valentine's Day dinner of tea and crackers depressing? Hard to say. I really resisted buying into all that monogamous romance crap, even if it was in my face everywhere I went. I'd been in relationships before. They weren't great. In my heart of hearts, I knew I was much happier having a whole bunch of friends with benefits. Maybe some people were meant for marriage. Not me. Variety was my spice.

Too lazy to grab a spoon from the drawer, I fished the bag from my hot tea with my bare fingers. Dwight was probably eating ramen tonight. He was big on noodles. Sunita might be eating a wonderful meal, but she was eating it with a man she had no feelings for. Me? I had college students in my bed. And I was tired. Damn tired.

By the time Elio and Natalie came out of my bedroom, still naked and magnificent, I'd fallen asleep on the couch with a half-drunk mug of tea in hand.

"Thank you so much," Natalie said, giving me a hug. I smiled as I took Ramona's nude little sis in my arms, feeling almost maternal or something. She was glowing. So was her guy. They really were a cute couple. "We'll be sure to buy you some new sheets, since we got those ones all sexed-up."

"Don't worry about it. I have plenty of sheets. What I would like, if you don't mind, is a copy of that video."

The couple giggled in unison. Elio looked to Natalie. "I guess we should get dressed and check out of here."

"Why?" I asked. "Do you get into trouble if you're not back at your dorms by curfew?"

"Curfew?" Elio chuckled.

Natalie pressed her lips together like she was trying not to laugh at the old lady's outdated ideas. "No," she said. "They're pretty laid back. We just thought we'd get out of your hair."

"Oh, don't worry about that," I said, wanting to show them I was cool. "You guys are welcome to sleep here tonight. We can all share a bed, right? I promise not to molest anybody."

They exchanged amused glances before collectively shrugging their shoulders. "If you really don't mind," Natalie said. "Your bed is so much nicer than the straw sacks they give us to sleep on at school."

I laughed. She was cute. I wasn't sure I could keep my word about not molesting her. "I'm too tired to change the sheets," I said. "Hey, I know. How about I hook up your camcorder to the TV and we give your porn video a watch?"

Elio's eyes lit up, but he turned to Natalie before saying, "Let's do it, man!"

Getting what I took for a second wind, I set up the TV in the bedroom. Elio and Natalie curled up in bed. I pressed play, stripped down to my boy shorts, and snuck in beside them. The blankets were still warm.

I must have been overwhelmed, because the second my head hit the pillow I couldn't keep my eyes open anymore. I tried to stay awake. I tried to at least listen to the homemade porn, but it wasn't happening. I was barely conscious when I heard Natalie switch off the TV. "Goodnight Sexi Lexi," she whispered, kissing me on the cheek and wrapping her arms around me.

"Yeah, goodnight," Elio said from behind her.

I tried to respond, but my "goodnight" came out as a smiling sigh. Those two had no idea how happy I was to have them warming my bed. The one "relationship" thing I did often miss was feeling someone's arms around me as I drifted into sleep. Natalie had remedied that. She was right there behind me.

Artists' Wives

I'd always had a thing for artists.

What was it about them? Not their looks—that's for sure. Didn't matter what a guy looked like, whether he was embarrassingly young or decrepitly old, big or small in any direction. If he was an artist, I was into him. From afar. I never had the confidence to actually approach a guy. I figured I wasn't an artist's type.

So my friend Luxanne hooked me up with some work as a life model. She'd been doing it for years and told me what to expect. *Nothing.*

"You hear all this bullshit about painters seducing naked girls on velvet sofas," she said. "Pure romanticism. Never happens."

And if it never happened to her, there was no way in hell it would happen for me. Luxanne was slim and blonde, undeniably desirable. I was pretty much the opposite of that.

I gave it a shot nonetheless, with my hopes sky-high. A private session, too—none of that posing for a class of students stuff. I stripped bare, I laid my naked self out, but Master Reinhardt didn't take the bait.

He was all business, all brushes and oils. I could see it in his eyes. No lust there.

And I felt pretty crappy about that, even though he was rather old and not what most women would call handsome. None of that mattered. He was an artist, and that made me all butterfly-bellied the whole time I was sitting for him.

Even though he was looking at me completely naked, I felt like he wasn't really seeing me at all. Maybe he was gay. I secretly hoped he was, just so this wouldn't be a case of yet another man gazing right past me.

Why was I invisible?

The great master set down his brush and looked me in the eye. Would he make a move now? My heart raced. *See me! Love me! Want me!*

No such luck.

"I have business to attend to." His voice was dark and rough, like gravel. It made me tingle all over, especially below my belly. "My wife Ethel will bring your luncheon. Please pardon my absence. I shall return post haste."

"Okay, sure." He'd already left the room by the time I said, "No problem."

I wasn't sure where to go, or if this wife of his was bringing lunch to me. Hell, I couldn't even remember where I'd put my clothes! I definitely wanted to get dressed before some old lady came in the room and spotted me in my birthday suit.

Too late.

A wheeled cart pushed the studio door open, squealing as it entered the room. Behind it stood a young Asian woman with long black hair tucked behind her ears. She had on a tight black T-shirt and frayed jogging pants covered in paint.

"Hey." She sounded uninspired, like she'd rather be any place but here. "Lunch."

There was a spring salad on the cart, with cherry tomatoes and little bocconcini balls alongside grilled chicken. It looked amazing. So did she. I didn't want to admit my attraction, even to myself, but I couldn't deny that tingle between my legs.

Artists...they did it for me every time.

Still, I felt jumpy and weird with this stranger seeing me naked.

"Sorry." Should I cover my boobs and my bush? No, she'd think I was an idiot. "Master Reinhardt said his wife was bringing me lunch."

She raised an eyebrow, seeming unamused in the extreme. "Okay."

"You're obviously an artist too." I didn't know why I was talking. I felt so stupid. "Do a lot of artists work out of the house?"

"A few." She shrugged. "Students use the extra studio space in exchange for household chores, a little cooking and cleaning. It's a pretty good deal."

Ahh, so this girl was an art student! My pussy pulsed as I looked at the globs of paint coating her clothes. What was it about artists? God, there was even paint on her bare arms. She was irresistible!

Stretching out on the sofa, I said, "I'm Tara."

"Okay."

She turned, and I was sure she would leave, but she didn't. She locked the door! I couldn't believe it. My belly did flip-flops as she inched between the master's canvas and the lunch cart, coming toward me.

"You're naked," she said.

I could hardly breathe. The look in her eyes, that dark lusty look, made me feel jittery and scared. I didn't know why.

"That's quite a bush." She was staring at my pussy.

I was so embarrassed I just wanted to die! "I'm sorry."

She laughed and shook her head. "No, I like it. I'm sick of shaved pussies. You don't see a nice thick pelt very often these days. Girls are so ashamed of their hair."

Something inside me clicked from no to yes, and I lifted my arms to show her I didn't shave there either.

"Wow." She nodded, and the look in her eyes was so ruthless I really didn't know what would happen next. My guess was she was about to jump on me, but she didn't. She just looked. *Stared*.

I let my arms fall at my sides. The words came out of nowhere: "Do you want me?"

Her eyebrow went up. "Do you want me to want you?"

"Yes." I'd never been so forward in all my life. "I want you to lick me."

"Where?" She was playing with me, teasing, taunting.

I was too turned on to play games. With two fingers, I spread my pussy lips to show her the glistening pink inside. I'd been wet all morning. "Here."

She smiled, a half-smile, like half of her was deliriously happy and the other half was aching with desire. That's how I felt, too. I would have begged if she weren't so willing.

When I opened my legs, setting one bare foot up on the sofa, she fell to her knees like my pussy was a force she just couldn't resist. I wanted to feel humiliated that this beautiful student had commented on my pubic hair, obviously comparing me mentally with all the other women she'd been with, but instead I felt strangely proud.

She stared straight into my pussy as I held my lips open for her. My heart clamped as I awaited her reaction. I felt hot and cold in pulses. Waves of heat and ice soared through my body.

"Please." I couldn't wait any longer. "Lick me."

I watched her full lips open and her pink tongue emerge, soft as velvet. Her black hair shone like oil streams against her washed-out cotton T-shirt. It felt like millennia as her mouth approached my pussy, like she was moving in slow motion. Maybe she was.

And then her tongue met my clit, and I felt it like a sizzling streak through my core. Throwing my head back, I whimpered, trying not to buck up and smack my wet pussy against her nose. It was hard to keep still. My body wanted to move, wanted to rock and writhe against her face. She had so much to give me—I could see it in her eyes.

When she dove at my pussy, I gasped, struggling to hold my lips open for her. Were my knuckles pummelling her nose? Did my pussy taste good? Was it sweet or was it musky, or could she taste only my juice? So much it was dripping down my ass crack, probably soaking Master Reinhardt's sofa. I'd have a lot of explaining to do when he came back.

But right now all I cared about was this sensation, her tongue lapping my clit in quick strokes. I'd never been licked by another woman. The sensation defied belief. She wasn't slow and steady, not at all. She attacked my cunt like she was running out of time, like she needed me to come right now.

I felt all the energy drain from my shoulders. My hands went numb. So did my toes. It all gravitated to my pussy.

My clit felt full and huge, big as a cock, and when she sucked it into her hot mouth I felt like she was giving me a blowjob. I'd never in my life felt so wildly aroused. She gave me everything. Her mouth was my pleasure.

"Oh God!" I couldn't keep quiet. It felt too good. "Yes, please! Suck my clit, suck it harder!"

She did! My God, I wouldn't have believed it was possible, but she somehow managed to suck my clit and my pussy lips into her mouth and devour them en masse.

I couldn't keep quiet and I couldn't keep still. I writhed against her face, still holding my outer lips open for her, trying desperately not to scratch her cheeks with my long fingernails.

"Fuck yeah!" I didn't usually swear like that, not even in bed, but the naughty words came streaming out beyond my control. "Fuck yeah, suck it, baby! Suck my fucking clit. That feels so fucking good you fucking slut!"

I'd never called anyone a slut in my life. I don't know where that came from, but it worked! She growled and shook her head side to side, putting a delicious strain on my clit. I was nothing but a big throbbing pussy being devoured by a beautiful stranger, and that was fine by me.

The edge was so close I could taste it. My climax was an ache pounding at the base of my pelvis, almost in my ass. It swelled each time she sucked and each time I swore, but I knew what would put me over the precipice. I'd been there before.

With my free hand, I pinched the closest nipple and lost all sense of time and place. My feet started kicking above the head between my legs. I knew I was hollering like a fiend, but all I could hear was the rush of my heartbeat, like an ocean in my ears.

My legs began to ache, and I wrapped them around the girl's black cotton back, forcing my pussy flush to her wet face. I couldn't stop myself. I thrust against her mouth, her chin, her cheeks, tracing my pussy juice all across her face until she was dripping with the stuff.

All at once, the pleasure was too much.

I tried to back away, but she kept eating me, kept sucking until I cried out, "Stop! Stop! Oh fuck, you have to stop!"

That's when I heard knocking on the studio door.

For a moment, everything buzzed. The world became too real.

Then I heard Master Reinhardt's voice. "Ethel? Ethel, would you let me inside?"

The girl between my legs glanced at the door, looking rather more nonchalant than I felt.

"Just a sec." Drawing away from my pussy, Ethel murmured, "I wish he'd stay out longer. I never get a turn."

I hadn't moved when she opened the door—I think I was in shock. My legs were still splayed, my pussy dripping juice all down the sofa. I was going to get fired for sure.

But Master Reinhardt simply looked from the food tray by the canvas to me on the sofa. As his wife slipped out the door, he picked up his brush and asked, "You didn't like your salad?"

"It...I...I don't know."

I'd always had a thing for artists.

Now I have a thing for artists' wives.

Chef's Kiss

H olly didn't care if everyone thought she was crazy—she was going to get more than just an autograph from Chef Burley.

She'd arrived hours before the book signing, thinking she'd be first in line. She should have known better. Every horny housewife in town was queued outside the yet-to-open restaurant, drooling for a taste of the sexy celebrity chef.

"I can't get enough of Chef Burley," said one woman in the line-up.

"I know what you mean," another chimed in. "Every time I watch his show, it gets me so worked up I pounce on my hubby. Poor guy doesn't know what hit him!"

Holly hugged Chef Burley's cookbook tight to her chest. As far as she knew, the sexy celebrity was single, just like her. Those women didn't know how lucky they were, having husbands to warm their beds. If they realized their good fortune, they wouldn't be hanging around out here, discussing all the dirty things they'd like to do with the chef.

When the line finally started to move, Holly's stomach dropped. No, she couldn't do this. Come face to face with the man whose presence, even on TV, made her ache with want? No. No way.

But she didn't turn around. She didn't leave. As the line moved forward, so did she, step by step, until an assistant asked her, "Who would you like your autograph made out to?"

"To Holly," she said.

Without another word, the austere assistant tore the cookbook from her arms.

She was still three side-steps away from Chef Burley, but if she leaned forward and looked down the table, she could see him. He was right there, in the flesh! They were breathing the same air. Unbelievable!

Holly bit her lip to keep herself from squealing. She always squealed when she watched his TV show—squealed, and throbbed, and wished for just a few minutes alone with him.

When Holly's turn came up, her knees nearly buckled. She'd worn a push-up bra, just for him. Bending forward, she let her low-cut blouse fall open. *For Chef's eyes only!*

Chef Burley looked up, and his eyes bulged. A playful smirk bled across his lips. "Have you been waiting long?"

Holly giggled like a schoolgirl. Oh, his accent! He was so sophisticated, so unlike the blockheads in this town. She wanted to grab his white chef's jacket, pull him across the table, and kiss him until he couldn't breathe.

Instead, Holly tittered and chewed her nail while Chef Burley scrawled his signature across the front page of his book. Every day on her way to work, she rehearsed what she'd say if she ever met him. Now he was right there, close enough to grab, and she didn't know what to do.

"Thanks for buying my book," Chef Burley said, looking her straight in the eye. Oh, those baby blues! They made her feel faint. "I hope you enjoy it, Sally."

She giggled and nodded as a second assistant handed back her copy of the cookbook. Their gazes lingered while she backed away. She was so besotted she just about walked into the drinks table.

Wait... had Chef Burley called her *Sally*?

Taking a glass of white wine, Holly sat at one of the tables and opened her book. Sure enough, the inscription was made out to *Sally*, not *Holly*. That assistant must have given Chef Burley the wrong name. She thought to go back, but she didn't want to make a fuss. She was embarrassed, even though the mistake wasn't hers.

The afternoon passed in a haze. Holly leaned her elbows against her lonely table and gazed meekly at the celebrity. He was even more striking in person. His blondish hair was styled haphazardly, his face clean shaven, his features somewhere between chiseled and boyish. She wanted to see his arms, his chest, his whole body, naked. He was right there, and yet worlds away.

"We're closing up now," one of the assistants said, interrupting her hardcore fantasy of showering with the chef. "Thanks for coming."

"Oh, but... sorry, I don't want to cause any trouble..."

"Hey, now." Chef Burley walked over, looking supremely concerned. "What's the trouble? Sally, was it?"

Holly couldn't believe he remembered her name... even if it was the wrong name. She told him about the mistake, and saw genuine concern in his face. He said he'd correct the error. If she gave him her address, he'd send her autographed copies of all his books.

Holly couldn't help herself. She sprung up from the chair and wrapped her arms around his neck, saying, "Thank you, Chef."

Once she'd pressed her body against his, she couldn't move. Her breast swelled against the solid plane of his chest. Her whole body felt full, warm and tingling. She just wanted him to... *take her*.

"I can finish up here," Chef Burley shouted to his staff. "Good job, everyone. You can be off now."

Holly tucked her head against the chef's shoulder while they left. She knew exactly what those people were thinking, and it wasn't complimentary. But, oh, the scent of Chef Burley's skin sent her to heaven. The smell of a clean man, mixed with cloves and hearty meats, made her want to lick him all over.

"Now, then," he said once the place had cleared out. "How do you like my new restaurant? It hasn't launched just yet."

"It's nice." Holly could feel his breath on her cheek, and it made her weak. "Chef, I love your show. Some of my friends say you're mean when you're helping other cooks, but I know it's your passion talking. You really care about people, even people you've just met."

"That's very true." He pressed his large hands into the small of her back, holding her against his big body. "I care about *you*, for instance."

Holly jerked her head back, feeling her cheeks flush. "You don't. You're only saying that."

"The world is full of liars," Chef Burley said, looking boldly into her eyes. "I'm not one of them."

Before she could say another word, his lips were on hers. He pressed his mouth firmly to her mouth while he ran one hand all the way up her back. It settled at the base of her head, warming her neck as it caught her hair. She was so stunned she didn't react, at first. When she felt his tongue prying open her teeth, she felt sixteen again—never been kissed.

62

Despite her innocent reluctance, Chef Burley's hot tongue found its way inside her mouth. This was high romance mixed with sheer heat. It was a fairy tale that wouldn't involve just a magic kiss—it would end with him tearing her clothes off and fucking her hard without leaving this gorgeous restaurant. She hoped the last person out had locked the front door.

Holly kissed the chef madly, climbing him like a tree. She should be ashamed of herself, but she wasn't. When would she ever get another opportunity like this?

"You're my fantasy," she panted while he kissed the length of her neck. "I watch you on TV and imagine you in my bed. I bet all the girls tell you that."

"I don't care about all the girls," he growled. "All I care about is *you*."

"You probably say that to everyone."

"I don't say that to anyone." Digging his fingers into her bottom, Chef Burley boosted Holly onto the table. "But believe what you will."

"Why me?" she asked.

Rather than answering, he ripped open her blouse. Holly shrieked as buttons flew across the dining room. Her bra was exposed, and her breasts swelled in the white lace cups.

Chef Burley looked her straight in the eye. She believed him when he said, "I don't know why, Holly. From the moment I saw you, I just... I don't know."

As he went back to his fevered exploration, her whole body ached for his mouth. She couldn't hold out any longer. Grabbing his coat with one hand, she said, "You don't need to explain it. Just show me... show me hard!"

He growled as she pulled him closer. When their mouths met for the second time, it was fireworks. His tongue whipped against hers, battling for supremacy. This was exactly how she'd imagined his kisses: hot, hard, like he was barely in control of his actions. There was something about the chef that inspired fear in her, and in everybody, because you never quite knew if he was about to crack.

Holly's stomach clenched as she worried again if the restaurant was locked. Pulling away from the chef's forceful mouth, she said, "Wait, what if someone walks in?"

He smirked. "Then they'll find me sucking your spectacular tits."

Before Holly could process what Chef Burley had said, he pulled her satin blouse down her shoulders. She reached behind her back and unclasped her bra, struggling out of both garments while the chef dove at her breasts.

"My God!" He traced his cheek across her chest. "You've got the most gorgeous pair I've ever seen."

"You're just saying that," Holly tittered.

Chef Burley's unseen stubble itched Holly's nipples in the most wonderful way. They hardened to pebbles, as if they could fight off the burn. They couldn't, of course. His stubble blazed against her flesh as he rolled both breasts around his charming face.

"You could do that all day!" Holly moaned as he flicked her nipples with his thumbs. His hands weren't as soft as she'd imagined, but she liked their roughness. "Will you suck them?"

Chef Burley glanced up at her, still toying with her tits. "I thought you said I could do *this* all day."

"It's torture," she whimpered, closing her eyes. "Oh god, Chef, I want to feel your hot mouth all over my body."

"Everywhere?"

"Yes!"

"Here?" His lips landed against her sweetly puckered nipple.

"Yes!"

Holly guessed someone with Chef Burley's intensity would suck her nipples violently, tearing into them, leaving her bloodied and sore. She was surprised by the deft care he showed. His skilled tongue bathed her breasts in warmth. She should have known he would savour her body like a fine *repas*.

"Everywhere," Holly whispered. "I want to feel your tongue *everywhere*, Chef."

"Mmm!"

He didn't shift from her nipples, and part of her didn't want him to. She'd never experienced such full pleasure. With every lick, she felt larger than life. Her body seemed to expand, like a helium balloon, floating to the rafters. She watched the scene from outside herself, and warm desire gushed between her legs.

"Please," she begged. "Oh please, Chef Burley, lick me lower."

"Lower?" He teased her, planting kisses down her stomach, nipping at the curve of flesh that gave way to her belly button. "You mean here?"

Holly giggled, pushing his head away. His hair surprised her. On TV, it looked like it would be crispy and full of gel, but it wasn't. It was soft—soft and blond and beautiful. She wove her fingers through it, then made a fist. She expected him to wince, but he didn't. He only looked up at her, his eyes burning with desire. They seemed to say, "Don't go there unless you mean it."

But Holly was serious as hell.

"Lick me, Chef."

As their violent stares mingled, Holly wondered just who was in control, here. She got the sense, from his TV presence, that Chef Burley would never do anything he didn't want to.

Staring him down, she asked, "Do you like the taste of pussy, Chef?"

His eyes blazed, like the question made him angry. For a moment, Holly cringed. She had no idea what this man was capable of.

Chef Burley grabbed her thighs and spread them so wide her muscles ached. When her feet found chairs to rest on, she planted her heels in the seats. Her short leather skirt had ridden up, revealing the white lace thong that matched the bra she'd launched across the room. He seemed to like it, if the raw hunger in his eye was anything to go on.

"Eat me." It wasn't like Holly to act so slutty, but Chef Burley brought out her inner vixen. "Plant your face between my legs, Chef. I want to come on your tongue."

He looked up at her, seemingly in awe. Maybe he liked hearing the dirty talk as much as she liked saying it.

"What are you waiting for?" Holly lifted her ass off the table, just enough for the chef to push her skirt up past her hips. "You want my pussy? It's right here."

Chef Burley snarled like a white wolf, sending a shiver down Holly's spine. She felt like a rabbit, tempting the unrestrained canine, knowing from his ice blue eyes that he wanted to consume her.

"Go on," she ordered, hearing her voice echo through the rafters. "Eat me."

He dove between her legs, biting her cunt through the lace of her thong. She cried out because, at first, she wasn't sure if it hurt or felt orgasmically good. His teeth dug into her pussy lips. His mouth soaked the slick gusset of her underwear. If he'd looked wolfish before, now he seemed barely human. She kept waiting for him to rip off his kitchen garb and transform into some kind of half-man, half-wolf. The idea would have made her laugh if she hadn't been so turned on.

"Lick my pussy. Lick my *skin*!"

His teeth pressed her swollen lips against her clit, arousing spikes of pleasure she couldn't tamp down. No one had ever eaten her like this before. It was positively savage! He was an animal, devouring her flesh with no regard for anything but raw sensation.

Reaching between her legs, Holly pulled her thong to the side, exposing her naked pussy. She'd shaved bare, just for him, on the off-chance she worked up the nerve to seduce him. Now that it was happening, she couldn't believe it was real. Chef Burley, the sexy celebrity every woman in town lusted after, was licking her smooth, wet pussy with a tongue so soft and huge it felt like a pink velvet pillow.

"Yes, Chef!" Holly's fist tightened in his hair while he worked tirelessly between her legs. "Lick my sweet clit. It's all fat and hot and aching, just for you."

"Your pussy is mine!"

She never thought this would happen. Not in a million years.

"Yes!" Holly lifted her ass off the table, feeding him hot pussy. "Suck it! Make me come hard."

Pussy juice dripped down the chef's chin. His face gleamed as he looked at her, an expression somewhere between ferocity and petulance.

Holly's muscles shook as she held her body aloft. She needed him to grab her ass, support it, and then dive in and eat her like a watermelon.

Chef Burley's calloused hands cradled her silky smooth cheeks. Her folds spread, like they had a life of their own, beckoning his mouth. When his tongue flattened against her clit, a sizzle passed through her body. She writhed against his face, feeling the meat of his tongue lapping her heat.

Holly watched him, beyond the quivering swell of her breasts. He seemed close to ecstasy just licking her cunt, but Holly knew what would put her over the edge. "Suck my clit."

Growling unrepentantly, Chef Burley plunged deeper between her legs. Driving hard, he drew her bud between his lips and sucked it the way he'd sucked her nipples. Oh, if only she could reach up and squeeze her tits right now, but both hands were pressed firmly against the table.

A bolt of hot pleasure raced through Holly's core, swirling around the spot that housed her orgasms. She was so close she could taste it. She had everything she'd ever wanted, and still she wanted more!

"Yes! Make me come, Chef." Holly's clit felt huge as she fucked his mouth, rubbing her wet pussy against his glistening lips. She bucked uncontrollably. It should have embarrassed her, the way her tits swung and her hips jerked, but she didn't stop. "Yes, please! Yes!"

She wasn't in control of her body anymore. Her need for climax took the reigns, driving her up, up, and over. Grinding her pussy against the chef's mouth, she released a string of words she didn't know she knew. Holly was a dirty girl now. She was every bit as dirty as the chef. Maybe even dirtier.

Holly's legs trembled. Her arms did, too. Her clit throbbed so hot and hard she couldn't bear any more pleasure. She couldn't even hold herself upright. Collapsing on the table, she buried the Chef's hands and he grunted in pain.

"Oh god, I'm sorry!" Holly hiked her bum off the table so he could retrieve his hands. "Did I hurt you, Chef?"

"I'm perfectly fine." His lips were bright pink, as swollen as her pussy, and glistening with the same wetness. Her juices actually dripped from his chin as he rose from the floor. "Come with me. I want to show you something in the kitchen."

She hoped that "something" was his cock, and without thinking, she said so!

Chef Burley smirked. "My, my, dear Holly. You are insatiable, aren't you?"

"Not usually," she confessed. "It's you, Chef. Seriously. There's something about you that makes my pussy throb and my mouth want to work overtime." She couldn't believe she'd just said that.

"You flatter me," Chef Burley said, with sincere politeness. He grabbed a napkin from the next table and wiped his face.

"It's true. You make me horny as hell. I don't usually say things like that, but there's no other way to describe it."

He offered a frisky grin, and then winked. "I know the feeling."

"I bet you get horny every time you look in the mirror!"

Chef Burley rolled his eyes. Taking her naked shoulders in his hands, he gave her a playful shake. "I'm talking about you, daft girl! Do you seriously think I travel around the world fucking strange women?"

"Probably." Holly looked away.

"Holly!" There was a smile in his voice, but she could tell that he was serious. "My eyes are up here, Holly."

Her gaze shot from his crotch to his steel eyes, and her cheeks burned. "Sorry, Chef."

"I'm not one of those men, Holly." He clutched her shoulders so tightly that Holly worried what was next. "I'm not like that."

"You just seem like you would be…"

Chef Burley released his hold on her and backed away. Was he angry? He was so hard to read. Why couldn't he scream at her, and swear, like he did on TV?

When he just stared at her with those piercing blue eyes, Holly's irritation peaked. "Well, what do you expect me to think when every woman in the world wants you in her bed?"

"What do I care what *every woman in the world* wants?" Chef Burley shot back. "I'm sure every man in town wants to bed you, but I assume that doesn't mean you've surrendered yourself to them all."

Holly's heart beat faster. She tried to feel upset, but all she could hear was his compliment. The chef found her attractive, though she certainly wasn't.

"Or am I wrong?" Chef Burley muttered when Holly didn't respond.

He didn't wait for an answer before storming into the kitchen. Had he just accused her of being a tramp? Her stomach dropped, but her legs found their prowess.

Slipping from the table, Holly stormed across the dining room, totally unashamed even though she was mostly naked.

Kicking open the door with her fierce heels, Holly howled, "How dare you?"

The kitchen was huge, full of gleaming, brand new steel. Chef Burley leaned against a six-burner range like the cat that had eaten the canary. "How dare I what?"

"Call me a slut," Holly shot back. "I don't sleep around. That, out there? That was the first time I've been with a man in... well, I don't need to tell you how long, but... it's been a while, okay? I'm not a slut."

"Neither am I," the chef replied, with a simple shrug.

That wasn't at all the response Holly had expected. She thought he'd yell and scream and start smashing dishes. But he'd said his piece, and he'd made his point. Now, he looked at her so disarmingly she hardly knew what to say.

Stepping forward, Holly placed her small purse on the stainless steel island. She unzipped it slowly, feeling his gaze warming her fingers as she pulled out a condom. "I don't know why I brought this. I really didn't think we'd... you know..."

"But you hoped?"

"Well, obviously." Holly bit her lip. She couldn't look at him as she slid the condom packet across the gleaming steel surface.

He took it from her, touching his fingers to hers, and she felt strange vibrations flowing through her hand.

"Holly?"

She looked into his face, and her pussy pulsed like it had its own heartbeat. He was *sooo* handsome...

"What's the most important component of a relationship?"

"Trust," she replied. She didn't even have to think about it.

"Trust," he said, nodding. "Come here, my dear."

"Where?" she asked, though the answer was obvious.

"Right here. Come close."

She walked around the island, pulling her skirt down, which was really rather silly when her breasts were still bare. She let him curl his big body around hers. Pressing his chest against her back, he pushed her hips forward until they met the oven door. Her heart raged and her pussy pulsed as he breathed in her ear.

"Do you trust me?" he asked.

She swallowed hard. "I... I... guess so?"

Grasping her wrist, he held her open hand firmly over one of the spider burners. "Do you trust me?"

Holly's throat ran dry. "What are you doing?"

"You've no reason to trust me. We've only just met."

She didn't struggle, because she wasn't sure how he'd react. "Please don't hurt me."

"I won't," he said. "You have my word. But that's the issue, Holly—do you trust my word?"

Holly gazed at her hand. It wasn't shaking, and that surprised her. "I do trust you. I don't know why. You're right—I have no reason to. We've only just met."

Chef Burley held her wrist firmly, yes, but there was nothing preventing her from pulling away, or at least trying. She didn't struggle against him. She didn't want to... until his other hand made a play for the knob.

Holly tried to yank her hand away, but the chef's grip tightened around her wrist. He pressed her palm down until it met cold black metal. Her heart beat a mile a minute.

"You've no cause to trust me," he said as he turned the stove on.

Clamping her eyes shut, Holly listened with horror for the hiss of gas, the click of ignition, and the whoosh of a blue flame. She prepared herself to be burned.

But nothing happened. No hiss, no click, no whoosh. Only Chef Burley's big hand around her small wrist as her palm sweated against the cold metal.

"The gas line won't be hooked up until next week." His breath scorched her ear. He let go of her wrist. "No chance the fire would light."

"I should have trusted you," she said, her throat dry as cotton.

"No, Holly. People think they know me because they've seen me on television. You don't *know* me—not yet. Trust must be earned. It takes time."

"You're right." And, because he was right, a seed of doubt sprouted in Holly's mind. "Do *you* trust *me?*"

His breath came on hot and slow. When she pressed back against him she felt his erection like a steel rod against her backside. If it wasn't for the huge stainless steel appliance in front of her, she'd have fallen to the ground for sure. She felt dizzy with lust as his hands rode her sides.

Finding Holly's breasts and crushing them together, Chef Burley pressed hot kisses into her neck. His cock rode slowly up her skirt, and she wished to god she could feel his hugeness inside her pussy. She was so wet for him. She wanted him now.

"Fuck me," she begged. "God, I need it."

"So do I, Holly." His voice sounded tortured by lust.

"Open your shirt." She wanted to feel his hard chest against her back while he fucked her. She saw him shirtless on TV once, and it turned her on so powerfully that she almost went crazy.

She watched over her shoulder as Chef Burley tore out of his white chef's jacket. Under that, he wore a white T-shirt. He ripped that off, too. His chest was clean, hairless, and every bit as chiseled as his jaw. Holly tried to speak, but she couldn't. Her body was just a pulsing pool of lust. Arousal had taken over. She was speechless.

Holly licked her lips as Chef Burley shed his pants. He had on dark blue jockeys, but he took those off, too. His cock sprang toward her, spanking her ass. She couldn't wait to feel his hot cock against her skin. She wanted it to burn her, brand her, so she would never forget this day.

Though, how could she possibly forget? This wasn't just some guy—this was the notorious Chef Burley. He was a celebrity and he wanted her!

Tearing open the condom packet, Chef Burley fitted the latex around his dick. Holly couldn't stop watching. The condom hugged his cock tight, and she wondered if she should have bought a larger variety.

"My god, the size of that thing!" Holly pulled up her skirt. "It'll never fit. Never in a million years."

"But I gather you're willing to give it a go." Chef Burley eyed her thong as she pushed it down her thighs.

"Well, sure." Holly winked over her shoulder. "Never know unless you try."

Chef Burley's sheathed cock kissed her ass cheek while he took hold of her wrists. She had to admit, she liked the way he gripped her and pressed her body down on the range. His chest pushed against her back, driving her down until the mean metal burners cradled her breasts.

"What are you doing?"

"What am I doing?" Chef Burley teased her with laughter. "Have you never made love in a kitchen?"

"Not like this!" Holly gasped as the chef's celebrity cock tickled her pussy lips. "Not ever, actually. That's the honest truth."

"Ah, so this will be a first for you?" The chef slapped her with his erection, igniting sparks in her clit. "First time in a kitchen?"

"Yeah." Holly struggled to laugh. Everything seemed dead serious when she was this aroused, like the world might crumble at her feet. "Please, no more teasing. You're killing me."

"I hardly think so." He traced his cockhead up her sopping pussy, navigating the folds of her lips, ending squarely on her asshole. When she clenched, he laughed.

"Oh god."

"Don't panic." Chef Burley retreated to her pussy. "I'm only teasing you."

"I can't take it." Holly set her cheek against the range. The dark metal felt cool as it pressed into her blazing skin. Cool, and rough. "Fuck me. Please just fuck me. I've wanted you for ages."

"Have you?" His cockhead found her wetness, filling it up, mushrooming inside. "Your pussy's certainly ready for me."

Holly opened her legs a little wider, feeling her thong digging into her thighs. "My pussy's always ready for you, Chef."

"Always?" He slid his cock deeper into her cunt.

He was huge, but she was ready. "Always."

Chef Burley lunged forward, bottoming out in her pussy, driving her breasts deeper into the spider burners. It was a little like medieval torture, as far as Holly was concerned. But in a good way.

"So, if I happened to be passing by the pretty little house I imagine you living in—" Chef Burley pulled back and then thrust forward, burying himself balls-deep in her cunt. "—when you come to the door, your pussy will be wet and ready for me?"

"My pussy will smell you coming, Chef." Holly heaved into the saddle of his hips, giving herself completely. "Every time you think about me, my pussy will tingle, my clit will throb, and I'll know you want to fuck me as bad as I want to fuck you."

"Mmm..." He gripped her hips and drove into her wetness. "I can't believe how wet you are."

"After eating my pussy, you still can't believe it?" Holly closed her eyes and pictured Chef Burley's chin dripping with juice. That image turned her on so intensely her pussy clamped down on his dick. "Oh god!"

"What are you doing to me, Holly?" Chef Burley fell against her back, his slick chest coating her skin with a sweet smear of sweat. "Fuck, I can't even think!"

As his ferocious fucking crushed her against the spider burners, Holly bore his weight gladly. He covered every inch of her skin, like a sauce. His breath was hot on her ear as he panted and moaned. Holly's noises were higher-pitched, but equally uncontrolled.

"Fuck me! Fuck me! Fuck me *hard*!"

With the racket they were making, she wouldn't be surprised if someone burst into the restaurant to make sure she wasn't being murdered.

"I want you to come, Holly."

"I will," she cried, hugging his erection with her tight pussy muscles. "God, I'm gonna come so hard. I'm gonna come all over your cock!"

"Do it."

He fucked her so rapidly she had to shield her head with her hands. His force was driving her against the range. Her tits would definitely be bruised from the spider burners, but that was fine. No one else would see them, and they'd remind her of the chef.

"Come for me, Holly."

"You first." She groaned as he pounded her cunt. "God, I want to see it."

Her flesh throbbed as he fucked her, and she knew she couldn't hold back. Some women said it was impossible to come just from a good fuck, but Holly knew the truth: everyone was different. She loved a good clit massage, and she'd had that earlier when the chef ate her pussy, but on rare occasions, when the fucking was intense and the cock was nice and huge, she could come without getting her clit stroked at all.

"Fuck!" Holly tightened every muscle in her body. Her head spun like a top. "You bastard! God, you're making me come! You're making me come so fucking hard!"

Like she needed to tell him! It was pretty obvious from the way her pussy clamped on his dick, from the way her thighs shook and her fingers clenched. She arched and screamed, milking his cock, trying to gauge from his appeals whether he was coming.

"I want to see!" she cried as he pressed harder against her backside. "Let me see!"

She didn't really expect him to pull out, but he did, so fast her pussy ached. She could never get enough.

Tearing off his condom, Chef Burley asked, "Is this want you want?"

His big hand encircled his shaft tightly. Leaning back against the stainless steel island, he jerked himself off so hard Holly's pussy clenched just watching him. His fist strangled his cock, gliding its length in raw, stilted motions.

A gush of saliva filled Holly's mouth. If she wasn't careful, she'd be drooling all over him. That's when the gift baskets at the far end of the island caught her eye. They must have been presents from well-wishers, congratulating the chef on his new book, or his new restaurant. Holly didn't take the time to read the cards. She just pulled out a bottle of olive oil, popped the cork, and poured it down Chef Burley's perfect chest.

"Holly!" the chef cried, laughing. "Do you know how much a bottle of that oil runs?"

"I have absolutely no idea." She set it down and ran her hands along his front, feeling every ridge of his belly, feeling the pink points of his hard nipples.

"Well over a hundred dollars, I'd say."

Holly's jaw dropped as the oil made its way to Chef Burley's pubic hair. "Then I'd better not waste any!"

Throwing herself at the chef, Holly licked him all over. The olive oil had a light virgin taste and texture. She'd never had anything like it—you could drink the stuff like wine!

Falling to her knees, Holly wrapped her oily hands around Chef Burley's expanding cock. They cradled his dick as she inched forward, taking just his tip inside her mouth.

Chef Burley threw his head back and moaned as Holly shifted his hands aside, taking more of his cock in her mouth. He was huge, but she didn't care.

This hundred-dollar olive oil was well worth the price. She sucked every drop from his beautiful shaft, then licked his balls, searching for more.

He gasped. "Isn't that something?"

She assumed he meant the oil. "Mmm... oh Chef, it's so good!"

"*You're* so good!" He toyed with her hair, tossing it over her shoulders. "The mouth on you, Holly! I've never felt anything like it. I want you to suck me forever."

"Anything!" She licked him, searching for more golden oil. "Anything for you, Chef!"

Holly swallowed his cock as he wrapped his hands around her head, fucking her face. She gagged and pushed back, wrapping her fists around the base of his shaft. His measured pace showed he didn't want to hurt her, but he just as obviously wanted to come.

Unzipping her skirt, Holly undressed completely before arching forward. She grabbed the olive oil and poured it across her breasts. Chef Burley watched in awe as she massaged the gorgeous oil into her skin. It dripped down her belly as she wrapped her tits around his dick. With her pussy lips bare, the oil kissed her clit.

Chef Burley released an animal growl.

"You like my tits, huh?"

"God, do I ever!"

She steadied herself, which was no easy task in heels, and fucked his surging dick with her breasts. They looked beautiful like this, all oiled and shining in the light from the sunroof. Holly and the chef both watched in awe as his cockhead popped between her breasts.

Chef Burley's hands met hers and, together, they cradled her tits around his throbbing cock. "I'm going to come again if you keep this up."

"I sure hope so!" Holly smirked. She loved the way it felt when his cock reamed her tits. It was like a breast massage, complete with hot oil. His thumbs found her nipples and he flicked them while he fucked her.

"God, that feels good!" Holly forced her tits against the chef's pelvis, making him moan.

His cockhead glistened every time it peeked out between her tits. She couldn't resist. Bending forward, she licked his tip. He ran his hands through her hair, thrusting into her cleavage, looking for her mouth but not finding it.

Her tongue put him over the edge. Hot cream splashed across her neck, and then down her chest. She trapped his cock between her tits as he pumped cum against her breasts.

Holly watched in awe while the chef spilled his seed on her skin. She'd never thought of ejaculate as beautiful before but, sprayed across her skin, it looked like art. If only she'd remembered her camera!

"Fuck, I can't take anymore." Chef Burley pulled his spent cock from between her breasts, giggling somewhat. "It's so sensitive that it starts to tickle."

"Does it?" Holly smiled. "I never knew that."

The chef looked her up and down. His eyes followed her shapely legs down to her black heels, then back up to her breasts. She looked a mess, and she loved it. Her heart felt huge and hot. So did her clit, for that matter.

"All this kitchen needs is a shower." Chef Burley leaned against the island as he scanned the room. "Oh, of course! Holly, stand over that grate."

There was a drain in the floor, and Holly went to it, though her knees threatened to buckle with every step. Chef Burley pulled the hose out from the sink and turned the water on, casting a warm spray across her chest.

Holly shrieked, though she really should have seen it coming. Of all the things she'd never expected to do in a kitchen... well, this was certainly one of them.

Chef Burley shifted closer to her, bringing the nozzle with him. He cast the spray over both their bodies, like watering a garden. The nurturing image made Holly smile. She traced her hands all over his body, and he tittered when she reached his cock. Chef Burley was actually kind of adorable. That side of him was never broadcast on TV—his childlike side, his impish side. Holly was glad to see a piece of him most people never would.

Though the water was warm, the cool air of the kitchen drew Holly's nipples into tight buds. Her shoes were getting wet, but in that moment she couldn't have cared less. She had everything she'd ever wanted. How had this happened?

"Towels, towels, towels..." Chef Burley turned off the water and searched for something passable. There were tea towels in one of his gift baskets, and he pulled them out, laughing. "Think this'll do?"

Holly chuckled as he dried her off. It was so telling, the way a man touched a woman in moments like these. Chef Burley's large hands guided the towel against her soft skin. He was forceful, but he wasn't rough.

They were both rather slick from the olive oil, but that made Holly feel wonderfully luxurious. With any other man, at any other time, she'd have been bashful, even mortified, standing naked in an industrial kitchen. Christ, she didn't even know if the door to this restaurant was locked.

"I would offer to cook you a little something, but, as you know—"

"The gas isn't hooked up," Holly finished. A niggling doubt twirled in her belly. He was going to ask her to leave, wasn't he?

"Oh, before I forget..." Chef Burley slipped his pants on and found a pen and paper. "Will you write down your address for me? I'll have my publicist send you a signed replacement copy of my book. In fact, I'll have her throw in some DVDs of the show, and whatever else is lying around her office."

Tears welled in Holly's eyes. She felt stupid and used. She vowed not to cry. "Are you paying me off? With DVDs?"

Chef Burley appeared shocked. "What? Are you bonkers, Holly? You think I'm going to love you and leave you?"

She tried to keep it together, but tears cascaded down her cheeks. "I'm sorry. I don't know why I'm crying."

"Sure you do." The chef set his pen and paper down on the island and wrapped his arms around Holly. His chest was still bare, and it warmed her cold nipples, sending waves of bliss through her naked body. "You think I've had my fill and now it's on to the next girl?"

Holly nodded against his shoulder. "You're a celebrity. Everyone wants you."

"Yes, but I don't want *everyone*." Chef Burley rocked her like a baby. "I knew you didn't believe me when I said it before. Seducing beautiful young women isn't part of my daily routine."

A blush spread across Holly's cheeks. "I'm sorry."

"You still don't believe me," he said, holding her close. "But we'll work on that."

Holly leaned back and looked into the chef's eyes. They were sky blue, like a sunny afternoon. "Work on it. How?"

"Tonight, for instance." He slid his hands down her arms and grasped her hands. "I finally have an evening free of publicity, investors, cameras. I'd planned on watching television in my hotel room, and maybe devouring an entire bag of kettle chips."

Holly laughed. "Wow, that's classy."

With a smirk, the chef said, "Now that you're in the picture, perhaps we could check out the competition, see what the other dining establishments in town have to offer. Get to know each other a little better?"

Holly's cheeks must have been beet red. She couldn't believe this was happening. "Sure. I'd love to. As long as... well, you're not going to be mean to the owners if the food isn't up to snuff, are you?"

"I assure you, my attention will be devoted to you and you alone." He winked. "Unless our meals are absolutely atrocious."

"Maybe we could just grab some fish and chips on the boardwalk and take a stroll along the beach?"

Chef Burley smiled like he couldn't be more pleased. "That sounds perfect."

They stood together, gazing into each other's eyes like a couple of lovesick teenagers. If anyone had told Holly she'd end her afternoon naked in a kitchen with her favourite celebrity chef, she'd have called them crazy. And this wasn't the end. There was more to come. Crazy!

"Now, then." Chef Burley squeezed Holly's hands, and then let go. "Let's see if we can't find your clothes."

Someone My Own Age

For as long as I can remember, my parents and I have spent two weeks every summer at my aunt and uncle's cottage in the Kawarthas. The one thing I forget every year is how much of a strain it is, being cooped up for all that time with a bunch of adults. It's a funny thing to say at age twenty seven, but living in close quarters with four people in their sixties makes me feel like I'm five years old again. Living alone, I'm not used to answering to anyone.

After a week and a half of doing just about everything alongside my mom, dad, aunt, and uncle, I needed some space. I threw a bit of change in my pocket, called out to my parents that I was taking a walk—alone—and began the long hike to the payphone by the marina. Too much family time left me with an itch in need of scratching, and I knew a guy who was an excellent scratcher... even by phone.

The walk itself calmed me down, which was good preparation for the surprise I received when I got to the payphone. The damn thing only accepted credit cards and phone cards, neither of which I had on me. It didn't take change at all.

As I stood there wondering if my phone sex dude would accept the charges for a collect call, three people walked by: one elderly man, one elderly woman, and a beautiful boy. A grown-up boy, I should say. A boy who looked a bit younger than me, but close enough to consider him my own age.

I watched him in awe. He had a mess of dark curls and a firm body under a T-shirt and shorts. I was staring, I admit. Ogling, even. I couldn't help it. I'd been cooped up too long. If I couldn't get in touch with my phone scratcher, why not get scratched in person?

When he looked over at me, I met his gaze straight on. I smiled. He smiled. I said, "Hi," but he looked down at the gravel, then up at the old woman. Were they together? No way. She could be his grandmother.

They went into the marina shop together, but the boy came out alone with a popsicle he promptly broke in half. Banana. When he held out half for me, I laughed and said, "Thank you." Now I really felt like I was five years old.

Over banana-flavoured ice, a conversation blossomed. Every thought we'd kept to ourselves in the past week and a half came spilling out. His name was Liam and he was staying with his grandparents who'd just gone out in the boat. He'd planned to go with them until he saw me checking him out. We were both desperate for contact with someone—anyone—under age sixty.

"I guess if your grandparents are out, that means you've got a cottage to yourself," I said, flirting shamelessly.

"For a couple minutes, yeah," he replied.

That was good enough for me. Liam was cute and young and I knew I would keel over if I didn't kiss him soon. Like teenagers, we snuck back to his cottage. It was just a small cabin, but I was more interested in Liam.

I nearly attacked him with a kiss. He led me to his tiny bedroom where I tore off my shirt and bra. No hiding what I was after. I set his hands on my breasts so he could feel me up while we kissed. The heat of his palms on my tits felt incredible. That's one sensation that's impossible to reproduce: a guy's hands squeezing and moulding my breasts while he thrust his tongue in my mouth.

When he bent forward to lick my nipples, I nearly came on the spot. I felt like a sixteen-year-old, but I didn't care. He took my tits in his hot mouth and I had to stifle a moan. Like a pro, I unzipped his shorts and pulled out his cock. I wanted it in my hands, to stroke and caress. He rubbed me through my jeans, pinpointing my erect clit with no trouble at all.

Wrapping my hand around his erection, I sat on my knees while I pumped his shaft. He pulled me to him and placed his head on my shoulder, stroking my pussy, back and forth in a quick motion, then in slow circles. I would have fucked him then and there if either of us had brought condoms.

His fingers brought me to climax in less than three minutes, and he cried out as I traced precum around his cockhead. I touched him gently at the tip, then harder around the shaft. I got rough with his cock, pushing his face on my tits while he worked his fingers against my denim pussy. He stroked, I stroked, he sucked, and I considered doing the same until my hand job got the better of him. He panted and whined like a puppy, then yelped as he came in hot spurts.

Supremely self-satisfied, I put on my bra and my tank top as Liam fell back on his bed mouthing, "Wow" again and again. It was such a hormone driven, wild, teenaged thing for a pair of adults to do. We laughed about our youthful desperation, making no promises or future plans. It was just something that happened, but it put a huge smile on my face as I made my way back to the family cottage.

Max Doesn't Steal (Anymore)

Max used to steal women's underwear, but he doesn't do that anymore. The first pair of panties he stole belonged to his sister. Max doesn't like to think about that, because he was reprimanded so sorely when his mother caught him.

"Those are for girls!" she'd howled as she walloped his bottom. "For girls, not for boys!"

After that, he started stealing off neighbourhood clotheslines. The whole town buzzed with rumours of a pervert who stole little girls' underpants. Max was sure his mother knew it was him, just an innocent little boy, but she never gave him up. She was probably too humiliated by his antics.

As an adult, Max began stealing from girlfriends. He'd take a pair, a clean pair, just one, from a woman's dresser drawer. He'd take it home and squirrel it away until the compulsion came on strong. Then, he'd slip them on and, ooh, they'd pinch. They were so tight around his thighs, cradling his cock, barely concealing it. He'd snap the elastics around the waist. They'd be shot in no time.

But he never stole from stores. Never. Not even once.

He thought about it, sure. He thought about it every time he bought batteries or washer fluid from the discount department store. It would be easy enough to shove a pair of panties down the front of his pants and walk out with them.

No, he never could. The thought loomed too large, of being caught, of being punished, banned, called a pervert. It was easier to just break down and buy a pair. Cashiers at those big faceless stores didn't care what you bought. They could be a gift for a wife or a girlfriend. In fact, Max opted for a fancy lace pair that first time, to give the impression the panties were a gift.

Walking into a specialty lingerie store? Well, that was a different story. He couldn't do it in his hometown. He thought about it a lot. The idea of going in there and being surrounded by all those panties, so many panties, oh god all the silk and satin and cotton and lace... he shuddered with excitement.

When he was travelling on business, freedom took hold. He strolled by a boutique store on his day off, and couldn't believe his eyes: a lingerie store for plus-sized women! He'd never imagined there could be such a place, but there it was, full of undies that wouldn't pinch his thighs.

A bell jingled over the door, which was the last thing Max needed. He didn't want to draw attention to himself. Why couldn't he just be invisible for a little while?

Thank goodness there was no one in the store but a pretty sales associate with frizzy brown hair. She smiled so big Max considered running away, but she shot across the shop and locked the door. Max watched her flip the latch and apologized, though he didn't know why. She laughed—oh, that smile!—and took his arm, guiding him around the store.

"I'm looking for a gift," Max stammered. "A gift. For my wife. A gift."

"Ahh," she said, but he could see in her eyes that she didn't believe him.

"Why did you lock the door?" he asked.

"Because you're here," she said, and then tossed her hair to one side and laughed again. "Every customer is my only customer."

"Good policy." He nodded, though he felt unsettled by the ardour of her joy and the heat of her body next to his. "I'm shopping for a gift."

Her smile was huge. "Yes, you mentioned that."

She guided him around the boutique, picking panties off the rack and slowly brushing the fabric along the back of his hand. She owned the store, she told him, and that explained why she was so knowledgeable about every single product. Her name was Andrea. He'd have guessed she was a Jessica, but no. Andrea.

"Do you need a bra?" she asked.

"No." He shook his head ardently. "Just panties."

Oh, that knowing smile. She could read him like a book, which was really humiliating in one sense... but actually kind of comforting in another. Andrea had locked the door. She trusted him. He wasn't a pervert, not to her.

"These," Andrea said and plucked a slinky pair of panties off one of those teeny-tiny hangers. She smiled as she told him, "There's a fitting room in the back."

No sense trying to convince her of his lie. He let her escort him to the booths at the back. They didn't have doors, just thick velvet drapes. She opened one, ushering him inside.

"I'll be just here if you need anything," she said and left Max alone.

No doors, no locks. Just Max behind a velvet curtain with a silky pair of panties. He could feel Andrea breathing out there. She was listening as he shuffled out of his pants and into the little mauve undies.

"How's the fit?" she asked. "Did I pick a good size?"

"Yeah." They cupped his bulge so perfectly he shuddered.

"Open up. Let me see."

Max froze, picturing those eyes, those curious, caring, honourable eyes. For anyone else he'd have said no. But Andrea was a perfect stranger. Perfect.

He opened the curtain and was greeted by a pleasant smile. Andrea glanced down at the mauve panties and nodded. "Very nice."

"Thank you."

Her eyes were all it took to get him hard—her eyes and the panties she'd given him to try on. She stepped closer and asked, "Do you mind?"

"Mind...?"

"If I..." She moved a tentative hand forward, and then grabbed him boldly. He arched and took two steps back, colliding with the wall.

She followed him inside, led by the hard cock she would not release. Max was a dog on a leash, and Andrea his benevolent master. She would give him what he needed.

"Do you mind terribly?" she asked, stroking his erection over the silky underwear. "I can stop, of course, if you really want me to."

"No." The word was out before he could catch it. "No, that's fine. This is fine."

She smiled and her throat made a satisfied "hmm" sound, which built his arousal even higher.

The elastic waist was strong enough to keep his dick from escaping, but he was so hard his erection struggled this way and that, trying to find a way out.

"Feels good, doesn't it?" Her palm smoothed down the length of his shaft, pressing the silky fabric against his skin. He drank up the sensation, the smoothness of the panties and firmness of her pressure. Up and down, she rubbed his cock, concentrating on the centre of his shaft rather than the extremities of his tip or his balls.

"You're close, aren't you?" she asked, and Max nodded vigorously. She seemed so pleased with herself, like she got off on the power of understanding.

"Would you stroke the head?" Max begged. He closed his eyes, unable to meet the gaze of this woman who was so eager to please him. "And my balls, too. Would you squeeze my balls?"

And she did! She did it all, pressing her palm to his cockhead and cupping his nut sack through his panties. Oh, his legs almost failed him. His knees were jelly. He couldn't take much more of this, this terrible pleasure.

Max just about fainted under the heavy knowledge that the woman getting him off was a complete stranger. He had no idea why she was doing this. What was in it for her?

Then he opened his eyes and saw her enjoyment, and her loving warmth flowed through him, from her hand to his dick to his heart.

"Thank you," Max said, though his throat was tight and the sound barely audible. "Oh god, thank you!"

Andrea rubbed Max up and down. She clenched her glorious fingers around his balls, and that was it. That combination of hard and fast put him over the edge and he yelped as his cum flowed, filling the mauve panties with heat and cream.

"Yes," Andrea whispered, like she could feel it too. "Yes, just like that. Just like that."

His cum soared in endless streams, soaking the silky fabric. He could tell when the wetness of it met Andrea's skin, because she purred like a kitten. She had lovely lips—pink and full. She had makeup on, but not too much, and Max liked that. He'd never been big on cosmetics, or even flashy clothes. Panties, he liked—something hidden, something private. Something pretty.

And he'd just ruined these ones.

"I'll buy them, of course." He felt awkward looking at her. "I'm sorry."

"Don't be." Andrea sniffed her palm, where his seed had soaked through the panties, and very deliberately, very slowly, she extended her tongue. Max watched in rapture as she licked the trace of cum from her flesh. He nearly passed out at the sight.

She wouldn't let him pay for the mauve panties. She wouldn't even let him wear them back to his hotel, all gooey and wet as they were. Instead, she gave him a fresh pair of panties and wouldn't let him pay for those either, no matter how much he insisted.

When Andrea unlocked the door, Max had to pass close by her seductive form to get out. She smelled so good he wanted to make a swift one eighty, but he felt so odd about everything that had happened that he thanked her without turning around.

"Come back any time," Andrea called to him. "You're always welcome here."

Max's throat went thick with gratitude, and he did turn then. She waved and smiled, and he did the same. And did he come back to visit Andrea's little lingerie boutique for big, beautiful women?

Oh, yes he did.

Wedding Heat:
Two in the Bush

"**P**lease just leave me alone," Irene mumbled. She'd avoided eye contact, but the short guy in the pinstriped pants and fedora was making his way over. "Oh, perfect."

"I like your dress," the boy said with a tip of his hat. "Very rockabilly, the red with the polka-dots. Looks great on you."

Irene's heart pounded with the compliment, and when she finally met the boy's delicate gaze she laughed. He wasn't a boy at all. Wait, was he? Irene followed the dark line of suspenders down a crisp white shirtfront. No, there were definitely breasts underneath. Her stalker was just another lonely girl.

"Well, thanks." Irene brushed imaginary wrinkles from her skirt. The crinolines made it poufy, but she liked that. "My sister said I was gonna look like Minnie Mouse in this thing."

"More like Bettie Page," said the girl in the fedora.

That made Irene laugh again. "I'm a little too fat to be a pin-up model."

The girl smirked but she didn't argue. "Hey, so I'm Vanessa. I'm Maggie's cousin."

"Nice to meet you. I'm Irene. Maggie and I work together."

They both nodded, and Vanessa rolled up her shirtsleeves. She had tattoos all up her forearms, but Irene always thought it was rude to ask people the stories behind their ink. Some things were personal.

"You want another drink?" Vanessa asked. "I sure do."

When Irene asked for a pina colada, Vanessa stumbled toward the bar. The last thing that girl needed was another drink, but who was she to judge? Alcohol played a huge role in Irene's weekend plans. No way she'd ever work up the courage to hit on Brian unless she was buzzed, and he probably wouldn't take the bait unless he was completely plastered.

Where the hell was Brian, anyway? He said he would come to the Boathouse, as this building was called, when he'd finished doing his hair, but that was twenty minutes ago. It made her anxious when she didn't have him in her sights. He was so damnably handsome. Part of this weekend's scheme was to keep other women's paws off his delectable body. She wanted it all to herself.

"Here you go, doll." Vanessa swept in out of nowhere to hand Irene her slushy drink.

"Oh, thanks." It suddenly occurred to Irene that this girl might be hitting on her, and the thought burned a hole in her chest. Maybe she should say something, to clarify. "I'm just waiting for someone, for Brian, this guy I like."

Irene's throat just about closed up once she'd said the words, and she took a swift sip of pina colada to cool the sizzle. She'd never told anybody except her sister that she liked Brian. Who *could* she tell? Most of her friends were co-workers, and they would squeal to Brian in a heartbeat. God, she'd be so embarrassed. Sometimes she wondered if they could tell she liked him by the way her body went all unsteady when he was around, but no one had ever said anything.

"So you work with my cousin, eh? What's that like?" Vanessa's body seemed a little more rigid than it had been before. She sipped on some kind of manly drink, like whisky or scotch. Irene wasn't a connoisseur of liqueurs.

"Good." Irene couldn't really think of anything more to say that wouldn't bore someone outside the office. "Brian works with us too—the guy I like. He's in accounting, but he isn't boring. People always think accountants are boring, but he's not. He snowboards."

When Vanessa didn't respond, Irene followed the girl's focused stare and realized it was fixed on Maggie. The bride to be was doing the rounds with what's-his-name, Ed, and she looked just dazzling.

Irene had always been jealous of Maggie, with that honey-blond hair in neat curls, the big boobs and tiny waist. She was like a human Barbie doll. Thank god she'd never been interested in Brian, or Irene wouldn't have stood a chance.

"You and my cousin must be close, I guess." Vanessa took another sip of amber liquid and made a face. "The hotel and resort fees are a lot of money to spend just to come to a co-worker's wedding."

"Well, yeah." Irene could feel a blush coming on. "But I'm sharing a room with Brian, the guy I like. Two beds, but... you know, I'm hoping..."

Vanessa's expression changed, and she smiled like she hadn't heard anything up until now. Leaning against the railing overlooking the dark lake, she turned her focus to Irene, and this time the attention felt nice. Too often, Irene was the invisible woman.

"You're trying to get this guy in the sac, eh?" Vanessa grinned, then shook her head as she looked down into her drink. "That's a good feeling, keeps you alive sometimes. So where is this dude? Point him out to me."

"I don't know. There are so many people here." Irene scanned the boathouse, but everywhere she looked felt like an information overload. There were so many faces she didn't recognize. "Aside from Pippa—she's one of the bridesmaids—Brian and I were pretty much the only ones from the office who came out for the weekend. A few others will drive up just for the ceremony on Sunday, but you're right, this resort is expensive. I had to talk Brian into coming. I still can't believe it worked."

"Well, good luck getting him into bed. I don't know how any guy could resist you." Vanessa paused a second then looked at her glass. "Fuck, I need another drink."

Irene wanted to clarify that it wasn't just about sex, but Vanessa had already shuffled toward the bar. With a sigh, Irene settled back against the railing and did another scan of the Boathouse. The room wasn't huge. If Brian were in here, she'd be able to find him. Maybe she was just looking from the wrong angle.

Shifting away from the railing, Irene walked the planks. The wooden flooring and walls in this room had the same convincing faux-rustic appeal as their hotel room, and if she had her choice she knew where she'd rather be right now: alone with Brian, rolling around on one of their two queen-size beds.

Where was he?

Nobody but Maggie and Pippa—and now that girl Vanessa—knew who she was, so nobody stopped to chat. That was just as well, as it let Irene focus all her energy on skulking around the crowded Boathouse bar in search of Brian.

And then she saw him.

Irene's throat closed up. She pressed her cold drink to her blazing heart both to cool her chest and keep the glass from slipping out of her hand. Brian was kissing another woman...

How dare he? *How dare he?*

Who was this floozy Brian had his arms around? Whose thick, dark hair cascaded across his shoulders? Whose hands squeezed his butt cheeks? This wasn't fair! They'd come all this way together, a long blissful drive up granite-lined highways, talking about anything and everything, really getting to know one another.

And then he runs off and starts making out with some random slut?

How *dare* he?

Irene bolted from the Boathouse to the resort hotel, racing up the stairs when the elevator took more than three seconds to find her. It wasn't until she was secured within the swaddling warmth of her room that she noticed she still had her pina colada in hand. Oh well, good thing. Saved her raiding the mini-bar. This god-forsaken trip was already dipping into enough of her savings without the added cost of hotel alcohol.

There were two chairs by the window looking out on the lake, and Irene fell into one of them. She could see the Boathouse from here, and sipped on her cold drink while she watched the smokers hanging around outside.

She kept the lights off, the windows closed, but that didn't stop the muted sounds of chit-chat and laughter from filtering in. Across the lake she heard a splash, and she looked in that direction. A group of skinny-dippers, maybe? It was too dark to know for sure.

"How dare you?" Irene asked Brian, though she was staring at her own reflection in the black window. "There's a spark between us. Can't you feel it?"

It was stupid to talk to him when he wasn't there, but she never could say the words when he was in the room. Why was it so easy for other people and so hard for her?

The door opened, and Irene spun around in the chair, stiff as a board. A blast of light from the hallway cast two figures in shadow as they stumbled into the room, hanging off each other from the looks of it. Kissing.

When the door slammed shut, the room fell again into darkness and the figures tumbled into the bed closest to the door—Brian's bed. He growled the words, "I'm gonna wreck you, bitch."

How could Brian say a thing like that? Irene wanted to cry, but she couldn't move. She couldn't breathe. Suddenly she felt sorry for the woman she'd held in such contempt earlier. Wait, was this the same woman?

Whoever she was, she didn't seem to need Irene's pity. "Yes, wreck me," she panted while Brian sucked her neck. "I want your cock in my cunt, pretty boy."

Irene covered her mouth with both hands. The moonlight must have gotten brighter, or maybe her eyes had just grown accustomed to the low light, because she could see them now. She could see them well. The woman was beautiful, Spanish-looking with that dark hair and golden skin. Her dress was already half off and Brian had worked his way down to her bare tits. Was she really not wearing a bra? What a total fucking whore! Why would Brian do this?

"You gonna suck my fucking tits, pretty boy?" The crass bitch had rolled on top of him now, and she rammed her breasts against Brian's face. "Yes, they taste good, don't they?"

"Mmm-hmm!" Brian sounded like he was suffocating under there.

"Your cock better be fucking huge," the bitch grunted as she writhed against his smaller frame. "Because I want you to destroy me. I want this to make me sore all weekend."

Shock melted into sorrow, and before Irene could catch herself, she let out a bloodcurdling scream that sounded like, "Stop!"

The woman looked up first, Brian next, and sheer humiliation took Irene by the intestines, twisting them in knots. Tears like lava stained her cheeks, tumbling quickly down her neck and soaking her red dress.

"No," Irene whimpered. Her head felt like a helium-filled bowling ball. She wanted to let it fall, but it wouldn't. "No, please." Each word sprang from her chest like a sobbing hiccup. "Please stop."

"Irene? Sorry, kiddo, I thought you were at the party." Brian did about the worst thing possible and snapped on the bedside lamp. "Oh... you're crying," he said, like that wasn't already obvious. "This is Denitsa. We were just..."

"Yeah, obviously," Irene snapped. God, she'd never felt so angry in her life. Every muscle in her back and shoulders had tensed beyond recognition. Her hands formed fists and her arms started shaking. "How dare you? How dare you, Brian? How could you be so stupid?"

Everything was a blur, but Irene distinctly saw Brian look up at Denitsa like he didn't know what the problem was. Why did she love him? He was such a stupid idiot!

Denitsa rolled off Brian and then off the bed, and Irene was sure she would leave discretely, but that's not what happened at all. Denitsa tucked her loose tits back inside her chocolate-coloured dress. She plucked about a hundred tissues from the box by the bed and rushed to Irene's side.

"Oh, you poor sweet girl!" Denitsa pulled the other chair over and sat so close to Irene their knees touched. "Tell me, why all the tears?"

"Sorry about this," Brian said, but Irene had a sinking feeling he was talking to Denitsa, and that made her instantly sadder and angrier.

As much as Irene wanted to hate the beautiful brunette with the great big boobs, Denitsa had offered a shoulder while Irene was crying. She fell against the woman's body, sobbing so hard her chest heaved against Denitsa's. When she hooked her chin around Denitsa's shoulder, she knew her tears were falling into that great bush of hair, and she pictured each brave little teardrop sliding down a brunette strand until it traced a path to the woman's bare back.

"Thank you," Irene whimpered between sobs. Strange to be thanking the woman Brian had obliviously chosen over her, but it was so rare for anybody to show Irene such tenderness. "I'm sorry. I'm so stupid."

"No, no, no." Denitsa kissed the side of Irene's head, and that tiny act of affection warmed her immeasurably. "No, you are not stupid, my dear. You are... in love?"

Irene pulled away to blow her nose, but it never seemed to stop running. She stared down at the shimmering gloss in her tissue as she nodded. Even after this insane show of emotion, she couldn't say the words. She couldn't even look at Brian.

"Do you two know each other?" he asked from across the room.

"A woman knows a woman's pain," Denitsa said, cradling Irene's head against her chest. "We are all connected in some way."

"That is so true," Irene whimpered, rocking with this stranger who showed her superhuman empathy. "Oh god, I've been such an idiot."

"No, no, no." Denitsa rested her cheek against Irene's head. "A man is never worth such pain, my angel." The warmth of that woman's hand rubbing up and down her arm made Irene want to cry all over again, but she was tired of the tears.

"Anyone feel like telling me what's going on?" Brian finally asked from the bed.

Irene looked up at him, almost without thinking, and when she met his confounded gaze she wondered why she'd placed him on such a high pedestal. He wasn't a god. He was just a guy from the office.

Denitsa tsked. "She loves you, pretty boy."

Brian's expression didn't change. He still looked confused. Of course, Irene couldn't breathe. All she could do was sit across the room from him and wait for another emotional beating.

"Oh, Reenee, I love you too, but not that way. You're like a sister to me. You're great, you really are, but..."

"Stop," Irene whimpered. "Please, just..."

Denitsa took over, pulling Irene up from her chair and sitting her on the second queen bed. "Look at this beautiful girl." Denitsa tucked a strand of Irene's black hair behind her ear, and the slight brush of the woman's hot fingers made her shiver. Shifting in so close her breath was hot against Irene's cheek, Denitsa asked, "What is your name, beautiful girl?"

"Irene." She looked to Brian. His eyes went wide and then clouded with dark lust as Denitsa leaned in to kiss Irene's neck. Irene froze, despite the sizzle of Denitsa's full lips on her skin. "What... what are you doing?"

"Keep doing it," Brain said before Denitsa could answer.

Irene gulped past the lump in her throat. She couldn't take her eyes off Brian, stretched out on the bed in dark trousers. His shirt was half pulled out at the waist, and his tie hung loose around his neck. She could see why

93

Denitsa called him "pretty boy," with his light blonde hair and schoolboy smirk, but he was the handsomest guy Irene had ever met.

"You... want to watch?" Irene felt stupid saying the words, but her intense emotion rendered her utterly inarticulate. All she knew was that she'd do anything for Brian. More than that, Denitsa's lips on her neck aroused an aching pulse between her legs. As much as she'd like to deny it, she was already so wet she could feel pussy juice seeping down her thighs.

Denitsa asked Brian, "Want to see us kiss?"

"God, yes." There was a tremble to Brian's voice, like he couldn't believe this was happening.

Even though Irene and Brian were on different mattresses, he was close enough that she felt his pull, like he'd hooked her heart and was unconsciously reeling her in.

"Have you ever been with two women, pretty boy?" Denitsa rubbed her feather-soft cheek against Irene's. It was so much like a dream Irene couldn't believe this was actually happening.

"What?" Brian asked. "You mean like at the same time?"

Denitsa chuckled, a rumbling growl that resonated low down in Irene's core. "Yes, at the same time."

"No," he admitted. "But something tells me tonight's the night."

Please god, yes. Irene wouldn't have planned it this way, but she knew in her gut Denitsa wasn't the competition. If anything, Denitsa was greasing the wheels, playing the gorgeous fairy godmother. Was she even a real person? Maybe she was an angel or some sort of matchmaker fae. Irene had always believed other beings lived among the humans, and she'd been waiting all her life for one to make itself known.

That's what Irene was thinking when Denitsa kissed her.

The sensation was foreign and shocking, like the time she was knocked over by an ocean wave on a family vacation to Florida. She still remembered the bathwater warmth of the ocean, the salt stinging her nose and throat as she struggled to find the world again. That's how she felt now, except instead of fighting Denitsa's hot tongue, she allowed herself to drown.

Irene had never kissed a woman before. She'd always half wondered what it would be like, and now she knew. Now she turned herself over to that woman, trusting Denitsa's strength as she lay back on white hotel linens. Her chest felt tight, her dress felt tight, and all she wanted now was to strip and experience the hot press of Denitsa's great breasts skin to skin. A tiny thought hatched deep in her mind...*destroy me.*

Her hand took initiative. As Denitsa kissed her full and hot on the mouth, Irene reached up to touch one of those beautiful braless tits. The fabric of Denitsa's dress was slinky and soft, and it only accentuated the glory of those big round breasts. Irene's pussy pulsed like rapid fire as she took hold of both Denitsa's boobs, pressing them together, squeezing and toying. She'd never done this before. Denitsa's nipples were hard, as she tried to pinch them, but the fabric of that chocolate brown dress was too slippery to get a firm grasp on those tiny buds. She wanted inside.

"Oh god, you're killing me," Brian said in the most tortured voice Irene had ever heard from him. "I gotta see you both naked."

That word, *both*, made Irene's heart race. Alone she was invisible, but paired with Denitsa she was desirable. For now, that was good enough.

"Undress me, sweet thing." Denitsa arched away from Irene and stood beside the bed. She was still wearing dangerously high heels, which made the already tall woman look like a giant. "Come, my darling. Take off my dress."

"I'll do it," Brian offered, bouncing off his bed.

Denitsa pushed his shoulder with just the tips of her fingers and he stumbled backward onto the mattress. "The lady in red will do it."

Irene felt a blush coming on, which was pretty amazing considering how hot she was already. Sliding off the bed, she stood on wobbly knees, feeling all the crinolines in her Minnie Mouse dress. She sensed Brian's eyes burning a hole in her arms as she reached up for the straps of Denitsa's dress and then pulled them down over those golden shoulders.

"Wow." Irene watched breathlessly as the V-neck of Denitsa's dress tumbled down her breasts, hanging for a moment on her pursed nipples before slipping to settle against her wide hips.

"Holy Mother." Brian sounded choked, throttled even. "I'm gonna jizz my pants."

But Brian's voice was just background noise. Irene couldn't steal her gaze away from those golden breasts with their dark pinky-brown nipples. She heard their call, and she answered with her mouth.

95

In flats, Irene was pretty much at eye level with Denitsa's big bare breasts. She tilted her head just a bit, just so Brian could get a better look as she opened her mouth for Denitsa's nipple.

"Oh, my sweet little angel!" Denitsa hissed when Irene sucked her tit, wrapping both hands tentatively around her hips. Denitsa's skin was sweet, hot, and soft, an erotic contrast to the erect nipple pressing into Irene's tongue. "Wonderful, darling. You are so beautiful and so wonderful."

Irene's heart thumped wildly at the compliments. When she pulled away to say thank you, she saw that her lipstick had left a red ring around Denitsa's nipple. The sight made her knees weak. It was like a temporary tattoo that she'd placed on the other woman's skin. For some strange reason, it made her feel like she could do anything.

"Are you jealous of the lady in red?" Denitsa asked with a swift nod in Brian's direction. "You want to suck my tits too?"

Brian gave a breathy laugh, like he couldn't believe this was happening. "I'm jealous of you both!"

That unexpected sentiment flooded Irene's chest with warmth. Denitsa sure knew how to get a man excited. Hell, she knew how to get a woman excited just the same. The gusset of Irene's panties felt as wet as a slip-and-slide, and she'd give just about anything to be touched down there.

"Take off her dress and you can suck my tits." Denitsa snapped her fingers, and Brian hopped to it, closing in on Irene.

"Wait." He stopped with his fingers perched above the zipper. "Irene, is this okay?"

She turned back to meet the sweetness and care in his lustful gaze. He didn't want to hurt her. He would never hurt her. She was sure of that, now more than ever.

"It's okay," Irene said, her voice mousy and small. She tried again. "It's more than okay, Brian. It's what I want. I've wanted this for... god, I don't even remember how long."

"I didn't know," he said, seeming confused again, like he couldn't trust himself. "I thought we were friends and whatever. I didn't know..."

"Take off the dress!" Denitsa's commanding voice made Irene's heart jump, but she smiled when Brian took her little zipper between his big thumb and forefinger and slid it down slowly. When she felt his breath on her back, the pulse between her legs throbbed so hard she could hear it like a heartbeat.

"Oh... I think I did something wrong," Brian said.

"No, there's a clasp at the top." Irene couldn't help but smile. "See? It's just little."

He found it and unhooked the metal fastener, and her red polka dot dress loosened and shifted, the shoulders catching her elbows and resting there.

"Pull it all the way down," Denitsa said. "Take it off."

Irene could feel Brian's hands shaking as he took hold of her sturdy cotton dress and pushed it to the floor. The crinolines spread in a circle, rising in the middle, making Irene feel like she was standing on top of a circus tent.

"Red fishnets!" Brian clapped his hands, chuckling deep in his throat. "I don't think I've ever seen red fishnets before."

A smile bled across Irene's lips as she stepped out of her dress and climbed onto Brian's bed. She remembered what that girl Vanessa had said in the Boathouse, how she looked like Bettie Page. Right now, she believed it. She struck a pin-up pose right there on the bed, showing off her black bra and underwear. Her panties were the high kind that covered most of her belly, but with black lace across the tummy-tucking part, they had a classic look to them. Why should fat girls have to be ashamed of their bodies?

"Wow." Brian repeated that word over and over again, and then finally said, "You look amazing."

"Thanks," Irene chirped. She felt incredibly happy, like her heart was about to explode. Sensing his hot gaze on her curves was heaven on earth. If she'd ever felt any embarrassment about her body, that look dissolved it completely.

Denitsa stepped out of her dress too. Underneath it, her golden legs were bare and she had on a slinky little thong, which she promptly removed. Irene couldn't help staring into the black triangle at the apex of Denitsa's thighs. The Bermuda triangle. An unshaved pussy was a thing of mystery.

"And now you undress for us, pretty boy." With a smirk, Denitsa sat naked on Brian's bed. As soon as that foreign pussy came within range, Irene reached for it, stroking the cloud of dense black hair.

Denitsa breathed deeply, making her breasts rise and fall. Irene knew she ought to be watching Brian undress, and she tried, but there was something magnetic about Denitsa's big, round boobs. Finally, she gave in and sucked the nearest tit, making kittenish mewling sounds as Denitsa's hard nipple massaged the pad of her tongue.

Brian fell in beside her, sucking Denitsa's other tit. Irene looked at him and he looked at her, and they smiled as they suckled. Their faces had never been so close. Soon she felt his fingers weaving with hers, caressing Denitsa's bush, forcing Irene's fingers lower until she felt juice. Denitsa gasped, arching on the bed.

"I think we struck gold," Brian teased.

Irene rubbed Denitsa's clit in circles, slow at first, but Brian's insistence made her pick up speed. Their hands moved in time with one another, swooping in circles as Denitsa leaned so far back her beautiful breast popped out of Irene's mouth.

"Oh." Irene whined. "I was enjoying that."

Denitsa laughed, pressing her big tit up to her own mouth and licking its fat, puckered nipple. "And now I'm sucking it," Denitsa teased. Except it wasn't exactly a tease, because she really did wrap her lips around her own erect nipple and suckle. "Irene, you have a naked man right there and you ignore him?"

"No," Irene shot back, even though Denitsa had hit the nail on the head. She'd tried desperately to keep her eyes above the belt, but now they wandered and she found herself apologizing. "Sorry, Brian."

"For what?" he asked, standing on the other side of Denitsa's open thighs.

Now Irene couldn't help but look. His cock was large and fully erect, pointing up to the ceiling even with him standing upright. She'd never seen a dick do that before.

The throbbing marble look of the thing was so stellar that Irene had to touch it. Of course, she was still circling her fingers around Denitsa's engorged clit, but the other hand was free. She reached out, but she needed to get closer.

Falling between Denitsa's open legs, she pressed the pad of her thumb to the gorgeous woman's clit while she trailed her fingers down Brian's shaft.

They both arched, gasping, and Irene immediately sensed what power she held in her two hands.

Wrapping her fist around Brian's shaft, she looked up at him, suppliantly, and he mirrored that same look back. "I never thought this would really happen," she admitted as she rubbed his cock. "I hoped, but I never thought..."

"Beautiful angel," Denitsa cut in, opening her pussy lips with two fingers. "Come, show pretty boy what your mouth can do."

Irene sensed the lustful jealousy pouring off Brian's skin like metaphysical sweat, but she obeyed the beautiful woman she'd only just met. In truth, she was dying to taste Denitsa's pussy, and she wasn't disappointed. She held tight to Brian's cock as she pushed deep between those open thighs, licking the spot where her fingers had just been.

"Yes, more." Denitsa ran a hand through Irene's hair as if to grant Brian a better view. "Harder, little angel. Lick with force."

Irene buried her face even deeper into Denitsa's bush. Dark curly hairs tickled her nostrils as she pressed her nose into the arch of the Denitsa's fingers. Of course, Irene had no idea what she was doing, but she did what she thought would feel good, and it seemed to work. Denitsa squirmed and writhed under her tongue, and Irene nearly jumped out of her fishnets when she felt Denitsa's fingers against hers on Brian's dick.

"I love a hard cock." Denitsa took over pumping it while Irene's fingers cascaded down his balls. "You love cock too, my angel?"

"Uhh-huh!" Irene agree, nodding wildly against Denitsa's clit. "Uhh-huh!"

"I want to see you suck this cock," Denitsa instructed. "You love this man. Let him fuck your mouth."

Those words dizzied Irene. Still, she had trouble drawing her lips away from Denitsa's wet pussy. When she did managed to pull up, she could feel the juice running down her chin, and she considered wiping it away, but she thought Brian might appreciate the moist glisten of it as he looked down on her.

She looked up into his eyes momentarily, but her focus remained on his cock. Denitsa's hand, with those lovely long nails, pressed his hard dick down while Irene bent toward that fiery pink cockhead. She opened her mouth wide, extending her tongue, letting Denitsa feed Brian's hard cock to her.

Brian's precum spilled across Irene's tongue. Its sweetness, mingling with Denitsa's juices, flooded her taste buds, warming her with desire. She closed her mouth around his tip as Denitsa's lovely hand shuttled up his length, pressing his soft skin against her lips. When Denitsa's hand retreated down his shaft, Irene followed it nearly all the way to the base. Brian's skin tasted so fresh, so clean, that Irene sucked harder, searching for something.

For pussy.

Irene shifted back and forth between Denitsa's cunt and Brian's cock, unable to decide which she preferred. There was a newness to both, but Denitsa's body excited her because, well, she really didn't know this woman. At all! But Brian pressed all the right buttons. She'd lusted after him for well over two years now, loved him from afar, hoped and prayed one day her wishes would come true.

And now here she was in a hotel room with a strange woman and the man she adored, and she couldn't decide where to put her mouth? It seemed rather silly, but Irene didn't care. She ate Denitsa's pussy like a wild thing, then sucked Brian's cock with all her strength, letting him fuck her throat while the dark-haired goddess eased their motions.

"Fuck her for me," Denitsa said to Brian.

Irene gasped around Brian's cock. She felt suddenly faint, and hoped she wouldn't pass out before he'd found his way inside of her.

"Use a condom, pretty boy," Denitsa went on. "Keep our angel safe. And you, my dear, take off your panties but leave on the fishnets."

Brian dug into his luggage, searching for condoms no doubt, while Irene looked down at her lingerie. She'd worn her underwear under the fishnets, of course, which meant she'd have to take off the stockings, then the underwear, then put the stockings back on.

"Quick, quick," Denitsa commanded, and Irene hopped to it, leaning back against the other bed while she struggled out of her lingerie.

The fishnets had no real crotch to them, and the holes were quite large, so Brian should have no problem fucking her through the hosiery. The very idea made Irene weak in the knees, and she retreated to the warmth and safety between Denitsa's thighs, like that pussy had some magic control over her.

"Okay, pretty boy, take her from behind." Denitsa's voice was warm as butter, yet commanding as an army sergeant's. "Lift her by the fishnets, bring her to standing."

Brian's fingers wove through the slits in the fishnets, tugging upward, encouraging Irene to stand. Though she could hardly bear to pull her face away from Denitsa's hot cunt, she forced herself to look down past her naked tits with their glossy peach nipples, down to where the bright red fishnets criss-crossed her own black bush. The sight made her heart palpitate, and for a moment she wondered if she might die here today. At least she'd go with a smile on her face.

"Find her pussy with your fingers," Denitsa instructed.

Brian's touch landed softly against Irene's skin, following the curve of her ass down, down to where the heat was. Irene gasped when he found her pussy lips through the fishnets, exploring slowly, striking her clit. She turned her face to the side, setting her cheek against Denitsa's juicy cunt.

"Is her pussy wet?" Denitsa asked Brian. "Put your fingers inside and tell me how it feels."

Brian wasted no time pressing two brave fingers up inside Irene's slit, and she felt her eyeballs rolling back in her head with the sheer pleasure of it. Without thinking, Irene pressed two of her own fingers into the overwhelming wetness of Denitsa's cunt, feeling those valiant pussy muscles clamp down on her digits, then pulse and flutter. She wondered if her own pussy was doing the same thing to Brian.

"There," Denitsa cooed, already bucking her hips slightly to meet Irene's invasion. "How does that feel?"

"Hot," Irene and Brian said in unison. "And Wet."

"Yessss." Denitsa growled now, scouring her clit against Irene's cheek. Irene had never felt so dirty, but she loved the idea of another woman painting her face with pussy juice. "Now fuck our angel, pretty boy. Put on a show for me."

Irene wished she could see the expression on Brian's face as he pulled his fingers from her pussy and replaced them with his cock, but she couldn't tear her face away from Denitsa's hot cunt. All she could do was turn and suck the woman's pulsing clit while she fucked Denitsa with her fingers.

Brian's cockhead rested at the mouth of Irene's slit, like it was waiting for the perfect moment to thrust inside of her. "Oh god," she said around Denitsa's clit. "Just fuck me, Brian. Fuck me hard until I come!"

"She wants you to destroy her," Denitsa said.

"Destroy me," Irene echoed without releasing Denitsa's clit from her lips.

That seemed to be all the encouragement Brian required, because he pressed his mushroom head beyond the entry to Irene's cunt, forcing it deep into her wetness. She savoured the squelching sound of his cock moving in her pussy every bit as much as the taste of Denitsa's cunt in her mouth.

"Oh yes, my angel." Denitsa formed a rope of Irene's hair, wrapping it around her hand to guide Irene's motion. "Yes, suck my clit, dear one. Fuck my cunt with those precious little fingers. Harder, yes."

Irene had been afraid of hurting Denitsa, but now she realized nothing she tried would be harmful. Closing her eyes, she bit Denitsa's clit and fucked her as hard and fast as her arm would let her.

"That's right," Denitsa cried. "Oh yes."

Brian held the back of Irene's fishnets in his fists, which brought the front up tight against her flesh. As he fucked her from behind, he stretched the sexy red leggings until one of the junctions of that tight fabric struck Irene square in the clit. Maybe the sensation wouldn't have been so intense if her clit hadn't been aching already, but that slight rubbing sensation brought a familiar itch to her pelvis. If Brian just kept fucking her like that, just kept rubbing that itty bitty piece of fishnet against her clit, she would come like crazy.

The pressure in Irene's belly built as Brian's big cock shocked her cunt again and again. She could feel him everywhere, from the wet mouth of her pussy to the grasping muscles inside. He pulled up on her fishnets, driving that perfectly placed bit against her clit. She couldn't keep still anymore. Flattening her tongue against Denitsa's hot pussy, Irene shook her head sided to side, up and down, round and round in circles that made her dizzy, and that dizzy feeling seeped down to her core, swirling in her pelvis, egging on her approaching orgasm.

"Fuck yes!" Denitsa pulled Irene's hair, and it hurt, but the hurt felt amazing. "Yes, you darling bitch, you little cunt. You're going to make me come."

Irene would have said the same, but she didn't want to stop what she was doing.

"Come, come, come," Brian was chanting behind her, thrusting so hard he moved her big body, making her tits swing under her and whack against the mattress. "I'm gonna come, I'm gonna come!"

Squealing against Denitsa's cunt, Irene tightened her pussy muscles around Brian's cock, milking his erection. "Uhh-huh! Uhh-huh!" She was right there with him, hovering over the precipice, and she couldn't wait any longer for her fishnets to push her off the cliff.

Sneaking her one unoccupied hand between her legs, Irene found her clit and rubbed. Her reaction was swift, overwhelming, and when her fingertips struck Brian's sheathed cock, he obviously wasn't expecting it.

Sometimes it's the little things that put a person over the edge, and for Brian it must have been Irene's fingertips against his thrusting cock. He released her fishnets and grabbed her shoulders, ramming her hard from behind as she screamed into Denitsa's pussy. They were lucky all the other guests were down in the boathouse, or they'd surely have had people knocking at the door, wondering who was being murdered.

"Yes, yes!" Denitsa arched up on the bed so fast she drove Irene's head away from her crotch, but Irene was too caught up in her own pleasure to slow down. Pressing Denitsa back down on the bed, she sucked the woman's nipples, which were still lined in her own red lipstick. Brian fell on top of the heap, taking Denitsa's other tit and devouring it as all three panted and moaned.

Even after orgasm, Brian's cock was still half-hard in Irene's pussy. It twitched, and then Irene's pussy muscles twitched, and they both snickered, and then kissed, and went back to sucking on Denitsa's tits.

After what seemed like a long while, they let out a deep sigh in unison, and then they all burst into laughter.

"Wow, that was..." Irene couldn't think up a word that characterised what they'd just done.

"Amazing?" Brian asked.

"Decadent," Denitsa said, kissing Irene's and Brian's foreheads before rolling out from under them. "Ahh, my heart is so full of love for you both."

Irene watched Denitsa dress, conscious that Brian's gaze had fixed firmly on her fishnets. They were damp almost to her knees, and every time she moved she felt Brian's waning erection still lodged inside of her. When he pulled out, she felt incomplete, except for the assurance that he would stay with her all night in this very bed.

"Well, my little ones, I ought to see if my husband has arrived yet." Denitsa picked up her purse from the floor and slipped on her shoes.

Bolting up from the bed, Brian cried, "You have a husband?"

"No need to worry, my darlings. He is a very open-minded man." Denitsa smiled and opened the door, wiggling her fingers in a wave. "Goodnight, my dears. Kisses!"

Irene's heart pounded in her throat. "Did you know she was married?"

"No!" Brian squealed, pulling down the covers and diving under them. "Oh Christ, I bet he's a big-ass bodybuilder, too. He'll pound me into pudding."

Smiling gently, Irene eased out of her fishnets and joined Brian under the covers. Pulling him in against her chest, she said, "Don't worry. I'll protect you."

Chuckling, Brian nuzzled her breasts, tracing his warm hands up and down her belly. It felt so good to be lying there, just the two of them.

"I've never done anything like that before." It seemed funny now and she wondered if Denitsa might be an angel or a fairy. "Who was she, anyway?"

"I don't know, exactly. One of Ed's relatives, I think she said. It was kind of weird. I mean, she just came up to me and there was very little chit chat before she had her tongue down my throat."

Brian kissed Irene's neck, kissed her cheek. Irene responded with a kiss on the top of Brian's head, giggling. "You're just that sexy."

"Apparently." He laughed.

They lay in silence for a long time, and just when Irene started feeling nervous about that, she realized Brian had fallen asleep. Everything that had happened tonight... well, it's the last thing she ever thought would happen. But thank god it did, because without Denitsa's encouragement Irene probably would have just slept in her own bed while Brian slept in his. The weekend would have passed them by, and nothing would have happened.

Irene had wanted Brian for so long, and now she had him. He'd fallen asleep in her arms, and he'd wake up with her. And she'd wake up with him.

Perfect.

Could Have Been Any Girl

I guess a lot of people do stupid things coming off a break-up, but I wonder how many do stupid things with strangers.

After weeks of mourning the future I'd seen in Justine's eyes, I decided the only way to feel better about myself was to fuck a total stranger. The big problem? When I got to the only lesbian club I'd ever heard of, the sidewalk was lined with bad-ass dykes. No way in hell I'd go inside.

"Hey," one of the dykes called as I turned to head home. She was big and built, but the way she flicked her cigarette to the sidewalk irritated the hell out of me. "You comin' in?"

"I don't think so." I tried to walk, but I couldn't move.

She came so close I could smell the smoke on her clothes—a wrinkled shirt over compressed tits, dirty black jeans and a studded belt.

"Why not?" she asked. "You straight or something?"

Those words burned me like acid. That sneer, that smell, even her slicked-back hair made me want to punch her. And kiss her. And more.

God, why couldn't I walk away?

"If I were straight why would I be hanging around outside a pussy club?"

She sneered and said, "Maybe because you're a pussy."

Stunned, I looked to the other smokers, but their group closed off and they turned away. My heart pounded so hard I could feel it in my cunt. What if this big dyke stole me away, just threw me over her shoulder like a Viking and ran me down the street?

"I'm a pussy?" I asked when I'd regained my capacity for speech. "Does that pass for clever where you come from?"

"Do *you* pass for clever where *you* come from?" she fired back.

"What is this, Grade Three?" I couldn't believe this girl, and I certainly couldn't fathom my attraction to her. "You're just like those eight-year-old boys, where your mom says, 'He's teasing you because he likes you, honey.' It's so lame."

"If it's so lame, why is it working?" She raised an eyebrow, too cocky for words.

I couldn't move. All I could think to say was, "Fuck you."

"I'd rather fuck *you*," she replied, like she'd prepared for this, like she was reading a script.

"Fine." What more could I say? "Go ahead."

"Fine," she said. "Maybe I will."

But she didn't do anything, just lorded over me, tall and broad and heavy.

"Well? Are you gonna fuck me or aren't you? Make up your mind, because plenty of other girls would love a piece of me."

"Oh yeah?" she asked, like she'd run out of insults. "Well..."

She stood so close her chest bumped mine with every inhale. Each time her flattened breasts nudged me, a blast of juice swelled in my pussy. I wanted her fingers in there, fucking me relentlessly, unforgivingly. But she waited me out, casting smoky breaths against my face.

I didn't want to give in, but I couldn't stand the suspense. Tossing my arms around her hefty neck, I leapt against her, wrapping my legs around her waist and kissing her hard. She didn't react at all, but I didn't give up. I couldn't. I wanted what she had to give.

After a moment, she opened her mouth to mine and our tongues whipped and writhed together. She tasted like cigarettes, and that would usually have grossed me out, but not today. I needed it too badly.

Carrying me while we kissed, she backed up against the building and then turned so it was me against that callous brick. Her hands found my ass, and she ran hot palms over my bare cheeks while the wall dug into my shoulders.

Thank God I'd worn a thong, not to mention a skirt. The stranger's hands wandered unapologetically across my skin while I grinded against her belly, trying to strike my clit against her studded belt. It wasn't working.

"You gotta fuck me," I growled, crawling from her arms.

Until she glanced at the group of dykes watching us kiss, I'd nearly forgotten we were on a city street.

"What, right here?" she asked. Her voice was squeaky and high, and she cleared her throat before saying, "We got an audience, babygirl."

I didn't care. I turned around, leaned against the brick wall, and spread my legs. "Fuck me. Hard."

The dykes were all watching when my reluctant stranger shoved her hand between my thighs and shifted my thong out of the way. When the stiff night air kissed my cunt, I gasped. It felt so new to be exposed like this, out on the street before a group of gawking lesbians.

The stranger took her turn with me, and the moment those thick fingers slid inside my pussy I was a helpless.

"Yeah, fuck me," I moaned, bucking back at her hand, making her fingers move hot and fast. "Harder."

She grunted as she reamed me. Her gravel voice turned me on as much as the sloshing sound of fingers firing inside my cunt. The harder I thrust against her hand, the more forcefully she fucked me. She must have had three fingers inside, because my pussy felt full to bursting.

"Make me come!" I wasn't above begging at this point. I wanted to get off and I didn't want to wait.

"I'll make you come," she grunted. "I'll make you come so hard you'll feel it into the middle of next week."

Her words made me groan. When she wrapped one arm around my body, I knew I was a goner. She found my throbbing clit and rubbed it in quick, tight circles. I was so hot, so wet, so ready to come that her touch pushed me right over the edge.

"How's that, baby?" The stranger sneered, like she thought she'd won this game. "Tell daddy you like it."

My whole body pulsed with orgasm. I could feel it in my toes, my mind dizzy from the fall into bliss. Still, I wouldn't give that dyke the satisfaction. With my tits flush to the brick, I sneered, "You're not my daddy."

"Oh yeah?" Grunting, she scoured my tender clit so hard it hurt. She fucked me from behind until I couldn't stand the pleasure. I must have been whimpering, pleading, begging her to stop, because she said, "I will, babygirl. Just tell me you like it."

"I like it!" I burst. "I fucking *love* it, okay?"

"That's right you do." Sliding her fingers from my snatch, she slapped my ass and backed away. I leaned against the wall, trying to catch my breath. I couldn't remember the last time I'd come so hard. My knees went weak, and I let go, falling to the sidewalk with my skirt pulled up over my hips.

"Come on," the stranger said.

When I looked up, she and the group that had watched us fuck were heading inside the club.

"Get up, babygirl."

Nodding, I picked myself off the sidewalk, dusted a cigarette butt from my knee, and followed.

Office Sex

ISOBEL'S CONFERENCE call went overtime, as usual. While the Copenhagen team droned on, she dreamed up new and unusual sex positions, doodling them on the back of scrap paper. If she were to perch on the side of her desk, could she fit a man between her legs and still rest both feet against the wall?

Only if she kept her heels on, she guessed.

The door to Isobel's office was closed, but the blinds on her little window were open. Through those blinds, she spotted a flurry activity in the hallway. Everybody seemed to be walking, running by.

Must be cake in the boardroom, she thought.

Nothing mobilized the troops like sweets.

And then she noticed a distinct odour on the air.

Burnt popcorn?

Burnt something...

Ahmed threw open her door, and she bolted upright, shoving her dirty drawings in the bin under her desk. He looked to the phone first, and then to her. "Sorry to intrude, but Sassafraz is burning!"

"Sassafraz is burning?" Her spine straightened vertebra by vertebra. A cold tingle ran up it.

The monotone voices on the line didn't even pause for breath.

Ahmed clung to the doorknob. "You can see it from the boardroom. Everybody's in there."

"I have go," Isobel told the phone. "There's a fire. I'm hanging up now."

Usually she'd have waited for a response, but not today. She ended the call and raced from her office, catching the icy clean scent of Ahmed's cologne as she passed him by.

He closed the door with one hand and placed the other on her lower back, propelling her down the hall.

His touch sparked something, a fire in her belly. She half-turned to look at him, but second-guessed herself and concentrated on putting one foot in front of the other. She always did stupid things when she was aroused, and she often fell off her heels even when she wasn't.

That campfire aroma she'd caught a whiff of in her office increased tenfold when they stepped into the boardroom. Ahmed was right—everyone *was* there. Her boss, his boss, the owners, the assistants, her colleagues, their clients, even the cleaning staff were pressed like a heaving mass against the wall-to-wall window.

It was funny to see all these professional people smushed together, foreheads and noses flattened against the glass. Those farther back looked over the heads and shoulders of the front row.

Three of the younger assistants climbed on the boardroom table to get a better view, but the owners snapped at them to get down. During the ruckus, Isobel and Ahmed snuck around the side, standing just behind Jin the receptionist.

People often say, "I can't believe my eyes," but Isobel really couldn't. She couldn't believe Sassafraz was burning. She felt numb, like she was in a dream, as she watched the orange flames soaring through a hole in the restaurant's roof.

They had an excellent view from their office tower—a helicopter view. Isobel could see burnt timbers breaking off from the black roof to feed the flames. They were huge. She'd never seen a fire so big.

"Have ever been there?" Ahmed asked without looking at her. He seemed as hypnotized by the flames as everyone else.

"No," she said. "I always figured it was too showy and expensive."

Sassafraz was a landmark restaurant, the place where celebrities dined when they were in town making movies or attending the film festival.

"Now I never will, I guess."

"They'll rebuild it," one of Connie's clients said. "It's the place to see and be seen. They'll *have to* rebuild it."

Still, Isobel felt queasy as she watched Sassafraz burning. She felt like she'd missed something essential, and now it was too late. It was mortality, this sensation, like death had her in his frosty grip. There were so many things she'd never experienced.

"I'm sending pictures to all the news places," Jin said, playing with her phone. "They pay you a hundred dollars if they use your shot."

"Are there any celebrities down there?" one of the young assistants asked. "Gossip magazines pay a thousand."

Everybody leaned forward, phones in hand, trying to get snaps of faces in the crowd outside the restaurant.

Is that Brad Pitt?

Where? Where? Where?

Are you kidding? That's a cook.

How do you know?

He's wearing that white top thingy like Gordon Ramsay.

Gordon Ramsay's down there?

No!

Isobel tuned them all out. Her focus was split between the flames, which were just starting to lick the adjacent building, and the heat coming off Ahmed's body. Her bare arm was touching his suit, and she could feel his warmth through the fabric. Her skin was getting goosebumpy even though she wasn't cold.

Something was about to happen. She could feel it in her bones.

Finally, sirens! What had taken the fire department so long?

They watched eagerly, but the first truck came one street over. Another truck arrived hot on its heels, and then a third and fourth, surrounding the building on three sides. They hooked up their hoses and pointed those huge things at the building.

Isobel expected an immediate abatement, but that wasn't at all what happened. So much water, and it seemed to have no effect. The flames burned bright, maybe a darker shade of orange, but still high, still licking the next building over. One of the hoses was trained on that building now, preventing a spread through the Victorian row houses that lined Cumberland Street.

Their hands were close, hers and Ahmed's. She could feel his skin against hers, rubbing gently as he breathed. She could hear his breath, and feel it, and smell it—minty, cool. She found herself tugging at his jacket.

Stepping away from the crowd, she waited for him to turn, but he didn't. He was staring into the flames, just like everyone else. She tugged his jacket again. When he turned, she pressed her finger to her lips and backed out of the boardroom.

Isobel wobbled down the hall in her high heels, hoping she wouldn't fall, praying Ahmed would follow. Ducking into her office, she leaned her bum against the edge of her desk and watched the door. The workplace was never this quiet, except after hours when everyone had gone home.

Even muffled by the industrial carpeting, the sounds of his footsteps rumbled in her belly.

He poked his head inside, grinning suspiciously as she leaned back. She knew she wasn't smiling, and when his grin fell, she knew that was the reason.

"What's wrong?" he asked.

"Come in." She didn't wait before saying, "Nothing's wrong. Just the fire. It's strange, you know?"

When he nodded, she really believed him. She didn't need to explain herself. He understood.

She felt oddly detached as she stepped toward him, so close her breasts pressed softly against his lapels. The satin texture of her top kissed the naked flesh above her bra, and she shivered. She could smell him, feel his heat, and, god, she wanted to taste him.

But first she reached around his back to close the blinds.

The door didn't lock. She'd just have to hope everyone stayed in the boardroom as long as possible.

"Isobel." His voice was a warm whisper against her neck. "What's happening?"

He tensed when she wrapped her arms around him, trying to smell his skin through his clothing. Why should she have to explain herself? Why couldn't they make love in silence, in this quiet, abandoned office?

"In my whole life," she said, "I've only ever been with one man. Can you believe that?"

She didn't expect him to answer, and he didn't.

"What if I catch fire like Sassafraz? What if I burn to the ground tomorrow? There are so many things I've never experienced."

Ahmed's heart pounded so loudly she could hear it over her own, but his cock also surged against her hip, begging to be touched, licked, sucked, fucked. They'd never done anything like this. The most they'd indulged in was a little office flirtation, a little brushing up against each other by the coffee pot, fingers touching, giggles.

Everybody did stuff like that. It had been innocent enough.

But Isobel had endured too much innocence already.

His breath was hot, hard, heavy. It rattled in his chest. She let her hands stray down his back until they met his rock-solid ass. Moaning, she pushed her breasts flush to his chest. Her cleavage rose beyond the upper limits of her satin shirt. If only he could see. She wanted him to look at her body, at her breasts.

She wanted him to *see* her.

Ahmed's cock pounded against her hip. His thumb met the base of her chin, and he used it to raise her head, getting her lips into position. The look in his eyes was new to Isobel. It wasn't innocent, wasn't sweet or kind or professional. His gaze glowed dark and hard, like he knew what he wanted and he was finally going to take it.

Grabbing her ass with one hand, Ahmed kissed her feverishly.

He released her chin and ran those decisive fingers down her front, cupping her breast over her satin shirt. Thank God she'd put special effort into dressing this morning, right down to her lingerie. Everything she had on was classy.

While Ahmed's tongue snaked wildly around hers, Isobel pushed her mother-of-pearl buttons through their slits, opening her top. He grabbed her shirt with both hands and tore it off, tossing it across the room. Blue satin landed on the ficus in the corner just as her posh grey skirt hit the floor.

"What do you think?" she asked, posing like a pin-up for his eyes only.

"I think…" Ahmed took a step back to fully appreciate Isobel in her black lace bra, matching panties, and heels. "I'm a lucky man, that's what I think."

Without taking his eyes off her, he slipped off his fitted blue jacket and hung it on the hook behind her door—over her yoga gear, but he didn't seem to notice.

With that sports coat out of the way, Isobel had a clear view of his cock pummelling his trousers. Just the outline of that massive erection brought a gush of juice to her pussy, and a rush of fluid under her tongue.

She wanted him everywhere at once.

"You like my bra?" she flirted, running her fingers under the straps, letting one of the two tumble down her arm.

"I like it." He cupped her breasts, thumbing her nipples through the fabric.

"It's lace."

His eyes darkened with lust. "I can see that."

They looked at each other, their breaths ragged, before devouring one another, mouth on mouth.

Scooping Isobel onto her thankfully clutter-free desk, Ahmed dove at her breasts, tearing down the cups of her bra before she could get it unhooked. The moment she felt his lips around her nipple, she hissed and arched her back. If Ahmed hadn't reached out to catch her, she'd have tumbled down hard.

"We have to move," she whimpered, scooting across her desk.

Ahmed barely shifted his lips from Isobel's nipple to ask the question, "Move?"

"Hurry!"

He followed her to the edge of the desk. She spread her legs in the place she'd been staring when she was drawing naughty pictures during her conference call. Sure enough, when he got between them she could easily rest her feet against the wall.

Isobel leaned back on her elbows, nearly knocking the phone to the floor.

Ahmed followed her down. "Let me at those tits."

She pushed his shoulders. "Lick my pussy."

He breathed in sharply through his nose, like he couldn't believe she'd just said that word. "You've still got your panties on."

She sure did, and he was trapped in a prison of her legs. The sight pleased her, and she smirked as she raised them straight up in the air. All those yoga classes were certainly paying off!

"You do the honours," she said.

The smell of fire hung on the air, heavier than it had been before. Ahmed's clean man musk impressed her far more. He pulled gingerly at her lace panties like he was afraid of putting a finger through them, so she helped him out, pushing them past her bum. He took it from there, surprising her by taking hold of her undies with his teeth and tugging them almost all the way to her ankles. Taking hold with both hands, he lifted the lace carefully over her heels and she let her legs trap him again.

"Now you can lick me. No excuses."

"No excuses," he agreed as he bent between her thighs.

He sniffed and then shuddered like her pussy was Heaven. Nuzzling at the apex of her thighs, Ahmed rubbed his whole face across her bush, back and forth, pressing his cheeks against her mound. Her old boyfriend never used to go wild over her cunt. Ben had reluctantly nibbled at her clit if she'd asked him to, but he'd never reacted like this!

"Does my pussy smell good?" Isobel asked, for the first time realizing she was naked but for her shoes.

In an office that didn't lock.

During regular business hours.

"Oh yes," he growled, rubbing his face in gaping circles all around her mound.

Just the sight of professional Ahmed going crazy for her pussy made her feel devilish and dirty. "You want a taste? You want to eat it?"

"Yes." It was a grunt and growl in one. He was almost beyond words. "Yeah, I want it."

Isobel cupped her breasts, staring down at the boyish face between her legs. "So eat me, Ahmed. Lick my pussy until I can't breathe."

The groan that came out of him resonated deep inside her belly. Her calves shook. She lodged her heels firmly against the wall. She tried to centre herself like in yoga, but the world was upside down—or at least on its side.

Ahmed pressed his lips against Isobel's mound, right above her pubic bone. At first, she wondered if maybe he couldn't find her clit, but when he kissed a meandering path through her bush, she realized he was just winding her up.

He slowed to a halt as he approached her throbbing bud.

116

She pressed her heels against the wall, arching her pussy up at his mouth. "Eat it!"

"Somebody's anxious," he teased, but Isobel was sure he wanted it every bit as much as she did.

She tried to keep her voice down, hoping to god everyone was still in the boardroom. "Eat me!"

Was Sassafraz still burning? Had the firefighters put out the blaze, or had it spread to the building next door?

When Ahmed licked her slit, the world beyond her legs disappeared. She closed her lips and moaned, trapping the sound inside her mouth like an angry bee. His tongue traced pussy juice to her clit, flicking the bud softly, barely touching it, driving her crazy.

"Lick it hard!"

Isobel's head was spinning. She had to lie back on her desk or risk falling.

"Please, Ahmed, you're killing me!"

He laughed: a hearty, heavy chuckle. Then, he sucked her clit between his lips. The pleasure was so immediate and so intense she gasped, arching up from her desk so fast her feet slipped down the wall.

Ahmed grabbed her legs before she could hurt herself, tossing both legs over shoulders. Her thighs contracted around his face, but that didn't stop him from going crazy on her clit.

The sensation of suction was much different now than it had been with her legs wide open. Everything felt concentrated, the pleasure pooling at the apex of her slit, making it pulse like her clit had a heartbeat of its own.

"I'm going to come if you don't stop," she warned him.

Ahmed seemed to take that as a challenge. He sucked even harder on her tender bud. It felt fat in his mouth, thick and pulpy. She wished she could cram her whole pussy into his mouth. She tried, but it didn't work.

"Suck my pussy lips," she begged. "Suck everything!"

He wrapped his mouth around her labia and clit, putting pressure on her mound in a way she'd never experienced. She couldn't keep still. The harder he sucked, the more she writhed against her desk, trying not to shove her pussy at his face and then doing it anyway.

The hot suction worked such magic that she came faster than she ever had with Ben. Whatever Ahmed was doing down there, it made her wild. She gripped his hair with both hands and tugged at those perfect black waves, squealing as she bit her lip. She didn't know what was going on outside her office door, but she couldn't make any noise. Maybe the fire at Sassafraz had been extinguished and everyone was going about their day.

"Can I fuck you?" Ahmed asked, unbuckling his belt before waiting for an answer.

"You'd better!"

Panting, she slid her legs down his arms, grabbing for his shirt and pulling herself upright. Her fingers found his buttons and brought each through its hole so she could run her hands across the muscled planes of his chest.

He dropped his pants as she leaned in to lick his flesh, and, god, she wanted look down, she wanted to see how big his dick was, how hard and huge it had grown for her, but a stream of bashfulness coursed through her. She couldn't steal a glance... but she *could* roll off her desk and then issue a coy, "Oops!"

"Are you all right?" he asked, his face all concern.

"Fine, I'm fine!" Naked on the carpet, she stared up at his cock. It was... wow. Wow! Her legs fell wide open to welcome him.

He reached for her hand, an offer of help, but when he stepped forward his feet caught the pants around his ankles and he tumbled. Isobel managed to look away from his hard cock just in time to see the terror in his eyes as he freefell on top of her. "Isobel!"

She flattened herself to the floor as he landed just short of crushing her, one hand on either side of her head, his body a plank. There was shock in his eyes, and she knew she must look equally surprised. Even as her heart thundered in her chest, the most intense sensation throbbed lower down.

His cockhead seeped precum onto her belly.

He was ready, she was ready...

"You're really okay?" he asked, the muscles in his arms quivering with strain.

"I'm fine, I'm fine."

His dick pummelled her belly, ready for action. "You're sure?"

"Yes, yes." She'd stashed her purse under her desk, and, miracle of miracles, it was just within reach. Yanking it by the strap, she dug inside the zippered pouch with one hand and pulled out her "just in case" condom.

"You have no idea how long I've been waiting to use this," she confessed, tearing the packet open with her teeth. Sliding the latex sheath down his hardened length was the perfect excuse to touch his cock. She shivered when she felt its steel heat in her hands.

Sinking down on her ready body, Ahmed said, "You have no idea how long I've been waiting for *this*."

When he slid inside of her, she felt his warmth throughout her entire body. His mouth crushed hers in the most explosive kiss she'd ever shared. He was everywhere, in her pussy and her mouth, melting her like butter. She was a glistening pool on her office floor, not even human anymore. She was wild heat, passion and desire, every want at once sparked and fulfilled by this man who'd always been so professional.

"More," she said. "Harder."

She planted her heels on the floor and bucked up at him. He caught her mouth again. Their hipbones banged and it panged, but not enough that she wanted to stop. He moaned in her mouth as their tongue whipped one against the other. He tasted like mint and pussy, a queer combination that stuck at the back of her throat as she returned his furious kisses.

It had been ages. Isobel hadn't fucked like this since... well, in truth, she'd never fucked like this: like a filthy animal on the carpet of her office. Her shoulders blazed. Rug burn was worse than sunburn. Or was it better? She could feel her upper back moving against the carpet, her skin grinding into those industrial fibres. It hurt while the rest of her body lost itself to bliss.

Ahmed fucked her hard, so hard she should be in pain, but she just wanted him so badly. A ball of tension tightened in her belly as she circled her orgasm. It was right there, close enough to touch, but no sudden movements. She didn't want to scare it off.

Sliding her hand between their damp bodies, Isobel found her pussy pulpy and wet. Her fingers brushed Ahmed's cock and he gasped, arching broadly.

"Are you going to come?" she whispered.

"Yes." His voice was high, barely audible. His face was pinched, muscles clenched, body strained.

Isobel touched her clit, which was still too sensitive to be played with. As she started to pull away, Ahmed drove his pelvis down on her hand, locking it against her clit, bringing a spike in her arousal and tossing her headlong into bliss. Her pussy contracted around his generous girth, and a sound came out of his throat, like a canine yelp.

Finding the root of his dick with her fingers, Isobel bit her lip to keep from screaming. Her clit throbbed beneath the heat of her hand as they both strained through climax. Isobel's toes curled inside her shoes. She pressed her feet into the carpet and raised her hips, taking him balls-deep and keeping him there, milking his dick with her pussy muscles until he couldn't handle any more.

He rolled to the side.

She watched his chest rise and fall. She couldn't speak, not even to tell him, "That was amazing."

They didn't move until the shadow of a coworker passed by the closed blinds. And then another. Isobel swallowed hard, scrambling to find her clothes and put them on. Her legs were jelly. She could barely stand.

"I wonder what happened to Sassafraz," Ahmed said. He was already dressed and looking decent while she was still buttoning her blouse.

Isobel's hands fell away from her half-done-up shirt. She'd forgotten about the fire, though the scent lingered.

"I wonder if it burned to the ground." Her stomach dropped as she imagined what that would look like: burnt rubble everywhere, all black, once a building, now charcoal. "I need to see."

Ahmed caught her hand as she grabbed the door knob. "How about buttoning your blouse first?"

She rolled her eyes and bit her lip, and gasped when he did it for her, sliding each button tenderly through its hole.

In the outside world of the office at large, things seemed to be getting back to normal. Isobel didn't stop to chat on her way to the boardroom. Ahmed followed her at a reasonable distance. They didn't want to arouse suspicion.

There were still a few stragglers at the window. The space felt eerily quiet as Isobel approached and stood next to a silent Connie. Her heart slowed. She looked down. The fire fighters were still on site, but their hoses were put away. There was a gaping hole in Sassafraz's roof. All she could see inside was black, but the yellow brick walls were still standing. It wasn't a pile of rubble. The restaurant was resilient.

She could feel Ahmed's presence at her back, and she whispered to him, "It didn't burn down, not all the way."

He set a hand on her shoulder and squeezed. "They'll rebuild it. A year from now it'll be good as new." Leaning in close, he whispered, "I'll take you there some day. I promise."

Isobel could feel Connie's glare like a blaze against her cheek, but she stared straight ahead and she smiled.

The Price of a Good Cup of Coffee

After topping my latte with a drizzle of caramel, Chaucer Girl passed the paper cup across the counter. She said, "If you show up one day at closing time and you're wearing a skirt, I'll know what that means."

I cluelessly replied, "I never wear skirts."

By her heavy smirk and lowered lids I knew she was coming on to me, but I couldn't unravel the precise connotation of her proposition. I was a complete and utter moron when it came to flirting.

"What would it mean?" I asked.

Glancing at the other cute barista—either to make sure he wasn't listening or to make sure he was serving the next customer—Chaucer Girl leaned in close. She smelled like coffee. Big surprise. She worked at a coffeehouse, after all.

In a whisper, she told me, "If you wore a skirt when you never wear skirts, it would be a signal that you wanted me to lift you up on this counter and eat your pussy 'til you squealed like a guinea pig."

I stared down at her sleeve. My brain buzzed. Was she going to laugh? Was this a joke? Because I wanted so badly for her to be serious.

"Do guinea pigs squeal?" I finally asked, but I'd waited too long to reply and she was off helping another customer. Good. Gave me time to think about all this before committing to anything.

You're probably wondering whether Chaucer Girl was just some random flirt or if I actually knew her. And you'd probably like to know how she earned the title of 'Chaucer Girl' and what she looked like and how I felt the moment I first laid eyes on her. No worries, all will be revealed.

I'd never had a crush on a girl before *LIN232: Syntactic Patterns in Language*. It was the second term of my second year at University, so I guess I would have been about twenty years old. I was a sloppy slip of a thing, still living with my mom. Back then, I wore jogging pants every day. What did I care what I looked like? I was at University to learn, not to impress anybody.

LIN232 was my Monday night class, 6-9 p.m. With classes all day, I always arrived at Sid Smith a little early, to eat dinner. I'd sit in the hallway opposite my classroom on the second floor, nibbling away at my sandwich or peanut butter crackers or whatever I'd brought from home.

One Monday, as I scrambled to finish my weekly reading before class, I got the feeling someone was watching me. I didn't want to look up in case it was some greasy guy, but I managed to catch sight of a pair of Mary Janes sprouting legs in thick black stockings.

Something about those legs made my heart jump into my throat. I buried my nose in my textbook, but that feeling of being watched didn't subside. It was like a supernatural force pulling at me, forcing my chin to elevate.

Sturdy calves in woolly tights led up to a brown corduroy jumper with two pockets in the front. Close to her chest, she held a large volume: *The Complete Works of Geoffrey Chaucer.*

The door to my classroom opened and the frenzied rush of math students broke Chaucer Girl's hypnotic hold on me. I rounded up my books before she got a chance to re-establish it. For some reason, as I hurried into my class, I couldn't bring myself to glance at her face even though I wanted so badly to know what she looked like.

What was I afraid of? What if Chaucer Girl was only a mirror held to my seeping desire? What if she wasn't a real person at all? From my lazy-student seat in the back row, I fixed my gaze on the doorway. An English major would never darken the doorstep of a linguistics class just to see me...*would she?*

No. I watched the door for three hours and didn't catch a glimpse of her. Well, that's not entirely true. Every person who entered or even walked by the room *was* her for a split-second. Even Professor Cuervo.

Chaucer Girl haunted my thoughts all week, though I'd never seen her face. She wasn't exactly a person yet, more like a feeling or an essence. *A projection*, the Psych students would have said. Whatever she was, I couldn't stop thinking about her. I couldn't keep my nose in a book for more than ten seconds at a time. I constantly sought her out, glancing up and down hallways. Where could she be? Maybe I'd never see her again. My only memory of Chaucer Girl would consist of Mary Janes, black wool tights and a corduroy jumper.

By the third Monday without a sighting, I'd just about given up hope. That morning my mom had asked why I'd dressed so nicely just to go to class. "Someone has a crush," she'd teased in her taunting-Evelina sing-song mom-voice.

I smiled behind my travel mug.

Chaucer Girl was nowhere to be found. Come to think of it, I didn't see a single student carrying a Chaucer book like hers. Maybe she just happened to be passing through Sid Smith that day, and her class wasn't even there. How would I ever find her? I could look up her course number, but the University treated course locations like State Secrets. They didn't want anybody auditing the cool courses, like Microbial Genetics, without paying the exorbitant tuition rates.

After a few more weeks, I downgraded back to my jogging pants. Chaucer Girl knew where my class was. If she'd wanted to find me, she could have. Easily. It was all so stupid, anyway. I didn't even know what she looked like.

That is, until I walked into the premium coffee shop near campus after *LIN322: Phonological Theory*. A whole summer had gone by, but I knew her the second I saw her. It was that same feeling I'd had in the hallway at Sid Smith. Really, I couldn't prove to myself or anyone else that the dark-haired, olive-skinned angel behind the counter was Chaucer Girl, but I knew she was. That's why I turned on my heels and ran all the way home.

"Oh my god, mom, it was Chaucer Girl!" I cried. "She works in the coffee shop."

"You found her?" my mom squealed, poking her head out from behind the shower curtain. "Did you talk to her?"

"No, I ran away."

"Well, what were you thinking, Evie? Get your ass back down there and give the girl your phone number!"

I laughed. "Nobody gives out their phone numbers anymore, mom."

"*Get with the times, mom!*" she imitated in that whiny girl voice that was supposed to sound like mine.

"I need time to prepare."

"Prepare what? Obsessing all summer wasn't preparation enough?"

"I don't know what to say," I admitted, grabbing the nail clippers from the wicker basket beside the sink.

"Start with, *Hi! My name's Evelina*, and go from there."

Gazing into the steamy mirror, I considered how lucky I was to have a mom I could talk to about anything. Sure, she teased me, but the mockery was loving. "But how do I let her know I'm interested?"

"How should I know?" My mom laughed from behind the shower curtain. "You're the lesbian!"

"Mom!" I whined, brushing nail clippings into the sink.

The water kept running. "Well, aren't you?"

I thought about it for what felt like a long time before saying, "I don't know. I feel like it's not real until you do something about it, right? Just talking about it doesn't make it real."

Mom turned the squeaky shower knob and the water stopped. As I handed her one of the new white towels, she said, "Well get out there and do something about it!"

That's when I knew I had the best mom in the world.

Next week after LIN322, I treated myself to the first of my weekly lattés. The cute boy with the flopsy bunny hair served me, but I caught Chaucer Girl's eye. I was pretty sure she recognized me. There was this intense energy between us, like a power line between two hydro poles.

I sat at one of the high chairs at the coffee bar, pretending to read the book open in front of me. How could I possibly be expected to concentrate with Chaucer Girl preparing drinks on the other side of the counter? She had the hugest, darkest eyes I'd ever seen, but every time she glanced in my direction, mine were back in the book. I read the same sentence over and over, never taking it in, until I could feel that she'd looked away.

Week after week I went back, taking her in without talking to her beyond the basics of, "Large caramel latté, please," and, "Thanks," when it was prepared. I always sat close at hand, watching her while she worked. The din of the coffee house blended into a muted soundtrack to Chaucer Girl's drink preparations.

One week, a woman with a nasty demeanour came in and pushed her way to the front of the line to order—demand, more like—a glass of ice water.

"Coming right up!" my crush replied with a saccharine smile.

When she turned in my direction to scoop the ice into a plastic cup, I tried to be invisible but it was too late. Direct eye contact. God, she had gorgeous lashes! And that smile, knowing and sublime like a Mannerist Madonna...

"That's way too much ice!" the cow in the hot pink windbreaker bitched. Chaucer Girl's smile faded into a cloudy grimace. She rolled her eyes. Leaning in close to my ear, she uttered the most beautiful statement I'd ever heard: "It's free, you stupid cunt! Take what you get."

I thought my heart would explode! Chaucer Girl had shared her innermost feelings with me. *She trusted me!* And now she'd put that phoney grin back on and fill the cup with water from a tall spout.

"It's hot outside; the ice'll melt," she told the bitchy customer.

"If you can't even get a glass of water right, I'll take my business elsewhere."

"One can only hope," Chaucer Girl grumbled as the woman strutted away.

As she helped other customers, I felt our connection deeper than ever. It was like there was a thread tied to my finger and to hers. No matter where she went, we were attached. She'd shared something with me. We were connected.

The very next week, that skirt conversation happened. I was bold. I told her I liked her little black military jumper. She said she'd like to see me showing a little leg, and it went from there.

So, to answer the earlier question of whether we knew each other when she offered to put me on the counter and eat my pussy... well, not in the sense that we'd had an actual conversation. I was a little worried. The more I thought about it, the less confident I felt in going through with it. Fortunately, I had my mom to egg me on.

For some, the preparation is half the fun. For me, it's half the battle. I've always hated getting dressed up and—wouldn't you know it—the two skirts I owned didn't fit, which was just as well because they were ugly as sin. 9:48

on a school night and I was trawling Mom's closet for something skanky to wear.

"My clothes are not skanky!" Mom said self-righteously.

Did I say that out loud? Wow. I was losing it.

"I don't have anything to wear," I told her.

"How about this?" She held up a long summery skirt.

"It's so flowery."

"This?"

Ugh. "Nothing with sequins!"

My mom set her fugly club attire down on the bed. "I'm sure this girl will like you no matter what you're wearing." Shaking her head, she went on, "I keep saying 'this girl.' What's her name, Evie?"

Blank slide. No disk. Please insert video. "Chaucer Girl?"

"Evelina!" I got the gruff mom-voice for that. "Ask what her name is before you..." Mom started up with a penis-in-vagina hand motion, running two straight fingers through two in a circle. When she realized that gesture wasn't the most relevant, she said, "Oh, wait, that's wrong." She waggled her tongue through a V in her fingers.

"Ew, Mom, don't be disgusting!" I threw my hopeless self into my mother's closet and came face-to-face with *the* perfect skirt.

"*Yeah, Chaucer Girl, just like that!*" my mom teased.

"This is it!" I cried, tearing the army green skirt from the rack. "Will you stop? You're grossing me out!"

"So-o-o-rry," Mom chuckled. "I'm sure you're just meeting up for a midnight poetry reading. Grab a jacket on your way out; it's getting chilly. And make sure to find out this girl's name before you do the nasty!"

Sometimes I was really glad there was nobody else within earshot when my mom said these things.

"Okay," I relented, and grabbed a jacket.

I walked five laps around the coffee house before I could bring myself to go inside. My stomach plunged as I opened the door. The cute boy who worked there rounded up trash while an Asian woman lifted the cash tray from the till. Chaucer Girl was nowhere in sight.

"We're just closing up," the floppy-haired boy told me. "Can I get you anything?"

"The girl who works here..." I stammered. *Where was she?*

"Oh, she isn't closing tonight," the boy said, lifting a bag of trash from the receptacle. I was already halfway out the door when he called, "Try Thursday."

As I walked out into the cold, I just wanted to cry. How could I feel rejected? Chaucer Girl wasn't even working that day! But I couldn't reason with myself. It hurt, and that was that.

I probably should have taken the subway home, but my feet were trying to run away from me. *Damn it!* Here I made this attempt, I was really going to go for it and... *damn it!* Why was I always losing this girl? This was only a small loss, perhaps, but I felt so abandoned. Of course she didn't close seven days a week. Why did I expect her to be there whenever I happened to show up? But *Thursday...* the boy said come Thursday. That gave me something to place on the horizon, like a stained glass window: something to colour the world between now and then.

Thursday was too cold for a skirt, but I wore that army green one again anyway. Too cold for a tank top, so I took my mom's advice *and* her black denim jacket.

Thursday, I was too cool for school.

Thursday, I couldn't get her out of my mind, couldn't study, couldn't eat, couldn't concentrate on anything but Chaucer Girl. Why did the day have to be so long? Why did it have to include a morning and an afternoon when all I needed was the night?

I squirmed in my chair, trying to keep my ass in that library until closing time, but my boots were made for walking. I could pretend to study just as well at the coffeehouse.

More man than mouse, I strutted through the door and there she was behind the counter. Her dark eyes seemed happy to see me, and a smile grew across her pouty pink lips when she said, "You're wearing a skirt."

Was this really happening? The lust in the air was palpable, thick as the last few sips of a blended iced coffee. God, I wanted to kiss her then and there, customers and all. There were no games with Chaucer Girl, not anymore. We'd been coy long enough. Time for action. How many minutes until I could lift that green apron over her head, unbutton that black blouse, kiss her lips, kiss her breasts? I needed to know.

"Are you going to keep your word?" I asked.

She leaned in so close I could feel her warm breath in my ear. "We had a deal."

Chaucer Girl made me a latté and wouldn't take a dime for it. The conversation was a haze interspersed between drink preparations. The words weren't important; it was all about the heaving heart sensations, the longing soon to be fulfilled, the excitement of what was new. Every sip of latté was a sip of her; she'd made it. Every breath of coffee aroma was an inhalation of her perfume. The minutes ticked on like ages. Would this place never close?

At eleven o'clock, the flopsy-haired boy shot me a knowing glance and peeled off his green apron. "You're okay to close up on your own?"

"I won't be on my own, but yeah." A lusty growl bubbled behind the words. When he left, she locked the door behind him.

She dimmed the lights until nothing but a dull glow emanated from the art glass sconces. I was hot all over, but my skin tingled with goosebumps.

I took off my jacket. As I slipped down from my swivelling bar chair, I realized I could see myself in the darkened storefront windows. I could watch Chaucer Girl's hips from behind as she swaggered toward me.

"Are you ready for this?"

"Yeah," I tried to say, but it came out as a breathy "uhhh," so I nodded my head to be clear.

She had the most incredible eyes, big thick lashes, skin almost blue in this light, and she was so close her breath warmed me. Her hands grasped my hips, my sides, my ass, as her tongue flitted like hummingbird wings between my open lips.

Hunger for Chaucer Girl overtook my senses and I grabbed her apron, kissing her with more heat than I'd ever kissed any guy. This wasn't some blasé interaction, it was a deep longing, a long time coming. It was a whole summer of hoping to see this girl again and for the first time.

As I took her head in my hands, turning her a bit, an image in the darkened windows made me tremble: the reflection of my shimmering tongue gliding into Chaucer Girl's mouth shone back at me. It was the hottest thing I'd ever seen. I'd never seen what I looked like kissing someone. Where could I buy the video? That image was one for the memory vaults. It swelled my passion and I kissed her again, watching our mouths, our bodies, our hands, in the window. I couldn't believe how composed I felt, like I was going to do this and it was going to be incredible and there was nothing to be afraid of...except...

"I have to pee."

"Do you?" Chaucer Girl asked matter-of-factly. And then she poked me in the belly.

"Hey!" I recoiled, back to the bar chair. Her gaze was playful, testing, like the cat that scratches the carpet just to see what you'll do about it. "I'd rather not go right here."

"Yeah, use the washroom like a normal person, ya little freak!" She poked me again.

My cheeks were burning bright red, and my lips looked bee-stung in the bathroom mirror. Tearing my gaze from my own petrified reflection, I pulled up my skirt and set my bum down on the toilet seat. Should I have gotten rid of this hair altogether, or was the trim good enough? Girls could be so judgmental...

My stomach leapt with doubt until I closed my eyes and saw that window-image of my glistening tongue slipping into her hot mouth. That snapshot memory was enough to pump up my confidence. When I strutted back into the coffeehouse, Chaucer Girl had drawn the blackout shades and lit the gas fireplace in the corner of the shop.

"Hop up," she bid. The metal-on-laminate tap of her rings against the coffee counter sounded out as she slapped her hand down on it.

"I thought you were gonna throw me up," I said, but that didn't sound right. "I mean, set me up there..."

Looking me straight in the eye, she grabbed my hips and pulled me close. Another of those crazy adrenaline rushes surged through me and I kissed her, our teeth clacking together because I guess she wasn't expecting me to be so bold. But how could I not?

Before I heard the words creeping up, I was saying, "God, you are so fucking hot I could swallow you whole!"

Growling like a vixen, she lifted my feet clear off the ground. With a bit of a hop and one foot on the bottom rung of the barstool, I made my way onto the coffee counter.

Chaucer Girl rolled my soft skirt up my thighs. Her hot tongue forged a glistening path to my slit as I set one foot on the coffee counter, the other on a barstool.

"Closer," she instructed, pulling me toward the edge of the counter. Her eyes grew wide. "No underwear? Nice touch."

"All the better to..." With all my blood flowing to my clit, I had no idea how to finish that thought. Wasting no time on formalities—like asking my name or telling me hers—Chaucer Girl dove at my pussy. My whole body surged under the wild assault. I had to grab hold of the counter's back edge just to stay upright.

Like a cat with cream, she licked my clit in even-tempoed tongue-thrashes until I couldn't resist closing my thighs against her olive cheeks. When she looked up at me with a hint of a dimple just above the corner of her mouth, my aching hunger spoke for me. "God, you're gorgeous."

A definite dimple pricked her cheek at the compliment, and she sank between my legs. Chaucer Girl waved her head madly, side to side. Her dark hair thrashed my thighs as she ate my pussy. As the waves of my first orgasm with another girl pounded up the beaches of my body, she grabbed my ass. I pretty much exploded at that sensation of flesh on flesh. I couldn't keep my mouth shut. "Oh, oh, oh my fucking lord, that's incredible!"

Smiling demurely, Chaucer Girl sat up on the bar chair. Her chin gleamed with my juices. Licking her lips like a wicked tease, she said, "Lean back."

I sank to my elbows on the coffee counter as Chaucer Girl grabbed a squeeze bottle and drizzled my thighs with caramel. The sticky stuff felt cool against my hot flesh, but her tongue sizzled against my skin as she licked the sweet mess. I watched her, entranced, as she consumed that tawny syrup, and wondered how it must taste: caramel combined with the salt of my skin, and the heavy aroma of pussy already on her tongue. It felt so naughty to be food for her, to be her serving dish and her meal all at once. She made growling *mmm* sounds in the back of her throat as she licked up the last traces of caramel, then planted heavy kisses across my thighs.

After coming so fast under Chaucer Girl's expert tongue, I wanted more. I was greedy for this girl, and for pleasure. I wanted to come again.

She must have known. She must have read my mind, because, nuzzling my clit, she licked through my pubic hair, chomping down and tugging with her teeth. Glad I didn't shave. Besides, pubic hair gives a pussy personality.

She ate me faster. Her full lips worked my tender bud with such wrath and precision they might have been the tip of a vibrator pressed square to my clit. It seemed beyond the range of human capability. I wanted to grab her head, press her gorgeous face against my cunt, trap her between my legs and never let go, but I couldn't bring myself to move. That human-generated vibration was so perfect I was afraid that if I budged, it would all fall apart. Even my throat was afraid the slightest noise might scare off that flaming comet from the realm of the screaming orgasms. But no, nothing could fight that thing off. It struck hard, blowing my body and mind into pools of pleasure.

I came so hard I thought I'd die. But I didn't. In fact, as I gazed down at the beautiful face between my thighs, I felt more alive than ever.

She kept going, even though I was now pulling her hair and trembling, writhing, bucking on the coffee counter.

I think I said "No."

I think I said "Stop."

But maybe I didn't.

Maybe I issued indecipherable cries and moans and shrieks and hollers.

Maybe I just pressed my pussy hard against her face, rubbing my wetness all over her lips, even against her nose and across her chin.

I'd never felt such an intense sensation—never in my life! I couldn't help my actions, even though it kind of embarrassed me to treat her face like some kind of living sex toy. My pussy was so wet, so hot, my clit so wonderfully engorged, that all I could do was let my body conspire with her mouth. She gave me pleasure I'd never known, and I went crazy with it until I really, really couldn't take any more. I pressed her away, begging for mercy, and finally she relented.

Chaucer Girl sank forward and, using my belly for a pillow, brushed her fingers down my thighs. I don't know how long we stayed like that, basking in comfortable silence. Really, what was there to say when your mind has just been blown apart? Besides the old standard, of course: "God, that was incredible."

She teased me. "Really? You didn't seem all that into it..."

"Bullshit!" I laughed, brushing her bangs from her eyes. "Should I...you know...reciprocate?"

"Not tonight." Chaucer Girl let out a pleasant sigh as she propped her chin against my stomach. "But if you ever want to return the favour, I can guarantee you so much free coffee you'll OD on caffeine."

When I laughed, her head bounced against my belly. "Wouldn't that make me some kind of coffee whore?"

"Yes it would." Her teasing smile sparkled like the night sky.

"God, you're beautiful. I don't know why you'd be interested in me."

"Oh, give me a break!" Chaucer Girl rolled her eyes, slipping out of the bar chair. "I only date girls who are hotter than I am. It's a little rule I have."

I sat straight up on the coffee bar and watched her saunter to the centre of the café. No point squabbling over who was better-looking. Neither of us could ever win that argument, even if she was the clear victor in my eyes.

"Date..." I stammered. "Do you date a lot of girls? Or...I mean...is there someone special in your life?"

"Yes," she said with an absolute nod. "There is now."

When a new smile broke across her lips, mine followed suit. Tonight I'd been bold to the point of numbness, almost. Now my heart seemed to be defrosting, and everything she did and said filled me with emotional wonderment.

"I've never dated a girl before," I admitted.

"I know," she replied right away. "I have a sense about these things. But I knew you had it in you. I knew that from the moment I first saw you."

'Which moment?' I wondered. 'Last year in Sid Smith, or this year in the coffeehouse?'

I sat perfectly still on the counter, hoping she'd go on, but she didn't. I'm not sure why, but I didn't want to ask the question. I just wanted her to tell me.

With a broad grin, Chaucer Girl meandered around the coffeehouse, tracing her fingers across the backs of chairs and the tops of tables. "So, you want to go out some time?"

I almost laughed because the order of operations seemed so off. Weren't people generally supposed to go on the date first and then have sex? Chaucer Girl had set me on the coffee counter and eaten my pussy, and I didn't even know her name yet! "Yeah, I want to go out with you. When were you thinking?"

"Tomorrow night?" she said. "A friend of mine is in a play at Hart House. Meet me at the theatre around seven?"

My heart fluttered. "For sure. I'll be there."

She smiled and nodded slowly as our gazes locked. For a deep moment, I watched her gorgeous face as she breathed. I really couldn't believe this was happening. After a summer of obsession, I'd found Chaucer Girl and she'd found me. Tonight she'd given me two orgasms and tomorrow we were going to the theatre together.

"Now get on out of here," she chuckled, "before I slap your ass with a wet coffee filter."

Dripping from the counter, I pulled my skirt down to cover the happy mess of my damp thighs. "Okay. I'll see you tomorrow." I hopped to the door on joyful feet, and pushed. It didn't open. I pulled on the door, but nothing, so I pushed again.

"Oh, sorry!" Chaucer Girl chuckled. "I forgot to unlock it for you..."

I pressed my back to the cool glass and she wove an arm around my waist for a sweet goodbye kiss. The sensuality of her embrace made me weak in the knees. Her tongue was silk, and her mouth tasted like caramel and me.

When her lips left mine, I thought about my mother, of all people. I knew exactly what she'd want to know when I got home.

Reluctantly, I asked, "Hey, so, do you have a name?"

Chaucer Girl stepped back with a coy look in her eye. "Maybe."

"Maybe you have a name?"

"Maybe," she repeated, flipping the key in the latch and pressing her body against mine to open the door. "When I see you tomorrow, I'll tell you whether I do or not."

When she kissed me again, I nearly melted into the pavement. She waved goodbye, but before she could lock herself in, I said, "Hey, be sure to wear a skirt tomorrow, will you? I want to start racking up those free coffee credits."

Biting her plump lower lip, Chaucer Girl nodded. "You bet."

And then she shut the door to finish closing up.

Bewildered, I stood there in the midst of a late-autumn chill, breathing in the musty scent of fallen leaves. My feet carried me half way home before I even began to process what had just happened. My heart leapt in my chest.

But nothing's ever complete until you've shared it, and cell phones were made for moments like these. I pressed number one on my speed dial. My mom picked up. "Well?" she asked. "How did it go tonight?"

"Oh my god, it was great!" My joy was her joy, and hers was mine. That's how it is when moms and daughters love each other without reservation. "I think I'm on my way to a lifetime of free coffee!"

A Bite For Dinner

I have a fantasy about this cute guy at the office...

Peter is slim and not terribly tall, with dark curly hair. He's always dressed to the nines in a three-piece suit with a flower in his lapel. He even has one of those old-fashioned hats like the debonair heroes of black-and-white movies.

Did I mention that Peter is gayer-than-gay?

Openly so; it's not just conjecture on my part.

This guy is quite a sight to behold, but my fantasy about him doesn't involve me at all, except in a voyeuristic capacity. What I'd really love to see is cute little Peter getting it on with my husband Ray.

It's pretty far-fetched, but this fantasy started up when I was working a lot of overtime alongside Peter. Ray would always call me at the office to make sure I'd grabbed a bite for dinner. He was always concerned that, if I was too busy, I'd skip meals. He would tell me I should make eating a higher priority.

I kept hoping Ray would show up at my office one evening with a picnic basket full of chicken, like the one Cary Grant and Grace Kelly share in *To Catch a Thief*. My mind would wander to Ray and I inviting Peter to share in our meal. I would see the spark between them the moment their eyes met. They'd look away from each other the way people do when they're uncomfortable with what they feel, but the air would be electric.

To give them a moment to get acquainted, I would suddenly "remember" that I needed to run to the printers before they closed. Leaving my husband alone with cute little Peter, I would race from the office just long enough for the boys to surrender to temptation.

Quietly, I would sneak back in and creep down the hallway, listening for their soft words: *Should we? Could we? But your wife... It's all right, she thinks it's hot...*

They'd shift to Peter's office, lock the door and shut the blinds.

I'd have to sink to the floor and peer inside to see what my husband was up to. If it weren't for those two knee-high broken slats, I wouldn't be able to see a thing.

My Ray's a pretty big guy—"big-boned," he would probably want me to clarify—so I picture him as the top. He'd be leaning against Peter's immaculate desk as my cute co-worker dug my husband's cock out from his unzipped jeans.

Somehow, in another man's hands, that familiar dick would seem like the most delicious thing in the world.

Sitting in his streamlined office chair, Peter would dive at my husband's erection.

Ray would release a great moan as Peter's lips closed around his big cock. I know how much my man loves a good blow job, and I'm happy to sit back and watch him get one from another guy.

Peter's head would move forward, taking in more of Ray's cock, then shift back and away from the open fly of my husband's jeans; toward Ray, then away from him. His pace would pick up like a locomotive pulling out of the station.

It would be almost as if Ray's stomach exerted some kind of magnetic pull on his head, because Peter would always pause for a moment when he was closest to my husband. He'd nearly have to pull his head away from my big man, until his lips caressed Ray's cockhead.

Then he'd swallow it up all over again.

Finally, the motion would become smooth and intentional, on both ends. Ray would grasp the edges of Peter's desk and thrust his hips, sending his cock deep into my cute co-worker's throat. Peter would reach forward and grasp the desk as well.

Even though one had his cock in the other's mouth, they would both be too timid to actually touch each other.

They'd get into a rhythm, Ray thrusting forward as Peter leaned in, and Ray withdrawing as Peter leaned away. They would be beautiful to watch, this cute guy and my sweetheart husband.

I would recognize when Ray was about to come by his unusual facial expressions.

His foot would tap wildly against the floor before he started thrusting in double-time. Peter wouldn't know what to do, so he'd just take the rampaging cock in his throat.

One, two, three slow-motion thrusts and Ray would throw his head back and howl like a beast.

At that point, I would rush to the office entrance and open the front door. Slamming it shut, I'd yell, "Hey guys, I'm back!" and walk slowly down the hallway to give them time to get decent.

I bet they'd start some nonsense conversation about "guy stuff" as they walked out of Peter's office. They wouldn't be able to look me in the eye, and they'd be wondering why I had such a huge smile on my face.

I'm not sure whether I would ever reveal what I'd seen to either Peter or Ray. I'd be concerned they'd feel embarrassed or apologetic, when neither of those reactions would be necessary for my sake.

They'd probably never believe they were acting out my most persistent fantasy.

Neither Love Nor Money

"How's Bernadetta feeling?" Jean leaned over Max's cubicle, wearing the familiar pouty-sad smile all female staff put on when they passed his workspace. "Doin' okay?"

Since when do you care how she's feeling? Max wanted to say. *You bitch about Detta more than anyone!*

But all he managed to mutter was, "Same as always."

Max held his tongue because Jean was holding a huge tub of chocolate peanut butter ice cream. As much as he loved Bernadetta, he wanted a bowl. The three o'clock lull hit hard and he needed a sugar rush.

When she didn't offer any, Max asked, "What have you got there, Jean?"

The creases around her grey eyes multiplied as she smiled. "I made poor Bernadetta a batch of my grandmother's special chicken noodle soup. Should lift her spirits some."

"Oh." Max had to admit, he felt a little disappointed there'd be no ice cream, but he couldn't deny the kindness of her gesture. "Thanks, Jean. I'm sure Detta will appreciate it."

It wasn't easy, carrying the damn thing home on the subway without spilling it all over somebody's fine Italian shoes, but nothing in Max's relationship had ever been easy. Bernadetta was the company's owner and figurehead, and she liked to remind staff that she'd built Detta Designs from the ground up. Everything they did, good or bad, reflected on her. She wasn't sweet or kind, and it didn't help that Detta was goddamn gorgeous. The women who worked for her told anyone who would listen that she'd slept her way to the top.

And, in a sense, that was true. But not in the way women like Jean were thinking.

"Honey, I'm home!" Max called as he stepped into her ornate condo apartment. Bernadetta was rich enough to buy one of those McMansions outside the city, but she preferred to have her finger on the pulse. She could also afford private nursing, but most healthcare workers wouldn't understand her unique situation.

"Nice day at the office, sweetheart?" She looked weak, a shadow of her formerly vivacious self. She kicked off about fourteen blankets when Max stepped into the room. Hot to cold, she went hot to cold, sweating to freezing.

Max put on a brave smile, despite feeling helpless. "Not bad. Jean made you some soup." He held up the ice cream tub.

Tilting her sallow cheek against the pillow, Detta let out a feeble laugh. "Chocolate peanut butter soup? Sounds delicious."

Her effort made him smile. "It's chicken noodle, apparently."

He checked on her five times while it heated up. Her dark hair had once been thick and lustrous. Now it was falling out in clumps. Her hands looked skeletal. Her face did, too, so much so that Max had trouble looking at her.

When she first hired him, Max couldn't look Bernadetta in the eye. Her beauty made his knees buckle. She'd been the source of hundreds of instant erections. All she had to do was saunter by his cubicle and—bing!—he was stiff as a pole. How many hard-ons had he rubbed out in the men's room? He'd lost count.

What is it about her? he'd wondered, back then.

It was everything: the long hair, the long legs, the round ass under those tight leather skirts. Her big tits burst out of tailored jackets, with only the thin ruffle of some see-through blouse separating her golden skin from her thin lapels. God, he wanted to bury his face in that mountainous cleavage. There was so goddamn much of it. He'd always hoped she might bend far enough forward that her beautiful breasts would cascade into full view.

And those were just the tangibles. He spotted a special something in her eyes, when he managed to look at them. They mesmerized Max, and scared him halfway to hell. A man could lose himself in those eyes. He got the feeling many men had, given the way she stared at him unsmilingly, then allowed a slow grin to bleed across her crimson lips. Many men had lost themselves somewhere inside her. Max was sure of it.

140

Thinking back, it was a typical night working late with the boss when he'd discovered Bernadetta's true nature. And when he found out—when he *realized* what she was—everything fell into place.

Max had always been good with visuals. Detta had asked for his help, for his "eye" as she put it. Her office was strewn with glossy pictures and panels of text as he helped her put together the following year's catalogue. He'd always wondered if she meant for this to happen, for any of it to happen, or if it was all some kind of near-fatal accident.

He was bent over the sideboard at the time, in part to get a closer look at the mock-ups, and in part to conceal his massive erection. She'd come up behind him, so close he could feel the heat of her front against his ass. That heat only got him harder. His dick slapped the edge of the sideboard, begging for something soft, something hot. Then rough. And he knew that's exactly what he'd get from Bernadetta.

Grabbing his sides, she dug her blood red nails into his flesh. She bucked her hips against his ass, like she could fuck him with her bones. In that moment, he wished she could. He wanted her to take him, just strip him bare and do whatever the hell she desired. He'd be hers if she wanted him. He'd give her anything.

Did she turn him around or did he do that himself? He couldn't remember anymore. Somehow he ended up facing her. She tore off his tie with one hand while she found his cock with the other. How did she manage to zero in like that? Just *wham*! She had it in her fist, stroking hard through the fabric of his trousers.

Max knew Detta wouldn't be gentle. He'd seen the violence in her, right from the start. She man-handled him, strong, tough, and she stood nearly his height in those fuck-me heels.

She only let go of his cock to bind his wrists behind him—and with his own tie, to boot. When she pressed him against the sideboard, he worried he might ruin one of the catalogue mock-ups, but if she didn't care why should he? So he pressed his head against the glossy board while Bernadetta tore open his shirt.

Buttons went flying, sailing to the floor in slow motion. Each mother-of-pearl droplet settled like rain on the industrial carpet. He was so mesmerized by the subtle shimmer that he almost didn't notice Detta ripping his belt from its loops. When she tossed it around her shoulders, it morphed into a black snake. Were his eyes playing tricks on him, or did his belt hiss while his boss opened his fly?

Max's pants dropped to the floor with the weight of his wallet, his keys, and his merciless arousal.

"Oh my God." Max didn't think he could speak, but the words spilled out when Detta pushed his jockeys down his thigh. "Oh my fucking lord."

His cock whacked his naked belly. The cool air was a relief against the blazing heat of his erection.

Bernadetta didn't even look at him as she grasped his dick, pumping the shaft in her fist. He'd never been this turned on in all his life. When his thick, swollen cockhead spilled streams of precum across his boss' fingers, the thought crossed his mind that this could be a trap. For a moment, he worried he'd be in trouble, maybe lose his job.

His boss answered his unspoken concern with a kiss so powerful it drove every ounce of energy between his legs.

Her mouth sweltered, sizzled, and when her tongue battled his, he fought hard but lost miserably. There was no winning with Bernadetta. She was too strong, too commanding to truly contend with. Max knew instinctively that they weren't on a level playing field.

And yet it was Bernadetta who bent at the hips, scratching his bare chest all the way down, until the pads of her fingers pressed into his pubic hair. His hips bucked uncontrollably when she touched him there, touched his pelvis, slipped those fingers around his balls. He hissed, then. God, she was rough. It hurt, the way she grabbed him, the way she squeezed. The pain was brilliant.

Slipping his belt from her shoulders, she wrapped it around Max's thighs, low down, almost at his knees. He watched in disbelief as she pulled the braided leather taught, so tight around his legs that it dug into his skin. He splayed his palms on the sturdy wooden sideboard. Danger sizzled on the air like electricity.

Max couldn't move. Though his position wasn't precarious in itself, he felt like if he budged even slightly in any direction, he'd lose his balance. But he knew, instinctively, that he couldn't move. Even if he had the inclination.

A dark haze took over. The edges of reality bled into something fantastical, something dizzy and delightful, but with an unshakably sinister underbelly. Something was happening, now. Something that had never happened to Max before...

"Bernadetta?" His head hung low, swinging side to side as she tossed that long stream of dark hair over one shoulder. The snake was back, black, hissing, squeezing his legs so tight he felt choked.

And then another snake, a pink one, tickled his cock. Her tongue. Her hot, wet, slithering, writhing tongue traced a slick circle around his tip. He shuddered. If he'd been able to move, he would have bucked forward, forced himself between her full red lips, but he couldn't budge. He was stuck, and dizzy besides. He couldn't keep his head up any longer. He tried to lift it, but it was too damn heavy.

Slumping forward, he watched her crimson lips part. Bernadetta's face blurred into green eyes and red lipstick on a golden canvas. Her nose, cheekbones, all her features disappeared as she swallowed him whole.

Max's knees buckled as his boss honest-to-god deepthroated his cock, right to the root. He'd never experienced anything like it, and he held his breath to keep from losing the moment. Her silky mouth enveloped his shaft. Her warm breath rustled his pubic hair. She squeezed his balls mercilessly.

And then, at an absolutely torturous speed, she leaned back, leaned away, and very nearly let his cock fall from her mouth. But not quite. She held him between her lips, sucking just the tip before swallowing him all over again. Faster this time. Faster next, until it became an in-and-out, a game, a race.

How could she stand like that, with her legs perfectly straight, in those killer heels? She bent at the hip, with her head tilted so he got a perfect view of her face. She sucked him hard. It was the sweetest torment, but what could he do? He wanted to thrust forward, drive the monster faster and deeper, but something held him in place, something beyond the physical restraints. He belonged to Detta in every sense.

Max wouldn't last long like this. His eyelids started to droop, feeling as heavy as his head, and he worried. Detta kept sucking, but he couldn't watch. He couldn't see. He tried to shift his weight to his hands so he could raise his hips, but it was useless. His muscles had once been thick ropes. Now they felt like dental floss. Despite his arousal, despite his desire to fill his boss' mouth with cum, his body lacked the energy required.

Couldn't he just lie down? On the carpet would be fine. He didn't mind. Just lie down, just a little rest...

Bernadetta sucked him hard, pumping his shaft with one hand, squeezing his balls with the other. Max felt a telltale trembling in his thighs, a quaking in his balls, but it was all so far away, like he was feeling somebody else's orgasm. His cum flooded her mouth, but the first surge sent him hurdling psychically backward, like the recoil on a pistol. Darkness consumed his peripheral vision. All he could see was the golden glow of his employer's face.

The shots kept firing, streaming from his cock to her mouth, sending him back even farther into the darkness. Farther, and farther still. Until everything was in shadow. Darkness all around. Nothing else.

He'd woken up in Detta's big bed, probably looking a lot like she did now. Over the hazy days that followed, as she nursed him back to health, she'd confessed her true nature.

In that strange dream-like state, it made perfect sense that Detta should be a succubus. Why not? It didn't even faze him when she admitted she could steal his essence. She could. All of it. She *could*. But she wouldn't, because she loved Max too much. That's what she said. This had never happened before, never in her entire life. As much as she wanted to suck the breath from his lungs, she couldn't. She really and truly loved him.

Max approached the bed with a bowl of Jean's soup on a tray. The succubus he loved slumped on her pillow, looking fragile, weak as a kitten.

"Bernadetta," he said.

She gazed up at him while his fingers tightened around the tray.

"You can't go on like this, Detta. Take what you need from me. Just take it."

"But I love you, Max. I can't impose this life on you anymore. Trust me, it's not as fun as it looks." She offered a meek smile. "And I can't take the force from strangers, the way I used to, because..." *Cough. Wheeze.* "Because everybody I drain is loved by someone the way I love you, the way you love me. How could I take that away? How could I take it from anybody?"

"A repentant succubus." Sitting beside her on the bed, Max placed the soup tray on her night table. "Now there's something you don't see every day."

He rested another pillow behind her head before spooning soup between her pale lips.

"It's good," she said. "Thank Jean for me."

Max watched as a blush of colour returned to Detta's cheeks. Max knew what she needed, and it was more than just soup. Couldn't she swallow her pride and take what he wanted to give?

Shifting the blankets aside, Max found Bernadetta naked underneath. She must have cast off her nightgown during one of her fever sweats. When he closed his eyes, he saw her body as it once was, and as it could be again: full and fleshy, bouncing and bountiful. He could give her that.

"Don't you think I love you too?" He traced his tongue down her chest. It was deliciously salty with sweat. He didn't stop until he'd arrived at her pert nipple. When he sucked it, Detta's chest bucked.

She gasped. "What are you doing, Max?"

"I would do anything for you," he told her, because she really didn't seem to understand how much he cared. "Detta, honey, I'd give my life for you."

"Please..." Her voice faltered as he kissed a path down her belly. "I don't want to lose you."

"I don't want to lose you!" He cackled like this was actually funny. "Let's get you a little stronger, then we'll find a way to keep you fed. We'll figure something out, Detta. Just please, please let me help you."

When the tip of his tongue met her pink folds, he could hear the lost lust in her cries. Her clit was hiding, but he found it. If he could get her started like this, surely she'd find enough energy to take what she needed. He just had to turn her on first—and judging by her hoarse moans, she was close.

She whimpered when he sucked her clit. He was getting her there—he could feel it. He had the power, and he worked hard at it. Damned if she wouldn't be screaming for mercy soon, her thin frame shuddering against the mattress, her pussy quaking under his tongue.

"Max!" she cried. "Max..."

When he looked up, Bernadetta waved in a come-hither motion. At first, he wasn't sure what she meant. And then she licked her lips, and they looked full, glossy and plump. Deep, deep red.

"Get up here," she said with a smile. "I want you in my mouth."

They were the greatest words of affection Max had ever heard, and as she wrapped those perfect lips around the head of his cock, sucking resolutely, all he could think to say was, "Detta, I will always love you."

Social Users

THE CRAZIEST DAY I'VE ever spent at the office had nothing to do with angry clients or a nasty boss. It was the day when Devi was typing away at her computer and, completely out of the blue, she looked up at me and said, "I don't know how some people wear butt plugs all day long."

I stared at her, thinking I must have heard wrong. "Did you just say you don't know how people wear butt plugs all day?"

With a dreamy look on her face, she said, "Yeah."

I looked around the office to see if anyone else had heard this bizarre remark. Everybody was going about their business as usual. It was such a weird thing to come out and say that I asked, "Who does that?"

"Don't look at me," she replied with a shrug.

I'd worked with Devi for nearly three years and that was the most random thing I'd ever heard her say. The look on my face must have given me away, because she continued trying to convince me. "I'm not talking about myself. I don't do it."

Wiggling around in my office chair, I thought how much more pleasant the workday would be with a big plug in my butt. It's not something I ever would have considered if Devi hadn't given me the idea, of course. I'm not the type to bring my sex life to work, but I couldn't stop thinking about shoving something up my ass.

"We should try it," I said in a tone that could easily have been mistaken for joking. I wanted an out in case she thought I was a total freak. I said, "I double dare you. We can walk over to Lovecraft at lunch and buy a pair."

Without taking her eyes off her computer screen, Devi replied, "You're paying."

Whoever thought to put a high-class sex shop smack in the middle of the business district deserves my undying gratitude. "Adult toy stores" aren't just for guys anymore. In fact, Lovecraft had a chandelier hanging in the entryway, and the window displays were always very attractive. So much better than those papered-over "Adults Only" storefronts you see all over the city.

They had a whole case full of butt plugs. I'd never imagined there were so many different styles. Some were glass, some wood, but most were synthetics. Some of them cost more than a hundred dollars.

Devi and I didn't get matching ones. She chose a slimmer plug with a jelly texture and silvery colour. Mine was thick and bulbous. It reminded me a little of an orange juicer. We picked up some lube as well—a bare necessity for anal play.

The matronly saleswoman shot us a sly smile as I paid for the plugs and lube. I almost wanted to say, "We're not lesbians. Really! We just thought it might be fun to wear butt plugs at the office today." But that probably would have sounded weird.

At work, we locked the washroom door so nobody would walk in as we washed our new toys in the sink. We headed into side-by-side stalls with our plugs in hand. There was only one bottle of lube. We'd have to take turns.

Hiking up my skirt, I wriggled out of my panties. Next door, Devi dropped her slacks. When they fell to the floor, I couldn't help but notice her creamy lace panties inside. She had a quick pee as I squirted my blue beast with lube.

Holding the butt plug flush against the toilet seat, I went all out and impaled myself on it. I tried to keep quiet, but I couldn't help grunting at the earthy feel of having something crammed in my ass. I'd never done anything remotely naughty at work. This was above and beyond.

When I passed the lube under the stall to Devi, I admit I listened pretty hard for her reaction. She didn't grunt about it. She whimpered. It sounded like she was having trouble getting her silver bad boy in there. Her breath seemed to jump and I wondered if she was playing with her clit.

She must have been.

The lube bottle made a squirting sound. She was using a lot. Was it going on the butt plug or on her clit as she rubbed it? If there was one way to loosen up a tight asshole, it was to give the pussy a good massage.

From the sounds of Devi's moans and groans, she was giving her pussy an *excellent* massage.

I could tell when she was about to take the plunge because she held her breath. As she shoved the plug up her ass, she gasped in a perfectly feminine way. I could feel my bum muscles clenching around my blue bulb as I eavesdropped on her. She seemed to be working it in little by little, until the whole thing was crammed inside her hole. When she let out an orgasmic squeal, I wished so hard I was watching her.

But that would have been weird...

Devi smiled when we stepped out of our stalls, but she didn't look at me. My guess was that she was embarrassed I'd heard her masturbating. Who was I to judge? We both had plugs up our asses.

As we walked back to our desks, Devi aimed her butt at me and whispered, "Can you see it through my pants?"

Our office manager Helena happened to be passing by at that moment. When she saw us examining each other's buns, she asked, "What are we looking at?"

Devi and I just shot her a pair of sheepish grins and sat down at our desks. My cushioned office chair had never felt so good as it did with a big bulbous butt plug warming my ass.

Balls to the Wall

THERE WASN'T ANY ALCOHOL at the party, which was fine by Kat. Drinking with co-workers wasn't exactly her idea of a good time. Especially when seventy percent of those co-workers were high school kids.

In truth, there *was* one guy she wouldn't mind drinking with. Edson took this fast food job to help pay for grad school, just like Kat. They'd been hired during the same group interview, where their manager kept asking if they were brother and sister. Like, hello! Edson's family was Korean and Kat's was Japanese, plus they had totally different last names. They didn't even look alike, apart from being Asian. In some people's minds, that was enough, apparently.

At the moment, there were half a dozen fourteen-year-old girls hanging off Edson like chimps at the zoo. "We're going to miss you so much! You're my favourite boy here! Will you text me later? Here, I'm putting my number in your phone."

Kat heaved a sigh as she observed the mist of pubescent hormones coming off the teens. Had she behaved that way when she was their age? She'd like to think no, but the answer was probably yes. Hard to remember. Ten years ago felt like another lifetime.

An artsy young woman with fiery red hair knocked on the glass door. Since Kat was leaning against it, she flipped the lock and said, "Restaurant's closed forever."

The woman laughed. "So I've heard. No, I'm just here to pick up my daughter." She pointed at one of the teens hanging off Edson. "Jeeze, that poor guy."

"Yeah, poor guy." Kat downed her cup of orange drink, suddenly wishing she had some vodka on her. It depressed her that this cool young woman was a teenager's mom.

"So, why exactly is the place closing down?" the cool mom asked. "My daughter was sketchy with the details."

"Reader's Digest version is the transit system bought the property. When they're finished building the new subway line, this'll be one of the stations."

The cool mom glanced back at the huge indoor playground their restaurant housed. "Kind of sad," she said. "I remember playing in that ball pit when I was a kid. This place has been here that long."

Kat turned to look at the enclosed plastic tube slide, ball pit and jungle gym. "Hmm."

"March of progress, I guess." The mom shrugged, but her smile seemed forlorn.

"Yeah," Kat said. "Progress."

The younger teens cleared out one by one as their parents picked them up. The older teens left as a group.

Maybe someone had spiked the orange drink, because Kat suddenly felt the kind of down that only took hold when she'd been boozing hard. The idea of walking out that door for the very last time made her depressed as hell.

When no one was looking, she snuck into the darkened indoor playground and climbed up the jungle gym.

Cool Mom wasn't the only one who'd been in a tube slide. Kat remembered that you could press the rubber soles of your running shoes against the plastic sides and stay like that, stuck there, causing a traffic jam when other kids came down behind you.

Kat camped out in the tube for God-knows how long. Until the restaurant lights extinguished. Until doors locked and cars drove away. Until she was utterly alone in an abandoned fast food chain.

She didn't want to leave and she didn't know why.

Her calf muscles ached from holding her in place. She was just about to let go when she heard footsteps in the distance. Her heart clenched as the playground door opened.

"Kat? You still here?"

"Edson?" Her heart melted, then raced. "I thought everyone left. I'm in the slide."

"I couldn't leave," he said. "I can't explain it. I just couldn't go, and I saw you sneak in here, so..."

She listened to his voice bouncing off the glass walls as he made his way up the jungle gym. When he poked his head into the slide, she said, "Hi."

"What are you doing in there?"

"I... don't know."

"Oh. Okay."

She could feel the hard plastic of the slide against each and every bump in her spine. This position was getting harder and harder to maintain, especially with Edson watching her. She should have felt embarrassed, hiding out like this, but for some reason she didn't.

"I was in the bathroom," he told her. "Not *going* to the bathroom. Just hiding out. Like you. But on the toilet."

"Oh."

"Sorry. That sounds gross."

"No, I get what you mean. A grown woman hiding in a children's slide sounds kind of gross too. Pervy-gross."

"Not for a girl," he said. "If a guy did it, that would seem pervy-gross, even if he didn't mean it that way."

She never knew what to say to him. He was so smart, and attractive enough that all the girls were drawn to him. Edson had the charisma of a boy band, all in one person.

"Get ready," he said. "I'm coming in."

Suddenly his feet were coming at her, then his legs were at her sides and she was somehow flipping upside down, dancing on the ceiling, landing with her face in his crotch as they slid down together. It might have been fun if she hadn't felt so humiliated. Sixty-nining fully clothed in a children's slide. What would her mother say?

Forget her mother—what would the police say?

They landed in the ball pit, her on top of him, both bodies sinking slowly. She struggled to get her face out of his crotch, but ended up falling to the bottom of the pit. Sure it was shallow, but the darkness of night made her heart palpitate. She shouldn't have been so scared, but she heard herself shrieking as she reached for Edson.

"It's okay," he said, catching her arm and pulling her against his chest. "It's okay. I'm here."

Moonlight streamed through the glass walls. Kat looked around. Everything was different at night.

"I've wanted to get you alone since the moment I met you," he said, his breath hot on her cheek, smelling of sweetness. "At that group interview where Natalia kept asking if we were brother and sister, I kept thinking how glad I was that you're not my sister. Because if you were, then I couldn't do this."

He kissed her. Kissed her! On the lips! He held her biceps tightly in his hands—wow, strong hands!—and kissed her in a way that wasn't nervous, no trepidations. Just a thorough, blazing kiss in the ball pit. A kiss she hoped would never end.

When it did end, she had to go and ruin it by asking, "Why did you wait so long to tell me?"

"Because we worked together. Weren't you at that sexual harassment seminar?"

"Yeah."

"I didn't want to make you feel uncomfortable in the workplace."

"Oh."

"So I waited until now, because you're going off to one location and I'm going off to another. We're not co-workers anymore."

"Oh my god, you're right," she said, clinging to him in the sea of plastic balls. "You're right. We're not co-workers anymore. When I go to work, you won't be there. When you go to work, I won't be there. We won't see each other five times a week. We might never see each other again!"

He laughed gently and held her to his chest to quell her panic. His uniform smelled like fries. A nauseating scent, on some men, but he wore it well. Oil and burgers and secret sauce, a hint of salt in the mix, a twist of lettuce.

She clung to him as they kneeled on the floor of the ball pit, like Tony and Maria if West Side Story had been set in a fast food restaurant. Kat then realized Edson had never seen her in a dress. He'd never even seen her in jeans. Only these black trousers and this uniform top, which was fitted without being flattering, just tight enough to get her sweating without the benefit of showcasing her breasts.

Of course, she'd never seen him in anything but his uniform and that didn't make a difference. She was attracted to him regardless. He looked good in his black trousers. They hugged his ass perfectly. Same went for his short-sleeved top. It hinted at the hardness of his chest while highlighting the breadth of his shoulders.

"We can decide to see each other again," he said. "It's our choice, yours and mine."

"True."

"And then, when we do see each other, it won't be because Natalia scheduled us to work the same shift. It'll be because we want to see each other."

"Oh my god, you're right!" Kat held his broad shoulders while she leaned back. When he folded his hands around her waist so she wouldn't tumble into the balls, his touch excited her as much as his kiss had before. Maybe more.

A ball pit might not sound like a romantic place to be, but with the lights out and the moon shining in, Kat could easily ignore the decals of cartoon characters on all the playground equipment. Anyway, it was the finality of the situation that infused the moment with such emotional largesse. This was the apocalypse of their restaurant. No more fries would ever be fried here. No more burgers would ever be grilled. No milkshakes shaken, no chickens nuggeted.

This was the end of days.

Kat traced her hands quickly up Edson's face and cupped his cheeks. Oh god, they were smooth. He must have shaved right before his shift. So soft, soft cheeks, soft lips. Oh, his full pink lips, so kissable. She planted peck after peck before knocking him into the balls and frenching him relentlessly.

She knocked the visor off his head. He did the same to her. She could feel her hair tie loosening, releasing her long black hair strand by strand.

Did he like her? Well, obviously. He said he wanted to keep seeing her, didn't he?

And he'd kissed her.

And he was kissing her now.

When he rolled on top of her and they sank into the balls, she felt the distinct press of an erection against her left thigh.

Light faded from view. She panicked when she realized she was fully under the balls. No wonder kids freaked out in here. It was scary, even for adults, like getting sucked into quicksand, if each grain was ball-sized and made of cheap plastic.

"Get up," he said, pulling her into a seated position. Her butt was on the base. His knees were on either side of her thighs. He was straddling her close when he said, "Let's get you out of here."

"No," she said, grabbing his wrists. "I don't want to leave."

"We'll get caught."

"Everyone's gone. It's fine."

"But the balls freak you out."

"Only when my head goes under. Just don't let my head go under. I'll be fine."

They were both panting madly when he kissed her again. Kat felt like her breasts were about to pop the three little buttons at the top of her uniform. Her boobs had never felt so huge. Her shirt could not contain them.

So she unbuttoned the fiddly little things while they kissed, and Edson took initiative, untucking her top and pulling it up.

Kat liked the way her skin looked in the moonlight: pale, almost blue. What some would call fat, she called rounded. She liked her curves, and Edson obviously did too because his hands moved across her skin like Hot Wheels, zipping here and there while she tore off her top.

Her white bra shone even bluer than her skin. Bright like the moon. She worried someone might see it through the glass, even though the giant windows looked out on the parking lot. There were no cars out there.

So she reached back and snapped the hook through the eye and let the straps slide down her arms. Edson backed off just enough to get a look at her breasts when she exposed them. Big breasts. Round and full, with soft pink nipples.

He took off his top, too, and she stared as his naked chest. Slid her hands from his hard abs up his smooth skin all the way to his shoulders. Almost no hair, which she liked. She could only hope he liked her hands on his flesh as much as she liked it when he cupped her large breasts and lifted them. Lifted them and squeezed. Squeezed and pressed them together.

Holding her breasts like his hands were the scales of justice, he bent down and traced his warm tongue in circles around one nipple. Then the other.

Kat buried her hands under the balls, trying to press her palms into the floor to keep from collapsing. Why was this so difficult? Balls kept getting under her hands, making her unsteady. She feared falling, but she refused to ask Edson to stop until she'd found her footing, as it were. She struggled and struggled, and lost the battle of the balls. She slipped and slid and her back met the balls and Edson came tumbling after.

She felt like Ophelia sinking into a river of balls while Edson hovered over her, suckling her breasts. His mouth felt so good. She couldn't believe how good. She stared at his worshipful face as balls covered hers. She watched him wrap his lips around her soft, sweet nipple and surrendered to the suck.

Closing her eyes, Kat allowed her head to sink until the only bits of her that were sticking up were her breasts, like two desert islands in the ball pit. Edson kneaded her flesh like dough, sucking one nipple, sucking the other, then pushing them both together and licking back and forth between the two.

How could she get her pants off with him on top of her? Maybe she couldn't. Maybe she'd have to start with him.

Her hands found his thighs and moved up, all the way to his belt. She wasn't great with belts. She slid the tongue through the metal, but got stuck on the pin thingy. That was the tough part.

Edson took over, unbuckling his own belt with no trouble at all, then undoing his trousers. They came down easily with the weight of his wallet and keys. Kat couldn't resist. She traced her fingers the length of his skin-tight underwear, finding his erection with ease.

He gasped and said, "You're not afraid of anything, are you?"

She was afraid of being under the balls, but she struggled not to hyperventilate. No sense ruining the moment.

Walking her fingers all the way up his cock, she found the elastic waist of his underwear and slid her hand beneath it. His hard-on popped out eagerly and he growled around her nipple as she wrapped her hand around his shaft.

God, was he ever hot! His dick blazed against her cool palm as she pumped him with both hands.

"You really know how to work it," Edson said as he moved from one breast to the other.

She felt like an explosion of boobs. Balloon boobs! Full of helium and floating up to the ceiling. If Edson wasn't sitting on top of her, she'd probably take off. Around the world in 80 days!

Kicking off his pants, he crawled up her belly and said, "Oh God, I gotta do this!"

Do what? She couldn't ask for fear that if she opened her mouth, balls would fall in and suffocate her. She just had to wait and see. Wait and feel.

He planted his cock between her breasts and pushed them together, forming a tight runway for his throbbing erection. How did she know it was throbbing? Oh, she could feel it against her breasts. She had no idea her tits were so sensitive.

His thumbs flicked her nipples as he pushed his dick in and out of the path he'd created. Who'd have thought it would feel so good? Almost as good as when he'd licked her tits.

When his big balls pressed against her sternum, she felt dirty and she loved it. She wanted more and told him so by moaning, closed-mouthed. "Mmm! Mmm! Mmmm!"

"God, these tits!" he said.

"Mmm! Mmmm!" Felt so good, the way he teased her nipples and mashed her breasts against his pulsing dick.

He grunted as he fucked her that way. The sound was so masculine and arousing it filled her panties with wet heat. She wanted him to squeeze tighter, driver harder, really ram the space between her breasts, but he backed off, saying, "I can't. I can't. I'm gonna come all over your neck."

"Do it!" she cried, popping out of the balls so fast she knocked him down on his back.

When she spotted his erection in all its glory, she couldn't help herself. She grabbed it with both hands.

Edson half-laughed, half-growled. "God, you're eager!"

"I never thought it would go this far," she said as she tugged his dick. "I'm glad it did."

"Do you want it to go farther?" he asked, almost shy but not quite.

Her hands slowed. Her grip loosened. Pre-cum leaked from Edson's dickhead onto her fingers when she said, "Want? Yeah, I want to but…"

He reached for the trousers he'd kicked off and dug into the pocket, pulling out a wallet. From the wallet, he pulled a condom. "But this?"

Was she really that obvious, or were they just on the same wavelength? "Yeah," she said. "That."

Releasing her hold on his dick, she wiped her hands on her trousers then undid her belt, her zipper. She pushed down her pants all in one go. Socks off, too. Totally naked in the ball pit. But where to fuck?

She crawled to the slide while Edson fitted on his condom. When she heard the latex snap around his hard-on, oh, her knees nearly gave out.

"Where are you going?" he asked, following behind her, sending balls in all directions. They made a hollow sloshing noise as he moved through them, which was kind of funny.

It occurred to Kat, as she planted her upper body in the tube slide, that she'd feel pervy about what they were doing if kids were ever going to play in this ball pit again. But tomorrow the bulldozers and wrecking balls moved in. No child would ever set foot in this playground.

Edson and Kat would be the final people ever to play here.

So they'd better make the best of it.

Planting her knees at the base of the ball pit, Kat hugged her bare breasts as she leaned her elbows inside the slide. Her panting breath echoed inside the plastic tube. When she looked up, she saw nothing but darkness. The slide wasn't straight. It had twists and turns. You couldn't see the top from the bottom.

"You're funny," Edson said, whacking her thigh with his sheathed dick.

"Why?" she asked.

"I don't know. All of this. I've never had sex in a ball pit."

"Same here." She glanced back, catching him ogling her ass. Moon ass. Pale blue in this light. "Bedroom sex is easy to forget. Sex in a ball pit? Now that's something you remember for the rest of your life."

Edson smirked. "No pressure, then."

She swallowed hard as he moved his cockhead up and down her wet slit. "Feels good."

"Does it?"

Her insides jumped when he touched his tip to her clit. "Yeah."

"I'm not even doing anything."

"You're doing more than you think."

He set one hot hand on her ass cheek and his skin blazed against hers. From inside the tube slide, she watched him concentrating hard as he found her slit with his tip. She wished she could see things from his perspective.

People were always saying men were the visual ones, and that pissed Kat right off because visuals turned her on too. She was desperate to watch Edson's dick splitting her in two, plunging between her swollen labia, moving in slowly. She could only imagine how hot it looked when his thick tip disappeared and her pussy gorged on his shaft, sucking in inch after inch of swollen wood.

Imagining the sight turned her on almost as much as the sensation of his dick moving inside her. She clenched her muscles and he groaned. "Oh, Kat. How are you doing that?"

"My special secret," she said, working those kegels.

The hard plastic slide felt cold against her breasts. Her nipples didn't get hard very often, but she could feel them doing so now. Cold plastic. Hot tits. God, this whole thing was dirty and ridiculous, like clown sex.

She laughed and he said, "What?"

"Nothing." But she couldn't stop laughing.

"What?" he asked as his dick moved deeper inside her. "What's so funny?"

"Nothing."

"What?"

"Clown sex."

"*What?*"

"Never mind."

Squeezing her ass with both hot hands, he said, "I always knew you were into some weird shit."

She laughed until he heaved his hard-on as deep as he could drive it, bottoming out. It hurt, and she clenched her pussy muscles around his dick, groaning unglamorously. Her voice echoed up the slide and then out of the slide and all around the playroom, a reminder of the pang deep inside her.

"You okay?" he asked, pushing the pads of his palms up her back, on either side of her spine.

"I wasn't expecting that," she said.

"What?"

"Nothing, just the..." She didn't want to tell him he'd hurt her. Anyway, the pain was fading fast. "Just... wow, you're big."

She could almost hear him rolling his eyes. But he didn't say anything, just drew back a bit and slammed her again. She tightened up inside so he couldn't hit so hard, and it worked. With the next thrust, she didn't wait. She bucked back into the saddle of his hips, feeling his balls recoil off the backs of her thighs.

He gripped her fleshy ass. She hoped his fingers would bruise her. She loved it when sex left marks.

"Good," she said, pressing her palms against the slide for leverage. "Yeah, good. Like that."

"Like this?" he asked, ploughing her pussy as he kneaded her ass.

"Yeah, like that. Keep going."

She gripped his dick with her pussy muscles, feeling hot friction moving through them. His heat made her thighs twinge and her toes tingle. Plastic balls bounced against their legs and recoiled with every thrust, every plunge. They worked together, groaning and growling, each seeking their own orgasm and helping the other along in the process.

Kat didn't need to touch her clit. All she needed was a good hard fuck, and that's what Edson gave her. He slammed her so hard she kept moving up the slide. He had to let go of her ass and hold onto the top of the tube. She planted her palms in front of her and pushed, driving herself down when gravity wouldn't do its job.

"Oh god," she cried into the hollow tube. "Don't stop! Don't stop! Don't stop! I'm gonna..."

He banged his hips against her ass, sending his dick so deep she shrieked in the slide. She lost control of her limbs, at that point. Her legs kicked out behind her and her arms flailed. She banged back at him, lost in the heights of orgasm while he let out a tortured cry. He must have been coming too.

She collapsed in the slide, and he got in there with her, hugging her naked body, struggling for breath.

"God," he said. "That was amazing. I've never had sex like that... ever!"

"I know," she panted. "Same here."

"In a ball pit," he said.

"In a slide!"

They stayed like that for a while—probably too long, considering anyone looking in from outside would see two naked butts sticking out of a children's slide.

When Edson pulled out, he said, "Bathroom" and collected his clothing.

Getting up was hard. Getting dressed in a ball pit was harder. When Kat had struggled into her uniform, she left the play area and zombie-walked behind the fast food counter. Nobody had cleaned up after the party. She poured some coffee into a paper cup, but it wasn't very hot, so she added soft-serve ice cream and mixed them to a drinkable consistency.

"I invented something," she told Edson when he emerged from the bathroom. "Mocha Milkshake. Or... Ice Cream Coffee. It doesn't have a name yet."

She prepared one for him and he raised an eyebrow when he'd tasted it. "Hey, not bad."

"I'm so much more than just a pretty face," she said, leaning forward on the counter.

Edson leaned from the other side and said, "Well, I knew that."

When he kissed her across their milkshakes, she felt like Betty... or Veronica—Betty's sensibilities with Veronica's style, maybe? Anyway, she felt old-fashioned. It was very sweet. Not what you'd expect from two people who'd just had sex without having been on even one date together.

But there was something sweet about them, as a couple. Not that they *were* a couple—not yet. They would be, though, once they'd gone on a couple dates. Kat was sure of it. Edson liked her. He really liked her. She could feel it in the way he'd fucked, in the way he'd kissed, in the way he'd pulled back and looked at her with that glazed expression of adoration in his eyes.

He liked her. She was sure of it.

Suffer

Every Sunday, Rex received his penance.

"I did it again, Sir." Naked, Rex kneeled in the centre of Mei-Xing's dark sitting room, his head hanging low. "I did it twice this week."

"Then you are suffering twice the burden," Mei-Xing reasoned. She was good that way, astute and compassionate.

Most people wouldn't understand why Rex classified the woman who punished him as compassionate, but Rex wasn't like most people. He felt things very deeply. Shame, mostly, and guilt as well. Those were at the top of his list. Love was up there, too. Mei-Xing understood that. She understood that his affair was more than just a fling. He really did love Josephine, every bit as much as he loved his wife.

"I couldn't keep away, Sir."

To some, it might seem strange that Rex called his Domme "Sir," but that's the way she liked it. Far be it for him to question her motives.

"I understand," Mei-Xing replied, her voice soft now, a mourning dove's coo. "Your body is weak. Your mind is weak. You are a weak man, a very weak man."

"Yes, Sir. I know I am." He shook his drooping head, clenching his fists behind his back. "If I were stronger, I'd never have started up with Josephine. I'd have stuck by my wife. Eventually, I'd have gotten used to being sexless and lonely—that, or I'd have killed myself. The trouble is that I'm in love with Josephine. If I left her now I'd break her heart, and break mine too."

"But if you left your wife, same thing," Mei-Xing added, standing very close behind him. "Despite the sexlessness and loneliness, you love her too."

Rex turned and looked up, looked way up. He met Mei-Xing's gaze, though he really wasn't supposed to.

Some would say Mei-Xing had a horse face, but Rex had never liked that term. And, yes, her face was rather long, but he liked it. The length made her seem stern. She wasn't a pretty girl like Josephine or a matronly woman like his wife, but maybe that's why Rex liked her so much. Mei-Xing was different. Her mouth rarely smiled, and it wasn't smiling now, but her eyes were. At least, they might be. Maybe. Mei-Xing was extremely hard to read.

"And if you left me?" she asked.

The question confounded Rex. "Why would I leave you? I *need* you. Without you, I'd just be a writhing mass of shame and guilt."

This time she smiled with her lips—a clear indication she was pleased. He hoped.

"Without you," Rex went on, "I'd have jumped off a bridge by now. I need my penance, Sir. I need to be punished."

"Good," she said. The word was like a gust of wind, explosive, and it made Rex's cock jump. He leaned further forward and hoped she wouldn't notice his erection.

Rex didn't come to Mei-Xing for sex—he got enough of that from Josephine—but he did find her punishment arousing. The trouble was that his arousal in Mei-Xing's living room left him feeling even more guilty than he felt coming in. It certainly didn't help that she wore these striking leather get-ups. Today it was a skin-tight black bodysuit with one zipper down the front and another up the back. Rex wondered how she did up the back one on her own. She was single, as far as Rex knew.

Did Sir ever get lonely?

"How do you choose to be punished?" Mei-Xing asked.

He liked that she gave him a choice, but he couldn't ask for his preferred punishment. "The crop left marks, just like the whip. My wife would never notice, not in a million years, but Josephine asked about them last time."

"What did you say?"

"I had to make something up, Sir, and you know what a terrible liar I am."

"What did you say?" Mei-Xing repeated, her tone noticeably stonier the second time around.

It was so stupid Rex didn't want to admit what he'd said, but how could he lie to the woman who doled out his punishment? "I said it was the guys at the gym, Sir. I said they were teasing me, cracking towels against my ass."

Mei-Xing laughed, but her grin remained canine and cruel.

"Josephine didn't believe me," Rex went on. "So I had to show her. After we got out of the shower, I dried myself off, then wrung up my towel and whipped her ass. I've never heard her shriek like that, and her eyes went so wide I thought they'd pop out of her head! I turned her around and told her to look at her ass in the mirror. She believed me after that. It was red as hell where I'd whipped her."

Mei-Xing sat slowly on the divan that was pushed up against the wall. It mustn't be easy to bend in that head-to-toe leather, but she managed.

"Here," she instructed, patting her lap. "We won't leave marks today."

"A spanking, Sir?" Rex crawled to her. "Sounds like just what I need."

Folding himself over her lap, he ensured his cock and balls hung between her thighs before she could close them. The tightness of those leather legs around his straining erection and full, tender balls made him ache. He wanted to thrust between her thighs. He wanted to fuck that warm, supple leather until he blasted the carpet with cum.

But he wouldn't do any of that. He'd hold perfectly still while she brought down punishment on his ass. He wouldn't move a muscle.

"Tell me what it's for, Sir." He braced himself for impact. "Tell me why I need to suffer."

"You suffer too much already. You bring your true punishment on yourself. That little voice in your head never gives you a moment's peace. What I give you is not penance, it's pleasure."

Mei-Xing didn't usually say this sort of thing before the pain began, and Rex didn't get to ask what she meant before her hand met his backside with a resounding crack. The first smack never fully registered. Its bark was worse than its bite. All he could feel was the blood whooshing to his head, which was down on the carpet. He felt dizzy already, and suddenly confused. His heart seemed to be pounding in his balls.

The moment he tried to lift his head, Mei-Xing spanked him again. He felt it this time. There was a sting, an unmistakeable bite that caught his ass when she struck it, and he hissed in response. Mei-Xing was strong. She could tear right through those lazy layers of flesh that sat in an office chair day after day, and make him faint. All that with just a smack of her palm.

164

Another smack. Was this one harder, or was his ass just getting more sensitive? He wanted to look back, see if it was pink yet. It didn't take long. After a few more spankings, his butt would be red as an apple.

Another and another! Oh god, it was starting to burn already. A slow tingle expanded outward from the point where her palm met his skin. Every spanking was a divine shock to his system. Each one gave him a jolt, propelled him forward. His forehead rubbed hard against the thankfully soft rug.

"Thank you, Sir!" Rex could feel himself squirming in Mei-Xing's lap, and before he could stop she brought down another clap on his ass.

"Thank you for what?" Mei-Xing traced circles around his butt, dragging her ruthless fingernails across his flesh while he writhed beneath her.

His cock strained between Sir's thighs. From his upside-down perspective, he could see a gossamer string of pre-cum streaming from his cockhead all the way down to the carpet. It was miraculous, like a spider web. The very sight made him forget all about Mei-Xing's simple question.

"Thank you for what?" she asked again, accompanying the question with a harsh smack. Mei-Xing never held anything back.

Rex cringed, grinding his teeth together, tightening every muscle in the lower half of his body. When Mei-Xing spanked him with all his butt muscles clenched, it didn't hurt so much.

Stifling a tortured yelp, Rex said, "Thank you, Sir, for punishing me."

Letting out a whiskey chuckle, Mei-Xing cast the most effective slap yet. It burned through him like fire, streaking across the topmost layer of flesh as it soared between his legs. His balls clenched so tight they looked like they'd shot back up into his body. When his cock jerked to the side, whacking his thigh, that crystal drizzle of pre-cum smeared across his flesh.

Mei-Xing tightened her thighs around his cock, trapping it in place. She said, "Nothing I do could be worse than the punishment you bring on yourself."

Rex puzzled over that statement while Mei-Xing traced her fingernails lightly down the backs of his thighs. It tickled when she got to his knee-pits, and his cock strained in light of that feathery sensation.

"What punishment, Sir?"

She spanked him and the echo of that clap resounded through the room. Again. Again. *Smack, smack.* Her actions were measured, deliberate. She never punished him in anger or ire; that wasn't her style. This was her job, her role in his life: to give him penance, to redeem him.

"You make..."

Smack!

"...yourself..."

Smack!

"...suffer."

Smack, smack!

His ass burned, truly burned, like he'd been sitting on a stove. His flesh was on fire, and the pain was nothing short of torture. His brain buzzed as he listened to Mei-Xing's words over and over again, repeating them to himself like an echo in a cavern.

You make yourself suffer.

You make yourself suffer.

His cock ached for release between those two leather thighs, but his body was the least of his concerns. Mei-Xing was right about his mental state, wasn't she? He made himself suffer, every day, with the guilt he held so tightly.

Suddenly, Mei-Xing snapped her thighs so tight together that they compressed Rex's balls, making him shriek with pain. When he closed his eyes, he saw stars, constellations blasting across the backdrop of his eyelids, brilliant as diamonds.

"That hurts?" Mei-Xing asked flatly.

"Yes, Sir."

"More than this?" She slapped his blazing ass, and the stars burst into pieces, streaking across his mind like shrapnel.

"No, Sir." He always told Mei-Xing the truth. "The spanking hurts more."

She smacked his raging red flesh, and he jerked forward, writhing now, trying to escape. It hurt so damn much he couldn't stand it, but how could he hope to escape with his cock trapped between Mei-Xing's thighs?

"What hurts more?" she went on asking, setting her palm down on his burning, prickling, hopping flesh. "A spanking on Sunday or the anguish you suffer every day of the week?"

Blood pumped loudly in his ears as his head rested heavily against the floor. His heart went into overdrive, sending gushes one direction toward his head and the other direction toward his throbbing erection.

He knew the answer to Mei-Xing's question about which anguish sat heavier on his mind. He told her, "Every day, Sir."

Sir traced her palm down his thigh, petting him gently while his cock ached for a release that wouldn't come, so to speak. Mei-Xing only gave one type of release: relief of his sins, temporary escape, a chance to let someone else beat him up for a change. He spent enough time beating up on himself. He did it every day.

"Have you suffered enough?" Mei-Xing asked.

The question surprised Rex. That was her call, not his. "What do you think, Sir?"

His muscles tensed. He was ready for anything. He waited for some twitch in her body that would tell him whether she would toss him to the floor or cast her palm down on his ass.

She sat still as stone, giving him no clue. His cock surged, ached, jerked forward as much as it could, but Mei-Xing didn't move.

Until she did.

Sliding her thighs open, she spread his legs enough to cast one small hand between them. Everything happened at once. Her hand landed flat against his tight balls. He yelped, trying to escape, but she had some magnetic hold on him. Rex stayed put, head on the floor, legs splayed, while Mei-Xing spanked his balls. It hurt like hell, and the pain shot through him like an elixir. He wanted to be sick when she slapped him again. He wanted to roll on the floor, curl into fetal position and give up. Instead, he let her smack his balls again.

His muscles clenched, from his calves to his shoulders. When he opened his eyes, he was staring his cockhead in the face. It seemed close enough to suck. That wasn't the case, but the image fucking his own mouth put him over the edge.

Mei-Xing spanked his balls, just softly this time, and it was all over. All over. His dick surged with cum, spewing white stuff directly at his face, creaming his cheek mere seconds after he'd closed his eyes. Another shot blasted the ridge of his nose, creeping hotly down to his forehead. After that, they struck the carpet. He'd pay for that mess as soon as Mei-Xing noticed.

Somehow, he ended up fully on the floor, rolling from his back to his front because his ass burned so badly. He'd come so hard he couldn't move, couldn't open his eyes as his cum turned cold against his face.

"I've never... never..." He stammered wildly, not knowing how to complete that sentence. "I've just never..."

Mei-Xing took a warm cloth to his face, and then to the carpet. She said, "You needed that, old soul."

He thought his pain was buried deep enough, but she always found it. She brought it to the surface, and today she gave him every kind of release.

How did she know what he needed before he did? How did she know things he'd probably never have figured out on his own?

With a compassionate smile, Mei-Xing read his mind and said, "Because, old soul, I've suffered, too."

$150 for the Half

They come to your house, $150 for the half, $250 for the hour. Brittany and Paige. Real original, but nobody cares about the names. It's the uniforms they're after. It's the pleated grey schoolgirl skirts and white cotton panties, pristine as fresh laundry in the sun.

Brittany wears a genuine Catholic School shirt, complete with authentic academic badge. None of the buttons are done up, and the tails are tied tight beneath obviously braless tits. You can already see puffy pink nipples hardening into stiff buds.

Paige is dressed in one of those Japanese sailor-girl tops, flaps grey like her skirt. You know she's got to be the naughtier of the two because she's wearing white thigh-highs with garters amply visible beneath the hem of her skirt. The stockings are rimmed with lace.

They come to your house and play just for you—play *with* you if you want, but it's almost better just to watch. They kiss. You can see their tongues mingling, so you know it's real. They fondle each other's tits, Brittany lifting Paige's top over her head and letting it fall to the floor.

Paige whacks Brittany's thighs with an old-school wooden ruler, pulls down her panties and slaps her ass. What's pinker, her tender cheeks or those drooling pussy lips that soon get their turn under the tongue? Paige has a tongue stud. See? Definitely the naughtier of the two.

$150 later, you're floating on a cloud of bliss and they're packing up to go. Paige asks to use the bathroom and you're so relieved you cleaned it this morning. Dirty girls though they may be, you make sure to treat them like queens.

Deeds of Mercy

If Mercedes had to sum up her ridiculously complex sex life, it would go a little something like this:

She used to date an older guy named Simon, who was married all the while to a woman called Florence. After years of hope and heartbreak, Mercedes broke it off with Simon and ultimately found herself engaged to a young guy named Anwar. Things were pretty solid until Mercedes met up with Simon again, purely by chance. She had no intention of hooking up with him... until he made her an offer of cold, hard cash.

With Mercedes' love of secrets, cocks, and infidelity, how could she refuse?

Mercedes' romantic world had grown into a man-eating monstrosity. She pictured it looking a lot like that giant plant from *Little Shop of Horrors*. She couldn't say why she kept seeing Simon. She really did love Anwar. It wasn't that she needed the money. Well, okay, the money was nice and it gave her a cheap thrill every time she added Sex-with-Simon cash to the Wedding-with-Anwar fund, but it's not like she was living at subsistence level. She didn't *need* it. But she liked it. She enjoyed the naughty thrill of prostituting herself to her married ex-lover while her husband-to-be remained oblivious.

Simon was very different as a paying customer than he'd been when Mercedes was his doting mistress. He'd been so careful before. Now he took all sorts of chances. He didn't seem to give a fuck about getting caught. Maybe that was a product of now being able to say, "What, this chick? I'm just paying her to suck my balls. Don't feel threatened, wifey."

Money made all the difference.

In the four years of their "couplehood," such as it was, Mercedes had never seen Simon's house. Never. She'd never seen his wife or his grown children, live in person or via any other medium. They'd been names, nothing more. In fact, his entire family was off-limits to her, though the rule itself remained unspoken.

That was then.

Now, when Florence left town to visit her parents for the weekend, Simon insisted Mercedes stay the night.

"At your house?" she asked.

"At my house," he replied.

"But..." Mercedes couldn't seem to locate the words required to express her trepidations. She wasn't even sure what, precisely, she was worried about. "A whole night? That's... a lot of hours. And we'll be... sleeping... together?"

Even over the phone, Simon sounded peeved. "The whole time we were together, you begged me to spend the night with you. Now you don't want to?" He let out an *humph* and then said, "I'll pay you per hour of sleep, if that's what you're so worried about."

"No, no. I mean, yes, thank you, but..." It finally clicked why she shouldn't be spending nights with her ex. "Anwar! What am I supposed to tell Anwar?"

"Are you suddenly living together?" Simon asked in his rhetorical voice. "No? Then what difference does it make where you sleep?"

Setting emotion aside, Mercedes looked at the situation from a business perspective: she could either spend Saturday night falling asleep in front of Anwar's TV, or go to Simon's house, get fucked, get paid, go to sleep, get paid, and probably get fucked and paid once again come morning.

"Okay," she said. "You're right. I'll make it work."

With a simple lie about a girls' night out, Mercy set off to visit Simon's house for the first time. Her stomach tied itself in knots. She felt strange, knowing she'd be fucking some woman named Florence's husband in said woman-named-Florence's house. She felt sleazy about it.

Florence.

What an old lady name. Who was this woman named Florence? And why had Mercedes never wondered about her before now? Why did Simon cheat? Did this woman drive him to it? Was she horrible? Demeaning? Lame-o in bed? That must be it. Why else would Simon pay Mercedes for sex?

When she arrived at his door, Mercy expected him to grab her by the arm and sweep her inside, whispering, "Did the neighbours see you?"

Well, that isn't how it went down.

Simon opened the door, casting a dark shadow across the stoop. He looked her up and down. Even as a dog-walking couple sauntered along the sidewalk, Simon smiled and told her she looked good enough to eat.

"I hope so," she mumbled as she crept inside.

She thought she'd be curious about this house of Simon's, but her present feeling was exactly the opposite of curiosity. Mercedes tried not to look anywhere or see anything. Her senses dulled as he guided her by the arm. She stared at her stocking feet as they traversed dark hardwood floors. Where were her shoes? She must have taken them off without realizing.

There were pictures on the walls, but Mercedes wouldn't allow herself to look at them, not even to distinguish whether they were paintings of photographs.

Why had she come here? Business, pleasure, or pure masochism?

Soon, they came to be in a bedroom on the second floor of the house. When had they ascended a staircase? Mercy's mind was muddled with desire for absentia intermingled with desire for Simon.

Despite her best efforts to find the man unattractive, she couldn't help being drawn to a body that defied age. Simon was always hard before his pants hit the ground, and his erections were thick and firm. When he fucked her, she always left satisfied.

Better than satisfied, in fact. Swollen and wet, sore, gasping for breath.

Now he seemed to be undressing her. No, scratch that. He seemed to have *undressed* her. Mercy's clothing hung over the back of a chair by the wooden desk. He was undressed too, but his clothes were on the floor. As always, his erection shot out in front of him like it was dowsing for wetness.

Yes, Mercy realized, she was dripping for him. *Dripping.*

Simon's hard cock swung side to side as he strutted to the bedroom door and closed it. His body gleamed golden in the low light of two bedside lamps, which cast Mercy's shadow up against the adjacent wall. The room was stark, she noticed. But she didn't want to notice—anything—so she focused her attention on Simon.

"How do you want me?" she asked.

He could do anything to her. They'd agreed on a flat rate for any activity, except for the hours of sleep, which would cost extra. He usually started with a blowjob and finished off fucking her pussy. On rare occasions, he fucked her ass. But he knew that hurt her and she really didn't like it all that much.

"I want to eat you," he said. His forceful gaze burned like the glowing embers in the gas fireplace across from the bed. "I miss the taste of your cunt. I want you on my tongue."

That statement should have excited her, but Mercy was too entranced by the fireplace. It seemed brand new. Why would a couple with a lousy sex life get a gas fireplace installed in their bedroom? It wouldn't be for heat. There were plenty of other ways to heat up a bedroom.

God!

Simon and his wife couldn't possibly have a healthy sex life, could they? If they did, why did Simon have had an affair with Mercedes? Why was he now paying her for the pleasure of eating her pussy?

But what reason, other than romance, was there for a new fireplace in a bedroom?

Simon lifted her off her feet and dropped her on the bed. She bounced. The quilt was too pretty to mess up with her juices, but too late now.

As Simon crawled up from the base of the bed, snarling like a wild thing, Mercy felt her inner thighs drench with juice. She crept back from him and drowned in a multitude of pillows. There was nowhere left to go. Only a wooden headboard remained at her back.

Simon smiled in a sneering sort of way. "Where are you going, Mercy? I thought you wanted me to eat you."

"I do," she said. Her heart fluttered as he grabbed her ankles and pulled her legs wide open.

"Nice work if you can get it," he teased as he propelled his body between her legs like a trench soldier. "You just sit back and enjoy my tongue on your pussy, and then you go home with your bra stuffed full of cash. Wish I could find a job like that."

His smugness would have pissed her off a few years ago. Now it turned her on. She couldn't bring herself to play the possession.

"It's too late for you," she replied. "Gotta be young and beautiful for a sweet position like this."

"Sweet position?" Simon chuckled as he dove between her thighs. He went right at it and obviously didn't plan on letting up until she came hard enough to wake the neighbours.

Back when they were a "couple," he'd been so dainty about eating her. He'd give her clit a few licks, she'd pretend he was God's gift, and then they'd move on to something else.

This was something else altogether. Simon was like a different person now that he was paying for sexual gratification. He tore into her like a beast.

Holding her thighs wide apart, he pressed his face firm against her pussy so his lips met her clit, planted his nose in her trimmed bush. Mercy could feel the stubble on his chin against the base of her wet slit. His bristled cheeks scratched her outer lips like as he took her clit in his hot mouth.

Mercy's whole body jumped. Simon sucked her clit like a tiny cock. This was something she'd never experienced before. Where had Simon picked up new material?

Was it something his wife had taught him?

No, couldn't be.

Mercy was convinced they had next to no sex life. She'd convinced herself.

Sensation melted Mercy's mind. She bucked against Simon's face. Now she knew why guys got off on blowjobs. As Simon sucked her inner lips in with her clit, she tossed her head back and grabbed his with both hands. She thrust her hips at his face until she felt the scratch of his whiskers against her slit.

His nose was flush to her bush. Could he even breathe down there? Mercy didn't give a fuck. She ran her pussy in tight circles against his muzzle. The prickle against her tender flesh generated an itch to fuck, and she hoped he'd get his cock inside her soon.

She'd have to come first, of course, but that was no chore.

The harder Simon sucked her clit, the harder it became to resist giving herself over to the looming wave of climax. She forced her clit into his mouth, nearly sitting upright as he splayed himself belly-down on the bed.

With his head in her hands, she pushed his face against her pussy the way porn star men do to porn star women when they're getting their blowjobs.

She felt almost guilty, treating him this way, especially when he'd be paying her in the morning, but she was so close to coming she couldn't stop now.

Finally, the urge to move was subsumed by the urge to receive pleasure. Mercy held Simon's face against her pussy and screamed as he sucked her.

When she finished screaming and could take no more pleasure or pain, Mercy closed her legs and fell back into the cluster of pillows.

Either her eyes were closed or she'd just gone blind.

Her orgasm had so overtaken that her she couldn't figure out which was the case. When she finally realized her eyes were indeed closed, she decided to open them. When she did, she saw two things: Simon looming between her knees with his long cock looking like it wanted to get up inside her; and, on the mantle behind him, a wedding photo. She must only have spent a few seconds looking at it, but she recognized a youthful Simon as the groom.

The woman in the white gown was obviously his wife.

Mercy was shocked by this photo.

Not because it was a wedding photo—she obviously knew Simon was married. This photo told her one thing she'd never known about the man:

His wife was pug ugly.

Worse than pug ugly! She had a face like a bulldog after a bar brawl. And in her wedding photo! A woman always looked her best on her wedding day. If Florence looked like that when she was married, imagine what she must look like now!

"I want to fuck you," Simon growled.

Slipping off the bed, he flipped her from her back to her front.

"I want it doggie style."

"Yeah, okay." She felt too distracted to sound sexy.

And then her gaze fell on another photo. This one sat on the night table right beside Mercy's face. It was definitely Florence—the face was an older, more wrinkled, and even uglier version of the one on the mantle. She looked like a Halloween hag.

Could this really be Simon's wife? Christ, no wonder he was willing to pay Mercedes for sex!

As Mercy lay staring at the figure in the photo, Simon climbed on the bed and splayed her legs as far apart as they would go. That action jolted her into the moment.

Her pussy clenched in anticipation.

She closed her eyes, but the image of Simon's ugly wife seemed burnt into her retinas.

When Simon grabbed her hips, Mercy raised her ass to him. He knew exactly what he wanted these days, and he lifted her up to the perfect height. After piling up pillows under her pelvis, he wasted no time going at her. He rammed her so hard it panged inside, but Mercy didn't care. The pang of a gleaming purple cockhead against her insides hurt less than the sting of resentment in knowing what Simon had stayed with throughout their years together.

He scratched her back with sharp little nails as he fucked her pussy. The pain felt wonderful. He smacked her ass cheeks until they turned red. That felt even better.

But why had Simon stayed with such an ugly woman when he could have had Mercedes?

As his cock raced in and out of her pussy, Mercy realized how ridiculously narcissistic she was being. Maybe Florence was the nicest, sweetest, most internally beautiful person in the world! Maybe Simon had a thousand reasons to stay married to her.

Grunting like a troll, Simon threw his sweating chest on top of Mercy's back. The pillows piled underneath her pelvis held their butts aloft, but Simon grasped her wrists and held them down as he fucked her. She felt trapped in his body now, as her mind was trapped in a cycle of, "Why her and not me? Why choose ugly when he could have beautiful? What's so great about Florence?"

Even as Simon grabbed Mercy's breasts and groaned, the pleasure of fucking couldn't dispel the multitude of questions.

Simon propelled his hips at Mercy's ass and bit down hard on her shoulder. Mercy screeched. Pain soared through her body. Her blood sizzled in her veins. She was sweating all over this pretty marriage quilt, and her pussy juice now graced a stack of throw pillows.

As her cunt clamped down on Simon's orgasmic cock, a series of words tumbled out of her mouth unhindered: "My God, Simon, your wife is one pug ugly motherfucker!"

The room went silent as Simon rolled off Mercy's back.

The bed bounced beneath them.

Was there any utterance crueller than the one that had just passed through her lips? She'd insulted Simon's wife! This was the woman he'd been married to for how many years?

And Mercy called her ugly.

Why would she say that? Was she jealous? Even with her engagement to Anwar, was she still subconsciously coveting Simon? Was she still in love with him?

Or was this wife of his simply unconscionably ugly?

"God, I know she is," he finally said. "And she always was. It's embarrassing, isn't it?"

With a growl, Simon pulled Mercedes down from her Princess-and-the-Pea stack of pillows. Tossing her onto her back, he rolled on top of her. His spent cock drooled forgotten spurts of cum against her leg as he took her breast in his mouth and sucked.

Everything he did to her was animalistic now. There was an intangible sort of brutality in his every move.

After the vicious nipple sucking, Mercedes asked, "Why did you marry her?"

Simon pressed Mercedes' breasts together. When he spoke, his voice resonated from somewhere inside her cleavage. "Back in the day, she used to be great in the sack." He laughed, and collapsed beside her on the bed. Grabbing a pillow for his head, he squeezed her in close to his body and closed his eyes. "Same reason I stick with you."

Mercy's heart froze in her chest.

When Simon pressed a cruel kiss against her temple, she tried to ease herself away, but he only wrapped her tighter in his arms.

The implications were too many, too jarring.

Her mind raced.

Sure, he was paying her to stay the night, but Mercedes didn't sleep a wink.

The Therapist and the Whore

"**L**ast week we left off talking about gender identity," Liesl said, scanning the scribbled sheets of lined paper in her tattered manila folder. "Has that been preying on your mind at all?"

Manny took her usual seat. She preferred the ratty leather armchair to the pristine sofa. It was *her* chair now, a signifier of their relationship prior to Liesl's move to the big office at the fancy address. Manny had been seeing her since Liesl was a wannabe-therapist heading up the LGBT support group in the basement of the University Health Centre.

"On and off, I guess," Manny replied. "But ultimately I have to ask myself, *Would I rather have a cock than a pussy?* No. *Would I ever give up my big tits?* No. But do I want my share of the power men hold in this world? Yes."

Nodding, Liesl said, "Sounds like your masculine style of dress and appearance is derived more from a desire for social standing than an attempt to align gender identity with presentation."

"Gawsh you talk awful purdy, doctor Liesl," Manny replied, slapping her knee in her best Aunt Jemima impersonation. "How long have you and I known each other? I'm not one of your snooty Yorkville clients. You don't have to impress me."

"Sorry." Liesl closed her folder and set it on her lap. "It's like Tourette's with me—sometimes big words just slip out at inappropriate moments."

"But, you know, the way I walk and talk and dress and act isn't only about achieving the social status a man is born into. No black girl's ever going to have that; it's useless trying. I think it's who I am now."

"Yup, you've mentioned that before," Liesl replied with a nod.

"And I really don't attach gender to it. I'm female—this I know—but I'm no girly girl. I'm butch and that's just...me. I think there are different ways to live your gender, and this is how I live my experience of being woman. I don't see myself as any less of a woman just because I don't wear dresses and perfume."

"That's a good point," Liesl said, still nodding. "There are as many genders as there are individuals."

"Exactly!" Manny smacked the armrest with her palm. "Exactly! See? You're the only person in the world who can read my mind."

"I don't know about that," Liesl demurred. "I think sometimes I'm just able to clarify your thoughts."

"You must be so bored with me, talking about the same dumb issues since university."

"Not boring at all," Liesl said. "It's obviously a matter you still think about from time to time."

Sliding from her chair, Manny walked over to the window overlooking the greenery of Hazelton Lane. She'd been trying to get this out for months, and she hated being messy about it. "Are you ready for something new?"

"I'm ready for anything you've got on your mind."

Was she ashamed of herself? Is that why she couldn't look Liesl in the face to tell her? Christ, it would almost be easier to tell Danica first, except that Danica tended to throw things. "I'm seeing someone on the sly."

"Another psychologist?" Liesl asked, mockingly. "I'm hurt."

"Oh, so now you're the joker?" Manny said with a smile, turning around to gauge Liesl's reaction. But Liesl never reacted to anything. "Her name is Star. Well, I'm sure that's not her name, but that's what people call her."

"And when you say you're *seeing* Star..."

"Yeah," Manny replied, leaning against the windowsill. "I mean, not *seeing* like we're in a relationship or anything. Christ, I can't believe how hard it is to say this word."

"What word?"

"Whore," Manny blurted. The hand of death took her throat in its skeletal grip, but Liesl's expression remained unchanged. "Star's a hooker... a prostitute. I don't know what to call her. I mean, I guess that's what she is. I pay her for what she does, but I don't see her that way. Not anymore."

Nodding slowly, Liesl opened the manila folder and clicked her pen into gear. "How long have you been seeing Star?"

Manny wasn't sure if she was in the doctor's office or the principal's office. She didn't want to answer, and that made her feel like a surly teenager. "I don't know. A while."

When Liesl looked up from her scribbles, she only nodded. She said nothing.

"Danica can't stand to see me naked anymore," Manny went on, partly in justification and partly to change the subject. "She darts from the bedroom the second I start taking my clothes off." It occurred to her that she sounded like she was blaming her girlfriend for her own indiscretions, and she didn't want to leave Liesl with the impression she thought that way. "I know it's not her fault. Shit, you must think I'm a total asshole."

"Do you think you're an asshole?" *Classic therapist move.*

"Kind of," Manny said with a shrug. "I'm cheating on Danica. She wants to look at buying a house, and here I'm spending our hard-earned cash on sex with another... woman."

Nodding, always nodding, Liesl asked, "If you don't like what you're doing, why are you doing it?"

"That's what you're supposed to tell me. I don't know!" For the first time this session, Manny felt exasperated. "Why am I paying a hooker to do everything Danica won't? To kiss me and fuck me... you know, with a strap-on... and just fucking *look* at my naked body?"

"I think you just answered your own question," Liesl replied with a nod.

All lies. Maybe next session she'd admit the truths.

EVERYBODY RECOGNIZED The Beach as the prettiest, most family-oriented area in the city. Who would ever have guessed the woman in the upstairs apartment of the mint green semi was what they would term a *lady of the evening*? With flowerboxes along the balcony, it looked like a little old grandmother's home.

"There's my lover!" Star cried in a cheery lilt when Manny arrived at her door. "Amanda, honey, you look like you could use some love. Come in and tell me all about it." Pulling Manny inside by the shirtsleeves, Star drew her into the kitchen's sunny breakfast nook. "I'll put on the tea. Would you like some tea? I would. But we can get right down to business, if that's what you want. It's whatever you want, sugar." Pressing the switch on the electric kettle, she turned to Manny and the feathers at the base of her pink vintage peignoir swished against her legs. "Do you want some sugar, sugar?"

Manny smiled. "You mean in my tea, or...?"

"Or...?" Star shuffled her low bedroom heels across the kitchen tile. Setting her fingertips against Manny's shoulders, she planted a luscious kiss on her lips. When Star tore herself away to gaze adoringly into Manny's eyes, she tasted berries. Star's shimmering, waxy lipstick always tasted sweet.

"Gosh, you're handsome," Star gushed. "Did you know that? You are very good-looking."

"You're the only one who's ever thought so," Manny replied, trying not to laugh. She recognized Star's sincerity. "Even when I was a kid, it was my brother who was the handsome one. I was the dark one. Can't be both."

"Well, *you're* both," Star replied, kissing her nose.

Her gaze was so giving, Manny searched for something to give back. "Did I ever tell you you're the only person in my life who's allowed to call me Amanda?"

"Yup!" Star replied, hopping away to pull teacups from the cupboard. "You tell me that all the time."

"Well, it makes you special."

"You're the special one, lover." Star poured boiling water into the teapot. "We'll just let that steep while you tell me about your week."

As Star sank into her lap, Manny paid close attention to the sensation of Star's ass on her thigh. She wasn't perfectly clear how it all got packed away down there.

"I had an appointment with Liesl," Manny said. "I told her about you."

"Aww!" Star kissed her cheek. "That's sweet. What did she say?"

"Nothing. She just listens. She never makes judgements."

Setting her head on Manny's shoulder, Star went uncharacteristically quiet. Times like these, Manny tried to assure herself this was just a job for Star, but she knew that wasn't the highest truth. In the silences, Manny worried. She was always afraid Star would make some comment about dumping Danica and moving in together. One day, Star would slip. Manny was sure of it.

"Tea should be ready," Star said in her most shimmering tone of voice. When the tea ran clear, she grimaced and lifted the lid on the pot. "Would you look at that? I didn't put any teabags in! Boy, I'd lose my head if it wasn't attached." Leaning against the counter, she asked, "Should I try again, or should we head to the next room?"

Rising from her chair, Manny placed her arm around Star's waist. "I love your use of euphemism. *The next room.* Is that sequential? The kitchen is the first room, the bedroom is the next room..."

"And the bathroom is the last," Star giggled, trotting across the kitchen in her heels. She slipped into the bedroom before Manny, and hid behind her closet door to take off her panties. After all this time, Manny had stopped wondering why Star was so mysterious about it. Manny used the opportunity to take off her trousers. She left on her buttoned-up shirt, despite the heat.

Star emerged in her peignoir and lace bra, absently stroking her cock as she looked Manny up and down. "You're binding every time I see you know."

Shrugging like it was just a big coincidence, Manny said, "I guess so." She tried to sound casual about it. "Why, does it bother you?"

"Of course not." Star approached at a snail's pace, all the while encouraging her erection with her fingertips. "Does it bother Danica?"

Manny breathed in sharply. It seemed so wrong when Star said her girlfriend's name. She had to be honest. "Yeah, I think it bothers Danica a lot. It really bugs her when we're out at a restaurant and the server calls me sir and I don't argue. She pouts through the whole meal."

"Does that happen often?"

"When I'm binding especially, yeah." Manny pulled her shirttails between her legs to cover her pussy. "It's an easy mistake."

Star gave her a generous smile. "Mistake?"

Manny couldn't keep from staring at the cock surging from behind Star's robe. She watched its swollen head pop out from between Star's fingers as she pumped it with her fist. She'd always thought its flesh looked much pinker than the rest of Star's bronze body, especially when all the surrounding flesh was so neatly shaved. Star had the gentlest-looking penis she'd ever seen. Not that Manny had a lot of experience with penises.

"What do feel like today?" Star asked. "Anal or..."

182

"I don't know yet." Manny didn't want to hear the word that would come next. "Can I just suck it?" She slid to her knees at the foot of Star's bed and waited for feeding time. "Let me suck it. Please."

With a chuckle, Star said, "Of course."

She drew near, smelling of flowers and soap. Taking the back of Manny's head in her hand, she held her cock by the base and ran its tip side to side across Manny's lips. Manny opened her mouth to suck, and salty pre-cum fell against her taste buds. She couldn't explain to herself why she loved the sensation of a cock firming up between her lips.

Would Liesl ask about the sex, if she made a full confession? No, Liesl never dug that deep. But she might. The chance was there.

As Manny ploughed her head back and forth, Star guided her motion with both hands. She sucked the shaft. She released, leaning back, back, back until just the tip of Star's cock remained between her lips. As Star looked on like a fairy godmother, Manny held her cock steady with the tips of her teeth and tickled the slit with her tongue. Star giggled and ran her pink fingernails down Manny's neck.

"Ooh, that feels nice."

For a butch dyke, Manny knew she was pretty damn good at sucking cock. Star didn't have to say it. She swallowed the shaft right down to the base. Her throat wanted to gag, but she wouldn't let it. She sucked and it settled. Cooing words of love, Star wrapped her peignoir around Manny's head until the light of day turned gauzy and pink. She grabbed Star's ass and squeezed her firm cheeks. Manny let her thrust her hips a bit, even though she preferred being in control of the motion.

Enough.

When she rose to her feet, Manny found herself trapped in Star's arms as well as her robe. Until she stood with her thighs closed, she didn't realize how wet she'd become. Who'd have thought giving head would be such a turn-on?

Manny stepped back, but they were closer to the bed than she realized. She fell back on the plush mattress. As she kicked the quilted coverlet to the floor, Star plucked a condom from the side table and tore the packet. Holding it wide open with long glittering nails, she asked, "Would you like to do the honours?"

Manny plunged her fingers inside and pulled out the slippery condom. Every time she squeezed the tip and slid the slick latex down the length of Star's firm shaft, she thought of green bananas and Ms. Kensington's health class. Little did that saucy teenager know she'd be using these things with a transsexual whore while her girlfriend worked extra hours at a retail franchise.

Whore? Why did she always use that word, even inside her own mind? It was unbearably crass and it certainly didn't do Star justice.

"What are you thinking?" the girl in the pink peignoir asked.

Danica liked that question too. Manny hated it. Inwardly, she refused to answer.

Gripping the base of her rock ready cock, Manny pulled on it until Star eased herself on to the bed. Straddling Manny's half-naked body, Star took back ownership of her sheathed erection. She unbuttoned the bottom of Manny's shirt, exposing her wet cunt to the sunny bedroom. Kneeling close, Star grasped the base of her shaft and smacked her with it. Manny leapt at the sensation of smooth latex flogging her engorged pussy lips. Star smacked her again and again, aligning her cockhead with Manny's clit. Manny's whole body surged with adrenaline and desire. She needed a good fuck. *God, did she need it.*

Slipping her fingers between her thighs, Manny pressed Star's slick cock down until the tip entered her slit. Everything seemed inconceivably wet. Manny couldn't believe her body was creating all that juice. Star must have slipped some lube up her cunt when she wasn't looking.

"You want it?" Star teased, pushing just the tip inside Manny's eager slit.

Manny thrust her hips hard to feel Star all the way inside her. "Aw yeee-ah!"

There was no other feeling like this one. She loved taking Star's firm cock in her snatch. Some days she couldn't do it. Some days she took it up the ass. Today she wanted the classics—penis-in-vagina sex.

"Give me your tits," Manny cried, anxiously, like she wanted to do everything quick before she came... like a man...

Star lifted her tits out of her bra and tucked the lace off to the sides. "Gimme!" Manny urged like a child. With Star, she was selfish.

Leaning forward, Star set her tits on either side of Manny's mouth. When she shimmied left and right, they slapped Manny's cheeks.

This is where their height difference came in handy. While Star grasped Manny's hips and fucked her from on top, Manny pressed her tits together and licked them from below. Sucking Star's nipples in alternation, Manny pressed her feet flat against the bed and drove her cunt upward to meet Star's raging erection. She sucked so hard Star squealed. This was good. This was *so* good. It never felt like this with a strap-on. *Cocks rock my socks.* Manny laughed.

Star offered a breathy but distracted chuckle. "What?"

Manny shoved a tit in her mouth so she wouldn't have to answer. Her mind said stupid things, at times. As she sucked, Star yelped. She held tighter to Manny's hips and pumped in double time, but she obviously couldn't fuck fast enough, kneeling. She flipped Manny onto her stomach. As she grabbed the good lube from the side table, Manny eased her knees underneath her body and stuck her butt in the air.

Smearing cold lube up and down Manny's ass crack, Star shoved her cockhead in Manny's hole and held tight. Manny looked back as Star ran her long fingernails down her ass cheeks. She loved the contrast of Star's tan thighs against her dark rear.

Leaning way down low, Star grazed Manny's clothed back with her erect nipples. Manny's asshole pulsed like it was trying to suck her cock in deeper. When Star rose up and flipped long dark hair behind her shoulders, Manny watched the pink feathers at the base of her sleeves shiver with delight.

Star pressed her cock deeper inside, pouting her full pink lips. Everything about Star shimmered. Even her skin glowed in the afternoon sun as it filtered through lace curtains. Manny eased her ass toward Star's hips as they picked up speed. God, she loved a woman who could give it to her. She wished she could give it right back.

Star rammed Manny. She went in deep, fucked hard until Manny's ass burned at the razor's edge of pleasure. Manny reached below and smacked her clit. She slapped it with her fingers to fill in Star's expressions of bliss with shouts of her own. Star was always loud, when she came. Noisy, sloppy, sing-it-from-the-rooftops. Delighted yips and growls as her cock pulsed in Manny. Pulsed and throbbed and rushed with fluid.

Even after Star pulled out, Manny continued spanking her cunt. Orgasms were weird for her, these days. She never felt fully spent until she's beaten herself up a bit.

They showered together while Manny's shirt dried out. As predicted, the pits were soaked with sweat.

It felt nice to be soaped up by Star, naked, skin to skin. As Star ran suds down her ass crack, Manny mulled over her compounded lies. "I told Liesl Danica won't look at me naked. I don't know why." She stared at the faint reflection of her dark skin in the white tile.

With a lilting giggle, Star rubbed the soap from Manny's cheeks. "Classic case of shifting the blame. You feel guilty for hiding your body from your girlfriend. You feel guilty for being here with me. If you pretend it's Danica who won't look at you, you have your perfect excuse."

"But I know it's not true."

"It becomes true the second you tell Dr. Liesl. You believe everything you say to her. When you lie to her, you're lying to yourself."

As warm water coursed across her flesh, the sudden insight brought Manny to a new level of nudity. Star washed and dried her, bound her tits and helped her on with her clothes.

After setting the kettle to boil, Star retreated to the bedroom to take care of her own binding issues. Manny opened the tea canister and threw two bags in the pot just as Star re-emerged in black capris and a flowery sleeveless top. As they sipped from matching mugs in comfortable silence, Star nibbled on arrowroot cookies and dried apricots. Manny reflected on her desperate attachment to these three women in her life—wise Liesl, stalwart and silent, Star, her glimmer of hope on the horizon, and Danica, simply her girlfriend. She saw their faces, Star's across the table, Liesl and Danica's in her mind's eye.

"I can't keep juggling like this," Manny said. "I can't keep lying to the people I care about."

With a slow nod, Star snapped a baby cookie in half and dusted the crumbs from the table. Her eyes were diamonds as she explored Manny's gaze. "Do you bind when you visit Liesl?"

The question brought bile to Manny's throat. Rising from the table, she took her wallet from her back pocket and pulled out Star's fee in cash.

MANNY TOOK A DEEP BREATH. "I'm sorry to leave like this, but things aren't working out for us. In the beginning everything was good. You understood me then. To be honest, I've been lying to you a lot lately. I don't know why. It could mean a lot of things, I guess. Anyway, there's no sense getting deep into it. I just wanted to say goodbye. I hope you don't think I'm a total cunt."

Liesl nodded slowly. "Do *you* think you're a total cunt?"

Bunny's Cowboy

Quinn's heart always beat a little faster as Bunny approached the car, especially on days like today when the rain was coming down in sheets. Her three-sizes-too-small tank top was already soaked to her skin, making her neon pink bra glow through the white fabric.

He tried not to stare, but it was mesmerizing the way her big breasts bounced as she ran through the downpour. Even her denim cut-offs were drenched, a much darker blue than usual, and he watched her long legs, all droplets of rain on smooth, tan skin.

Quinn couldn't imagine how she managed to run, let alone walk, in those platform heels, but she insisted they were part of the getup.

He panicked, checking his teeth yet again in the rear view mirror when she arrived outside the passenger door. He'd chewed four pieces of gum since lunch, but he cupped his hand against his mouth nonetheless and breathed against his palm.

Minty fresh—he wouldn't have it any other way.

When the door still hadn't opened, he realized Bunny was out there wringing the water from her thick black ponytail. Bunny had the most lustrous hair he'd ever seen in all his life. She was special in so many ways.

He bent across the front seat and pushed open her door, calling, "You'll catch pneumonia if you doddle out there much longer."

"Yes, mother!"

She was laughing as she fell into the leather seat. Her wet thighs made sloppy squelching sounds as she fastened her belt, but Quinn was too taken with her to say anything.

Once she'd buckled up, she slipped off her shoes, leaned way back in her seat and put both feet on the dashboard.

"Your whore has arrived," she announced, like it was something she was proud about. "Whatcha gonna do with me today, Cowboy?"

Quinn was surprised to find himself recoiling as she leaned over to tip his hat. There were times this arrangement damn well broke his heart.

"Well, now what's wrong with you?" Bunny pouted, crossing her arms in front of her chest, effectively pushing the perfect, heavy globes of her breasts together.

Quinn was just lost. He couldn't think of anything but those gorgeous mounds of flesh. "Huh? What? I..."

When she giggled, she smacked her knee. Her tits bounced underneath that wet top and bright bra. "Come on, Cowboy. Want me to take you around the world?"

Now he remembered what had irked him before, and he looked his beautiful Bunny straight in the eye. "It bugs the hell outta me when you talk just like a common whore."

A darkness fell over her bright expression, like a mourning veil, and she shot right back with, "Well, what do you damn well want from me, Cowboy? I am what I am."

The thick silence that overtook them had become increasingly familiar over the last couple weeks. This had been so easy in the beginning: just a good time, no strings. But now Quinn had fallen deep—so deep he couldn't climb his way out of it even if he wanted to.

"Ain't nothing common about you, Bunny."

He said it to ease the tension, but these days saying her name only made him ask questions. Was she always called Bunny, or only by a certain element of society? Did she use a different name with different people? Had this flower of his heart ever been to prison? The police weren't known to go easy on Native girls, around here.

"Let me take you to a nice hotel," he pleaded. "Get you into a warm shower and then a big 'ol bed with a fluffy feather duvet. Nothin's too good for my girl."

She rolled her eyes, but she smiled too. For a brief moment, he really thought she might go for it this time.

Then the darkness came over her again, and Quinn knew she was remembering something awful, something that had nothing to do with him and yet impacted every step of their relationship, such as it was.

"You know my rule, Cowboy. Let's drive down to the woods and park it in our usual spot, eh?"

The usual was better than nothing, he figured, and put 'er in gear, turning on the heat when he noticed Bunny's teeth chattering. "You cold, there?"

"No, I'm just getting my jaws all warmed up," she teased.

Bunny was a real kidder, and that was one of the many qualities Quinn adored about her. He didn't know much about her past—she was the type of girl who'd shut down when he tried to open her up—but she always did say if you want to laugh, spend your time around Natives, because they'd shed their fair share of tears already. Them who'd been persecuted generation after generation wouldn't last another lifetime if they didn't learn to laugh.

"If I got us a nice hotel room, you could warm your whole body up," he prodded, hoping against hope he might finally get her to say yes. "Same as if I took you back to my place. I got a nice little bed just callin' out your name."

She cackled, as always. "Yeah, I bet your wife would just love you screwing a hooker in her damn bed."

Shaking his head, Quinn made the same turn he made every day. "I told you a million times I ain't got no wife."

Pulling into their makeshift parking spot, he laced his arm around her wet hair, around her shoulder, and scooched in closer on the broad bench seat.

"Ain't it every day I tell you you're the only gal in my life?"

"Yeah, that's what you say…" She was looking down at his jeans, where his erection formed a stiff bulge in the denim. "But that's what they all say, ain't it?"

"Who's 'they all,' eh?" Quinn asked as she ran her nails up his thigh, brushing lightly across his shaft. Damn, but that felt good! "I thought you said I was paying you enough you didn't have to take no other tricks."

"Well, sure you are."

"And are you taking any other tricks?"

"You know I ain't, Cowboy."

"Just like you know I ain't got no wife," he said, leaning in to kiss her fragrant neck, her skin fresh like the rain pelting down through the trees.

She allowed it, if only for a moment, before pulling away and saying, "And you know kissin' ain't allowed, Cowboy."

"You know my name," he encouraged. "Say it."

She hesitated, pressing her palm against his hard dick and rubbing it against his thigh. He really thought she'd say it that time, and he was actually surprised when she didn't make a peep, just kept stroking his length through that thick fabric.

"Want me to suck it today?" she finally asked—and it was a good thing, too, because Quinn was already on the verge of jizzing his pants.

Just the thought of Bunny's pretty lips encircling his cockhead, that precious cat-like tongue lapping his preliminary fluids, made his cock throb between the denim and his thigh.

"Bunny, I want you to suck it every day, baby."

"I pretty well do," she replied as she snuck one hand under his jeans, shielding behind the fly so there was no way in hell anything'd get caught in there.

God, even just the back of her hand brushing his pubic hair made his pulse race.

He swallowed hard while she unzipped him and freed his engorged length.

Her hand on his cock was just heaven.

This girl knew how it was done, and Quinn didn't like to remind himself of the reason for that.

He stretched out like a cat in the sun, though the rain was coming down in barrels, placing both hands on the backs of the head rests, opening his body up to her. "God, you look pretty." He knew she didn't like him saying things like that, but he couldn't very well help it. "Pretty as a picture, you are."

"Bullshit."

A distinct blush blazed in Bunny's cheeks as she stared down at the cock throbbing in her hand. Though the car was cozy warm now, her nipples were hard, visible right through the cups of her bra.

Quinn felt his dick swelling in her hand as he gazed into her cleavage. "Take your top off, Bunny. You'll catch your death in those wet clothes."

Without question, she released his erection and tore off her clinging tank top, pushed down her unyielding shorts. Her panties matched her bra—a bright shade of pink—but both were off in no time, and when he caught sight of those heavy breasts culminating in dark nipples, those naked curves everywhere they could be, Quinn knew he needed more than a blowjob today.

But she was on him already, her nude body curled into his lap, her lips touching his cockhead ever so gently, and her little cat's tongue lapping there. His whole body shuddered, and he wished she'd let him take her somewhere he could throw her down on a bed, show her a little bit of luxury in life.

As it was, the sheer sensation of her mouth enveloping the blazing steel of his cock made him wild. He had to force himself to keep those hips still, because he knew if he let go, he'd be driving that dick straight down her throat.

Bunny's hand was wrapped tight around his shaft, pumping hard as her head moved on his dick. She sucked like mad, like his cock was her everything. Her wet hair fell against his thigh, spotting his jeans with rain. He resisted the urge to wrap it in his fist so tight she shrieked.

When she started in with those purring noises that always brought on an orgasm, he had to stop her there. "Bunny, Bunny, Bunny," he was panting. "You got condoms in that purse a'yours?"

"Course I do." Her lips were full and dark from sucking, almost as engorged as his cockhead. "Why? What're you after now?"

He let his head tip back, despite the desire to simply gaze into her pretty face. "I want to fuck you, Bunny. I gotta do it."

"Fine by me."

Naked, she fished a packet from her purse and tore it open with her teeth. Quinn always loved the way that latex snapped against his most sensitive skin. He loved watching her careful fingers rolling it down his shaft. That slick little barrier, that oughta hold him off for a while.

Bunny had splayed herself across the front seat, her back up against the passenger door, her hand moving south across her belly. Her fingers played in the wet down of her hair until they reached the pink and eased those glistening folds wide open.

"Come on, Cowboy. You gonna give it to me or what?"

"Not in here," he said, though, by God, he wanted to take her right this second.

The rain was still raging outside.

He opened his door and beckoned Bunny outside. "Ain't nobody gonna see us through the trees and all."

His boots were already sliding in the mud, but he stepped back as Bunny reluctantly inched forward across the seats.

She looked past him, into the trees, the rain coming down in buckets. The apprehension on Bunny's face gave way to freedom and she sprang from the car, slamming the door shut behind her before running barefoot through the mud.

"Where you headed?" Quinn called after her.

Bunny turned around, both palms flush to the white bark of a tall birch tree, her long legs extended, butt in the air, beckoning.

"Come and get it!" she called out against the thundering rain.

Naked in woods. How could he resist?

Quinn didn't take down his jeans, didn't unsnap his farm boy shirt, he just went straight to her, led by the thick erection he held in his hands.

"Oh, Bunny." His throat was tight. He could barely think as he watched droplets of water form a small stream that pooled at the small of her back. "Oh, baby..."

He couldn't damn well wait any longer. Grabbing her hip with one hand, he traced his sheathed cock down her slit, pressing into the thick wetness there until it eased and opened and swallowed him whole.

Despite the raging storm soaking his back and recoiling off the rim of his hat, he could hear every whimper, every grunt, every sigh as she bucked back against him. It was more of a rocking motion, at first, but when he started pumping faster, she had to set her forehead against the soft white bark of that tree to keep steady.

Bunny pushed back effortlessly, her muscles writhing, her bum rippling every time it met the saddle of his hips. His jeans felt tight and stiff now, and when he pushed them down a touch, they hovered above his knees. Bunny shrieked as her pussy milked his cock, and it felt almost like her little mouth sucking him—maybe even tighter!

The motion made him strain. His thighs were shaking already. He wasn't quite prepared for this, but his body was giving itself the go-ahead.

Leaning forward, he wrapped his hand around her hair just like he'd wanted to before, and he fucked her hard as she'd ever been fucked, he was sure. He rammed her again and again, his hips banging against her ass cheeks, their union sending rainwater splashing up and all around. Wet and wild fun, this was.

Quinn never would have expected it.

His balls seized tight, churning inside, his thighs trembling like they'd just seen a ghost. No sense in fighting it. Bunny's naked body lurched and spasmed, too, only encouraging Quinn's impending orgasm. He had to let go. He just had to. And as he did, she did too, crying out in the rain, singing her cowboy's praises as he spurted again and again. Everything was hot now, despite the cold rain running down his ass crack, soaking his balls, mingling in the spot where their two bodies converged.

When he pulled out, Bunny groaned, her arms now wrapped around the birch tree.

He chuckled at the sight of her. "You found your true love, there?"

She turned to him, still panting, but laughing too. "That was incredible, Cowboy."

He raised an encouraging eyebrow. "You know my name by now, I hope."

Nodding, straight-faced, Bunny said, "Quinn."

Just that one word, his name, was more than enough.

Walking around the passenger side of the car, Quinn yanked the condom from his waning erection. He rifled through the back seat to find the clean fleece blanket and set it on Bunny's spot to keep her warm on the drive back. Other guys teased him, seeing that he didn't drive a truck, but Quinn would always be a Cadillac Cowboy—if he wasn't riding horses or Bunny, that is.

"Get in there, nice and cozy." He showed his gal the nest he'd built her and she coyly entered in, wrapping the blanket around her bare shoulders. Her full breasts, her belly, her thighs, all disappeared inside.

Quinn was still wet in the driver's seat, and he fired up the engine to turn the heater on, but he didn't plan on moving.

"I'm just going to wait until this rain lets up a bit. That okay with you?"

A mere month ago, Bunny would have been clawing for escape, but they'd built a certain level of trust since then. She just nodded, closed her eyes, and sighed.

"Can I ask you one question?"

She opened her eyes and looked at him queerly. "Okay..." The word was suspicious and drawn-out. "But just the one."

"How's about one today, one tomorrow..." He smiled, knowing Bunny was less and less able to resist him when he did. "One for every day we're together?"

Bunny looked like she was trying not to grin, but not succeeding very well. "I guess that's fair, but if I don't want to answer I ain't gonna."

Quinn believed that, all right! "Where you come from? You ain't lived in the big city all your life, I'm guessing."

Her expression fell, and that dark veil came across her once again. "Why you wanna know?"

"Because I like you," he said, just like every day. "And I care about who you are on the inside. I know you don't like me sayin' it, but I love you, Bunny."

She flinched, as she always did, but she didn't go nuts about it like she had at the start. One day he was going to marry this girl—Quinn was sure of it—but before he got her to the altar, he'd have to get her into bed, and then get her into *his* bed, get her so she could think about trusting someone again. She'd been hurt bad, his Bunny, but Quinn knew that deep down in her heart she didn't want to be living hand to mouth like this. He could give her all the things she'd only dreamed of. All she had to do was wake up and see him there, see him smiling in his kindly way and offering her a hand.

After a deep breath, she said, "Fish Creek." Her voice was small now, like a child's but without the wonder or the joy.

"What tribe you got out there?"

She looked up at him, a flash of rancour blazing in her eyes, and she pressed her lips tight together. Just when Quinn was sure she was about to explode, she laughed and said, "That's two questions, Cowboy."

"So I'll use up tomorrow's today."

195

With a beseeching smile, she shook her head. Just when Quinn was sure she wouldn't answer, she said, "I'm Kainai—that's Blood Tribe. But I ain't been home since..."

Her gaze went far away again, and Quinn knew he was digging deep, but this was good.

"You were adopted, eh? Raised by white folks here in town?"

Bunny's eyes flashed again, bright as lightning, and then they opened wide as if to ask how he could possibly know. But Quinn always knew. That's something she'd be sure to find out about him, in time. He could look at a person and know in three seconds they were raised by people who weren't their birth parents. Those were the ones who were always searching, never knowing exactly who they were—maybe knowing details, tribes, origins, but never knowing the full truth.

Quinn, for instance, knew his heritage was a mix of Metis and Ukrainian. He knew because his adoptive parents had told him so. Unlike Bunny, he didn't look Native, so the world treated him a damn spot kinder. But he and Bunny, they were one and the same, on the same path to self-discovery, only she didn't know it yet and, just for today, he wouldn't push her.

"It's okay," Quinn finally said. "You don't have to answer, not right this second." He fished some wet bills out of his pocket and handed them to her. "That enough to keep you mine for one more day?"

She flipped through the bills and nodded, tears welling in her eyes. The rain was slowing up, so he reached for the key in the ignition. He sure was surprised when Bunny set her cold little hand on his.

"Wait. Can we just..." She shook her head and then smiled like she felt silly saying any of this. "In all this time you ain't never told me about you. So... if you wanna... I guess I could listen some."

She shrugged like it was nothing, but she must have known, after all this time, that her little hand on his meant a whole damn lot.

Saturday Night Sex Show

from the Wedding Heat series

"EVERYTHING'S READY," Pippa called from inside Maggie's cabin. "Bring in the bride."

"What's going on?" Maggie asked.

Gripping Maggie's shoulders, Vanessa said, "It's a surprise."

"A good surprise?"

Leaning closer, Vanessa took a long inhale. The fruity scent of Maggie's blonde ringlets got right inside her, right between her thighs. She wanted to trace her hands down Maggie's front and fondle those lovely, luscious breasts.

The door swung open and Pippa poked her head out. "What's the hold-up, you two?"

Blindfolded, Maggie stuck her hands out in front of her, grasping for her maid of honour. "Pippa, what's the surprise?"

"Oh, I think you'll like it." Pippa pulled her inside. "Guaranteed you've never been to a bachelorette party like this one."

Maggie's curls bounced and bobbed as she groped her way through the threshold.

Vanessa rolled her eyes, still not totally sure what Pippa had planned. A bunch of Chippendale stripper dudes, probably. *Ugh.* Naked men weren't exactly Vanessa's thing.

And, after the night they'd spent together, Vanessa knew the bride had a secret penchant for pussy.

All lights were off in the cabin. Even the blackout blinds had been pulled. No moon to guide them. No stars. God only knew how Pippa managed to lead them safely to the sofa in the dark.

"What is this?" Maggie asked. "What's going on?"

Vanessa's heart slowed. The air felt thick as she cautiously found a seat.

"Hello, stranger!" Shonette said with a laugh.

"Oh, sorry. Was that your lap?"

"You're not sorry at all," grumbled Kristen, Shonette's secret girlfriend.

Someone took Vanessa's wrist and guided her toward an unoccupied chair. When she'd found a seat in the darkness, Pippa said, "Okay, is everybody ready?"

"Ready for what?" Vanessa asked.

"Don't ask for what," Kristen said, with that faint Scottish brogue.

Shonette added, "Just say yes. All your bridesmaids are here, present and correct."

After that, the girls started whooping and hollering. Vanessa slumped in her chair. *Great. Male strippers.* Just the kind of show every lesbian hopes for.

But as soon as the thick, throbbing music started up, the atmosphere changed. Pulsations travelled up from the floor. Vanessa's chair pounded hard enough to make her wet. The room felt electric. As much as she didn't want to buy in to all this bachelorette bullshit, her skin buzzed and bristled. She felt cold on the outside and hot on the inside as the thrill of the unknown ran through her.

When the lights went up, the girls' screams reached a fever pitch. Even Maggie clapped and howled, and she still had her blindfold on. Vanessa tried to suppress her eagerness and tell herself she wasn't interested, but she followed the bridesmaids' gazes toward the loft, and...

"Wow!"

"What?" Maggie screamed over the thumping music. "What is it? Is it strippers?"

"No," Vanessa replied. "It's... it's..."

When Pippa ripped off the blindfold, Maggie's jaw dropped. "What *is* it?"

Giving Maggie's hair a playful tug, the maid of honour replied, "It's a live sex show!"

"Oh my god!" Maggie squealed, bouncing on the couch. "Is this legal?"

"Shhh!" Shonette hissed, playfully. "That's none of your concern."

The set-up blew Vanessa's mind. She'd seen some crazy shit in her day, but nothing like this. Maggie's rustic cabin loft was visible from the main space, where the girls all sat as spectators of this raunchy display.

The man was naked. The woman wasn't.

They both kneeled on the bed, which was pushed right up against the loft railing. They held one another as they kissed, pressing their beautiful bodies together. It was like spying a seduction in progress.

The guy could easily have been a stripper. He had that hunky male model look about him, all hard muscles and cut abs. His hair was a honey colour, cropped fairly close, but with a cute curl. He was lip-locked with a bright red mouth, which belonged to an Asian girl. Not model-skinny, oh no. This girl had tats to beat the band, raven hair all the way down to her ass, and more than a little meat on her bones.

Vanessa's skin erupted in goosebumps.

As the couple kissed, the guy's hands moved across the girl's rear, kneading her butt cheeks over her purple satin lingerie. Man, that was a cute outfit—teeny tiny shorts lined with pink lace, and a matching camisole that hugged her big tits like a set of loving hands.

Pippa whooped and hollered louder than the music. "Strip that girl, big boy!"

Maggie started the chant: "Take it off! Take it off!"

"Take it off," Kristen and Shonette joined in.

"Take it off," Vanessa said, quietly.

The models broke their kiss for a fleeting glance at their spectators, before again turning their attention to one another. With that look, Vanessa found herself totally entranced.

Vanessa's clit throbbed as she watched Maggie watching the couple. What was the etiquette for a live sex show, exactly? Vanessa had never seen one before. Could the audience plunge their hands down their pants and play with their pussies? Or would that seem pervy?

The other girls pumped their fists in the air. "Take it off! Take it off!"

Vanessa swallowed hard as her gaze moved from Maggie to the unbelievable scene in the loft. The guy turned the girl to face the audience.

Much better! Since he was hidden behind her, Vanessa could fancy those were *her own* hands slipping indiscreetly beneath the waistband of that hot chick's shorts. Under the silky fabric, big fingers moved against the girl's hot pussy. Vanessa could only imagine how wet it must be.

Was she shaved? Was she trimmed? Was she insanely hairy?

"Take it off!" Vanessa hollered.

The hot girl tossed her hair to one side, and the guy kissed her neck. Pippa and Maggie gasped so loudly Vanessa heard them over the music. God, that girl's skin looked soft. The warm lighting made their bodies glow, and Vanessa itched to see what was under the purple silk.

Those big hands glided across the girl's body like a sailboat over still waters. Then one clutched her big breast and she let out a seductive sigh. The other hand pulsed, returning beneath her shorts, making her lashes flutter and her eyes roll back in her head.

"Those must be some hands!" Pippa said to Maggie. "She looks like she's about to come."

"She's faking," Kristen replied, with a groan.

Shonette nodded. "Yeah, for sure."

"Shush!" Pippa swatted them playfully. "Ever hear of suspending disbelief?"

Whether or not they believed the performance, Kristen and Shonette's eyes were glued to the makeshift stage. It was strange, watching two flesh-and-blood humans get nasty with each other. And not on a screen, oh no. Right there. For an audience.

Vanessa would have preferred two women, but she had to admit this show was pretty sexy, even with a guy and a girl.

"Pippa?" Maggie turned her head, just slightly. "What are their names?"

"The girl's name is China. The guy is Brad."

"Fake names," Shonette said.

Kristen chuckled. "Obviously."

Vanessa hushed them. "You're being rude. Just enjoy the show."

Nobody said anything. Were they were looking at her? Vanessa couldn't tell, because her gaze had locked on the performers. Brad's face was lost in the curve of China's neck, nuzzling and kissing it like she was smothered in chocolate sauce. God, that looked good. Maybe it didn't even matter that Brad was a dude, as long as he could give the girl jaw-dropping pleasure.

"Let's see her skin," Vanessa called out. "Take off her top."

Oh, that Brad was a player. He wouldn't be forced. Teasing the audience, he pushed China's tits together, driving her nipples so close to the edge Vanessa could just about see them through the lace. What was that? A nipple or a shadow? Hard to tell at such a distance. Could they not come closer?

"Take off her top!" Kristen joined in.

"Yeah," Shonette shouted. "Take it off!"

Maggie giggled wildly, yelling, "Show us her boobs!"

The girls all laughed, and so did Vanessa. There was something really cute about Maggie begging to see a stranger's breasts.

Brad didn't acknowledge his audience in words, but he did lift China's camisole. She extended her arms and then cupped her hands around the back of Brad's head. Vanessa's pulse quickened as he teased the audience by lifting the purple silk, then dropping it down just a touch. Little by little, he worked his way up China's curved belly until... oh god, yes... oh god...

Boobs! Boobs! Boobs!

The girls fell silent as Brad slipped off China's camisole. He fondled her breasts forcefully, like he knew exactly how to please her. No desperate fiddling for Brad. He knew the path to a woman's desire. And China did nothing to discourage his advances.

Vanessa's breath grew shallow as the man upstairs pushed down his lover's silky shorts.

"Yesss," Maggie hissed as China's trimmed mound was revealed. "Pusssssssyyy..."

Biting her tongue, Vanessa observed Maggie's growing arousal. The air in the cabin had gone heavy with lust, making it hard to inhale. Maggie's breasts swelled inside her low-cut sundress.

"Fuck me, baby." China leaned forward, setting both hands on the railing.

Shonette gasped, covering her mouth. "She's gonna fall!"

"Shhh!" Vanessa sat forward in her seat.

"Don't shush my... don't shush *Shonette*," Kristen said. "This is dangerous. If he fucks that girl too hard, she could die."

Pippa chuckled. "You guys are nuts."

China's pendulous breasts swung as she welcomed Brad, doggy-style. "Don't tease me, baby. Fill me with that hot cock."

"This cock?" He whacked her with it and struck her asshole, judging from her reaction.

"Yeah, baby. That's the one."

"Yeah, baby," Maggie repeated, under her breath. "Yeah, baby. Fuck her."

Vanessa never imagined she'd be so hot for some guy's dick, but if Brad didn't ram that thing into China in the next three seconds, she might have to go up there and fuck him herself.

"Fuck her!" Vanessa yelled.

All the girls joined in. "Yeah, fuck her!"

"Give it to her!"

"Pound that pussy!"

"Fuck me." China's knuckles turned white as she clutched the railing. "Now!"

"Ooh, you really want it, don't you?"

"Can't you feel how wet my pussy is? That's all for you, baby."

Vanessa could have sworn China was looking at her, speaking to her, wet for her. Under the music, she mouthed, "I'm wet for you too."

"You sure you're ready?" Brad grunted.

"Yes!"

"Really?"

"Yes!" the girls shouted, like the audience at a British pantomime.

Brad guided his dick into China from behind. Vanessa could tell when he was inside her from the look on her face. Her hair cascaded over one shoulder as she tilted her head, forming a delicious O with her lips.

"That's good," Vanessa whispered.

This was some party: five girls sitting around, watching a hired dick give it to a plump sexpot. Vanessa couldn't catch her breath when that gorgeous girl let go of the railing with one hand and reached up to grab her swinging breast.

"Squeeze it!" Pippa shouted—she was really getting into this. Or maybe she was just trying to convince herself a live sex show was a good idea for a bachelorette party.

But Pippa didn't need to worry. It *was* a good idea. In fact, it was a great idea.

"Lick it," Vanessa cried. And in case China didn't hear her the first time, she echoed the command even louder. "Lick your tits! Do it!"

Pippa shot her a colluding smile. "Yeah, lick your tits. Good long licks."

Wow, Pippa! She'd always struck Vanessa as super-straight, but maybe not. Her energy and focus seemed different tonight. Maybe the maid of honour was ready to try something a little less than honourable.

Nobody else seemed to notice Pippa's raw lust. Maggie, Kristen, and Shonette were all staring at China as she brought her big boobs to her mouth and licked. A shudder of pure Sapphic joy ran between Vanessa's thighs, despite the fact that Brad was still ramming the girl from behind.

Just then, Vanessa realized she'd slept with every party guest but one. No wonder she was so drawn to Pippa—she always did see herself as something of a sexual conquistador. She wanted girls she'd never had, especially the ones who'd never been with another woman.

And China, oh yes, she'd fucked other girls. Vanessa could see it in her face. In *real life*, their porn model probably preferred girls over guys. She'd probably starred in lesbian porn. Even as China bucked into the saddle of Brad's hips, teetering precariously over the edge of the loft, Vanessa could imagine her sucking another girl's tits, kissing some hot chick's belly, and eating a soft, sweet pussy. *Devouring* that pussy, actually.

Oh yeah, Vanessa could totally imagine China's face between her legs, cheeks covered in juice, chin dripping, cheeks rosy with exertion...

"She's gonna come!" Shonette squealed.

Kristen clicked her teeth. "She can't come already, stupid. They're just getting started."

"No, I think she's really coming." Maggie didn't take her eyes off the couple in the loft. "Look how hard she's squeezing the rail."

"Maybe she's just afraid of falling," Kristen muttered. "I'd be scared out of my mind."

There was no mistaking the expression of genuine bliss painted all over China's beautiful face. Her red lips parted as she forced her large ass back at Brad. If he wasn't holding her by the hips, he'd probably go flying across the room.

He fucked her harder, really ramming her cunt from behind. She panted, then yelped, then screamed. Shonette was right—China's orgasm collided with Brad's cock as she jerked forward, then bucked back. *Dirty girl. Dirty, dirty girl!*

She hollered, "Yeah, baby, fuck me hard!"

Brad's next stroke propelled China forward so hard she sailed off the bed and over the loft rail.

Vanessa watched the woman flip over the railing like a circus performer. She had trouble convincing herself that what she was seeing was actually happening. It seemed like some kind of Olympic gymnastics move as her body flew over the rail with one hand and gripping tight with the other. China turned, mid-air, and spun like a top. Screaming her name, Brad grabbed her wrist at the last second.

China shrieked, "Don't let me fall!"

Reality kicked in. The girls froze in place while China reached for Brad's other hand. She swung slowly, trying to reinforce her hold as he lay on the bed, hanging precariously over the railing.

It was like watching an action movie, but in real life. The heroine's voice cracked with fear as she struggled to maintain her grip. Meanwhile, the hero's muscles strained while he attempted to pull her back up to the loft. No way. He couldn't manage it. He grunted and swore, but Vanessa envisioned another hero—a dapper dyke sent to save the day.

"Watch out," she growled, pushing the coffee table across the room.

"What are you doing?" Shonette asked.

Maggie's voice trembled with fear. "My god, Ness, be careful!"

Vanessa didn't respond as she climbed onto the coffee table, hoping it was sturdier than your run-of-the-mill hotel furniture.

"Help me!" China cried. "Somebody, please! I can't hold on!"

"I've got you," Brad assured her. "Don't worry, babe. Just keep breathing. You're gonna be fine."

Even standing on the coffee table, Vanessa's shoulders barely reached China's thighs. If only she was a smidge taller... but with the model's wet pussy hovering before her face, all thoughts of rescue vanished from Vanessa's mind. She didn't care that this woman was in a desperate situation. She didn't care that Maggie and three other girls were watching. Wrapping her arms around the model's ass, she brought her lips to China's swollen clit and kissed it.

China shrieked. "Holy hell!"

"What's wrong?" Brad asked.

Pippa's scowl rang out in her voice. "What are you doing to her?"

"Nothing, she's... oh!" For a moment, China's body ceased quaking. Her legs found their way around Vanessa's back and she locked them behind Vanessa's head. "Keep going. Don't stop."

Shonette laughed in the background. "You're not!"

"What's she doing?" Kristen asked.

"She's eating the girl's pussy!"

Kristen swatted Vanessa's thigh. "Stop that! Lose your balance and you'll both be dead."

Vanessa closed her ears to the heckling and concentrated her energy on China's luscious pink pussy. When she licked it, China froze, and when she licked it again China moaned. "Oh, that's good. Don't stop, baby."

The model's labia were plump and pulpy from being fucked. Her clit stood at attention like a hot little soldier. Vanessa couldn't resist sucking it, and when she did the dangling girl cried out like she was being tortured.

"Oh, my heart!" China cried. "It's pumping so hard!"

Vanessa sucked the girl's clit even faster, trapping it between her lips while the other girls yanked at her trousers.

"Get down from there," Kristen said. "If you're not going to help her, at least let us!"

"Oh, she's helping," China replied. "She's helping big-time!"

"You're going to get yourself killed!" Maggie screamed. "This is my bachelorette party and I say get the hell down, Ness!"

But Vanessa just kept swallowing China's musky juice, then going back for more. Her tattooed skin was soft as silk, just the way Vanessa liked a girl to feel. And her pussy? Oh, the taste could not compare: sweet, tangy, with just a hint of cigarette smoke and leather. Her muscles stiffened as she gnawed the girl's cunt, going crazy eating it.

"Oh my god, I can't hold on," China said, in a whining, desperate sort of voice. "Brad? I can't..."

"I've got you," he assured her. "Can someone get her down? One of you?"

205

Pippa came to the rescue, saving China from the big bad dyke. Kristen and Shonette helped her heave the couch close enough that China's toes nearly touched the back edge. Every spare hand grabbed the naked girl's body, guiding her, helping her away from Vanessa's evil tongue.

"Are you okay?" Brad asked from the loft.

China whimpered, and he raced down the stairs to check on her. All the other bridesmaids fluttered around China as she lay on the couch with her hands above her head. Meanwhile, Vanessa stood on the coffee table, staring at Maggie, who was staring back at her.

"Why didn't you help her?" Maggie asked.

"I did."

The bridesmaids clucked apologies for Vanessa's outlandish behaviour while Brad arrived at China's side, checking to see that there were no broken bones or dislodged joints or whatever injuries one might incur while hanging from a loft. Obviously Vanessa wasn't wanted in the mix. If she'd had a hotel room to herself for Maggie's wedding weekend, she'd have left the bachelorette party altogether.

Who did Pippa think she was, anyway? What kind of maid of honour throws a bachelorette party the night before the wedding?

Or maybe that was common practice. What did Vanessa know? Her friends were all the "fuck marriage" types, so she wasn't commonly invited to these gigs.

Where could she go?

Up to the loft. Why not? Nobody was using it.

When she climbed the stairs, that lingering aroma of sex brought back memories of the previous night: the night Maggie surrendered to their mutual attraction.

Now Maggie and the rest of those girls hated her. That was the problem with women: they got ridiculously jealous every time she fucked someone else. *Who cares? It's just sex.* If she was ever going to find herself a long-lasting relationship, Vanessa needed a girlfriend who didn't mind her philandering ways.

The Queen-sized bed was messed up from two people fucking on it, and Vanessa heaved the massive thing away from the railing with all her might. Whose bright idea was it for them to perform so close to the edge? Probably

Pippa's. Screw the idea of fucking the straight girl. Vanessa didn't want her anymore.

Collapsing on the big bed, Vanessa savoured the taste of China's pussy alongside the memory of seducing a beautiful blonde. A *beautiful blonde who was about to marry some dumb guy.* In that moment, Vanessa felt so many emotions she couldn't pin down just one.

"I wondered where you'd disappeared to."

Vanessa lurched straight up as Brad helped China to the bed. "I'm sorry. I just wanted to get away and..."

"Stay right where you are," China said with a kind smile. "I mean it. Don't move."

"Okay."

"What's your name?" she asked.

"Vanessa."

"*Vanessa...*" China gave her a long, hot stare and that lost throb returned between her thighs. "Don't listen to those other girls. You took my mind off the pain until they could get me down. That helped a lot."

An unexpected flush came over Vanessa, and she shielded her cheeks with her cool hands. "I couldn't help myself. Your body was right there and you smelled so good, like candy. I couldn't resist you."

"I'm glad you couldn't." China looked to Brad and said, "Why don't you head downstairs and play host to the bachelorette party?"

"Are you sure you don't need an ambulance?" he asked with sincere concern.

"I'm sure," she said as he helped her up on the bed. "Vanessa will take good care of me. Won't you, Vanessa?"

"Sure." Vanessa looked to Brad, who grinned and then rolled his eyes.

He pulled on a tight blue pair of underwear before heading to the stairs. "Scream if you need anything."

Looking Vanessa straight in the eye, China said, "If I scream, it won't be for him."

Vanessa laughed. Her heart was racing. Why was she so nervous? She'd done this a million times.

Raising both hands above her head, China sighed and said, "That's better. I guess my arms got used to being up. Now they don't want to come back down."

With a chuckle, Vanessa asked, "Is there anything I can do?"

"You can take off that dapper dyke gear, for starters."

Vanessa's heart hammered in her ears. "No, I... you can't... you obviously need some rest."

"What does it look like I'm doing?" Lying flat on her back, China wiggled her naked hips side to side. "Now take off your pants and sit on my face."

Vanessa felt her jaw drop, and she couldn't pick it up again.

"What's wrong? Cat got your tongue? Well I've still got mine, so get over here and let me lick your clit."

Throwing her head back, Vanessa laughed. "I knew you liked pussy. I knew it from the moment I saw you."

"From the moment you saw me kissing a dude?" China asked, raising an eyebrow. "I guess I wasn't putting on a very good show."

"No, you were! You did!" Vanessa hopped off the side of the bed and started undressing. "I just meant that I have a sense about these things. I usually know, just looking at a girl, if she wants to lick another chick, even if she's never done it."

"I'm the same way," China said as Vanessa tore off her pants. "I'm strictly straight-for-pay. Outside of the job, I always date women—though, sometimes I think anyone who goes out with girls must have a screw loose."

"Why's that?"

China smirked. "Because chicks are nuts."

"Spoken like a true lover of women."

"No, spoken like a girl who just got dumped."

Vanessa paused with her pants around her ankles, and gazed into China's dark eyes. They glittered so sorrowfully Vanessa actually felt China's pain. "I'm sorry. You wanna talk about it?"

China shook off the sadness and said, "I want to taste your cunt."

With her heart in her throat, Vanessa pulled her undershirt over her head. China's eyes glazed over when she got a look at Vanessa's naked tits, and then again when Vanessa pulled down her underwear.

208

"You've got some sweet ink," China said.

"Yeah, you too. We'll have to compare tats when you're fully recovered."

China rolled her eyes. "I told you I'm not hurt."

"I don't know..." Climbing across the bed, Vanessa paused to breathe in the musky aroma between China's legs. "I think some girl hurt you bad and you need to take your mind off it."

As Vanessa straddled her curvy body, China pleaded, "Stop teasing me."

"Or what?"

She smirked, then bit her lip. "If my arms didn't feel like they were floating right now, I'd roll you over and pin you to the bed."

"Oh, would you?" Vanessa toured the unfamiliar body, tracing her fingers over the girl's skin, always just a kiss away. "What if I suck your tits instead?"

China's throat squeaked. "Well, I guess I couldn't stop you."

"That's right." Vanessa leaned down and licked a nipple. "You couldn't stop me if you tried."

"Do the other one," China pleaded.

"Oh, so now you're eager?"

"It's not my fault! You made me want you."

Vanessa licked her right breast, then the left again. "And how did I do that?"

The model didn't answer, not in words. She threw her head to one side and moaned, like she'd never felt anything so good in all her life. For a brief moment, Vanessa wondered if the reaction was real. After all, this girl knew how to act. Was she putting on a show?

No. Why would she?

When Vanessa sucked her tits, China squealed. She writhed on the bed. Couldn't fake a feeling like that. The way she moved her body, Vanessa knew this was the real thing. She pressed China's sweet tits together and crushed her face against those hard little nipples. She dragged her lips side to side across one, then the other.

"Come up here," China said, in a voice close to orgasm. "Come and sit on my face, baby."

And abandon those luscious-as-fuck tits? How could she possibly?

"Please?" China asked, between moans. "Just turn yourself around and sit on me backwards. I need to taste your pussy, babe."

How could Vanessa resist? She straddled the model's head, but faced China's tits, belly, cunt. That way she didn't have to stop playing just to be played with.

The moment Vanessa's pussy landed on China's lips, the model went nuts licking and gurgling. By now, Vanessa knew the difference between a girl who liked eating pussy and one who just did it for the experience, or because she had to. Thank goodness the pounding music was still playing downstairs, because this was going to get loud. She could tell already.

"Oh my god," Vanessa cried. "Oh, that feels so good."

She'd spent the weekend seducing straights and sweethearts—the bride and two bridesmaids—but none of those girls were pros. China was the real deal. She knew what to do.

Grabbing Vanessa's hips, China forced her to rock back and forth. Fuck, that felt good. Every time she moved on the model's warm tongue, it struck her clit in just the right place, bringing her one step closer to a screaming orgasm.

China pushed and pulled on Vanessa's hips, taunting her with every quick thrash of the tongue. Vanessa responded by tweaking the girl's tits, making China cry out against her throbbing pussy. God, she was going to come quick. No question. Her orgasm rose up out of nowhere and shrieked through her chest like a banshee.

Was China as wet as Vanessa? Only one way to find out. Releasing one nipple, Vanessa slipped her hand between the girl's thighs, finding a wealth of juice right at the surface. She rubbed with her whole hand, rubbed that engorged clit, rubbed those swollen pussy lips, rubbed and rubbed until China was screaming against her slit.

"Fuck yeah!" Vanessa ground her pussy on China's mouth, harder and faster as they howled to beat the band. The music was loud, but no match for their shared climax.

Vanessa couldn't stop herself. She pummelled the stranger's mouth with her cunt, forcefully, relentlessly. She didn't stop until her pleasure peaked so hard it hurt. Then, she withdrew her fingers from between China's legs and fell to the side, crashing down on the bed, exhausted.

"Wow." China stared up at the ceiling. "That was…"

"I know," Vanessa replied, though she could barely catch her breath. Staring at the ceiling, she said, "Wow."

China sat up slowly and leaned against the headboard. "Weird that Brad didn't come to check on me with all that noise."

"Maybe he didn't hear us over the music." Vanessa sat up too. "Although, we were pretty loud."

"We were very loud." China eased herself off the bed and crept toward the railing. And laughed. "Oh my god, Brad!"

"What's he doing?" Vanessa asked, but she had her answer before the words were even out. "Holy shit! Would you watch him go!"

"I am," China said with a laugh. "This is a little different. Usually he's going at me."

Vanessa's post-coital jelly legs gave out and she folded down on the floor, gazing at the scene through the gaps in the railing. She didn't even look up when China joined her. She was too mesmerized by the three naked bodies climbing all over China's partner-in-crime.

"I always wondered what a reverse gangbang would look like," Vanessa said with a chuckle.

Downstairs, Kristen fought Shonette over who would suck Brad's dick. They both lost, because he buried it in Pippa's pussy. Every time he pulled out, the girls dove at his shaft, wrapping their lips around it or licking it like a popsicle before he could ram it back in Pippa.

"Dang," China said. "That man's got moves."

"You're looking at *him*?" Vanessa laughed. "I've got my eyes on another prize—well, three other prizes, to be exact."

"The girls are okay," China conceded. "But look at the ass on Brad. He is fine with a capital F."

Vanessa shook her head. "And you call yourself a lesbian."

China's brow furrowed. "I call myself a lesbian because I *am* a lesbian."

"Relax," Vanessa said. "I'm only joking."

"I don't think you are."

Springing up from the floor, China crossed the loft and pulled on her sex show lingerie. Vanessa knew she should probably say something, but she'd just met this girl and who knows? Maybe China was a little nuts. There were lots of crazy chicks out there. She didn't want to get into a whole thing with a stranger.

Instead of engaging, she watched through the rails as Brad held Pippa's light brown hips and thrust into her slick, wet pussy. The angle from above was pretty neat—not your typical porno shot—but Vanessa wished she could get the close-up view that Kristen and Shonette shared.

In fact, the only way Vanessa could tell just how juicy Pippa's pussy had become was by the voracity with which the other two girls cleaned his dick. Every time he pulled out, they were there like cats on cream.

When China sat beside her wearing a Gothic black dress, Vanessa said, "See those girls licking Brad's dick? I fucked them yester... wait, no, it was just this afternoon. Holy shit, I get around!"

China bumped her playfully, shoulder to shoulder. "You fucked them separately, or both together?"

"Together," Vanessa said. "They're a couple, but they're super-super-closeted. I bet they're just licking a dude to be like, 'Look at us! We're totally not gay!'"

China's brow furrowed for a second time. "I don't know. They look like they're enjoying themselves. You don't think they are?"

Vanessa looked again, watching the anticipation in their eyes as Brad slammed into Pippa. Pippa arched and cried out, though Vanessa couldn't hear her voice over the music. Anyway, Pippa always struck her as the demure girl who'd be quiet in bed. Good on her, having a fourway with a sex show performer and two bridesmaids.

When Brad pulled out, Shonette pounced, licking the pussy juice from his shaft. Kristen ducked down, disappearing between Brad's legs. At first, Vanessa couldn't tell what the girl was up to. When she saw the gasping look of pleasure on the guy's face, then she realized Kristen must be sucking his balls.

"Wow, you're right," Vanessa said. "They do look like they're enjoying it."

China shrugged. "I'm a dyke and I like dick. It's not that weird."

"Yeah, but it's different with you. You're paid to do it."

"Paid to *do* it," China said. "Not paid to like it. I like it because it feels good."

Vanessa didn't know how to respond. If a girl liked sleeping with guys, didn't that make her bi? How could China identify as a dyke and still enjoy getting hammered by cock? How could those girls down there, Kristen and Shonette, be in a long-term relationship and not identify as lesbians?

The queer world wasn't so cut-and-dried as Vanessa wanted it to be, sometimes.

"What feels good about it?" she asked.

China shot her a hot grin. "What, you've never tried dick?"

"No." Now she felt like a child, like an innocent.

"Watch." China pointed to the junction of Brad's cock and Pippa's pussy. "See the way he slams his hips against her like that? His dick is filling her right and his balls are slapping her cunt. That's why her legs are shaking. She'll probably fall on the couch in a second. It feels so good she can barely stand."

"Sounds like you're up for a little wham, bam, thank you ma'am." Vanessa wasn't sure if she meant that ruefully or if it was just a casual prod.

"I'm up for anything, any time," China said. "Honestly, I just love sex. And getting paid to put on a show? I don't know why anyone does the nine-to-five thing when they could fuck for a living."

"Hmm..."

Tilting her head, China asked, "Have you ever done porn?"

"Me?" Vanessa laughed more than was necessary. "No."

"You should! You've got the right look for queer porn. I mean, anyone could, I guess. It's really about enthusiasm more than appearance."

Vanessa couldn't believe her ears. "It's not all blonde bimbos and little licks?"

China let out a low chuckle. "You haven't watched a lot of porn lately, have you?"

"I watch porn all the time!"

"Well, then, not the right kind. Mainstream porn hasn't changed, except it's gotten rougher, but there's this whole new subculture of stuff made for queers, by queers. That's what you want to get in on."

"Do I?" For some reason, the thought of fucking on camera resonated so deeply it actually scared her. Scared her so much she looked away from China, and stared at the fuck party going on one level down. Suddenly, it dawned on her... "Hey, where's Maggie?"

213

"Hmm?"

"Maggie's not down there. It's *her* bachelorette party. Where did she go?"

China shrugged.

Pulling herself up from the floor, Vanessa raced halfway down the stairs before realizing she was naked. She found her clothes, pulled them on, and rushed away before her shirt was buttoned. She didn't even turn to see if China had followed her.

If they hadn't been in *flagrante delicto*, Vanessa might have asked the writhing heap what happened to Maggie. She wasn't sure what drove her out the door, but when she closed it behind herself, the rapturous night was filled by the hum of activity from the party tent. Other revellers, the guests who hadn't been invited to either Ed's bachelor party or Maggie's bachelorette, carried on in a drunken stupor. The DJ's sound carried all the way across the still lake at the centre of the resort.

But there were sounds coming from somewhere closer than the party tent, and they weren't terribly musical. Vanessa wasn't sure why she chose to approach the animalistic grunts, but they led her straight to the source: Maggie with her dress up around her hips and her chest pressed against the side of the cabin. Ed rammed her from behind, same way Brad had been doing Pippa indoors.

Pippa and Brad hadn't fazed her, but this sight did. Maybe because she'd been in love with Maggie for as long as she could remember. Try as she might to cast her lust aside, it clung to her heart like a hobo on a rail car.

She walked away in a daze, trying not to see what she'd seen and yet unable to cast the image from her mind. Her homeless heart ached for everything she would never have. It ached for Maggie.

When Vanessa returned to the front of Maggie's cabin, China was just stepping out with a cigarette in her mouth and a lighter in her hand. Cupping her fingers around the cigarette, she lit it quickly and took a long drag, like the nicotine had just saved her life. Puffs of smoke wafted out her nose as she asked, "Find the bride?"

"Don't ask."

China held out her cigarette and raised an eyebrow, but Vanessa shook her head. As China brought the blazing stick back to her lips, Vanessa changed her mind and cut in for a quick drag. Their cheeks met as she breathed in her salvation, regretting it only momentarily before finding Nirvana in the smoke.

"Maggie's fucking her fiancé," Vanessa said. "I guess she has every right to, but..."

"I know." China took another drag, then blew smoke into the night in a whispered shot. "Take me for a walk, Master."

Vanessa chuckled. "Where's your leash?"

"Left it at home, along with my collar." The girl in black led the way down the stone path, toward the man-made lake. "You ever done that? *Puppy play*?"

"Me? No."

"What are you into?" China asked, sauntering along the stones.

"Like kinky stuff, you mean?"

She shrugged. "Anything. What do you like?"

"I can be kinky," Vanessa said. "But I can also be pretty vanilla. Depends on my mood, and on her mood."

"*Her* who?"

Shrug, shrug. "Whoever *her* happens to be."

"You got nobody special in your life?"

Without meaning to, Vanessa looked over her shoulder, to where Maggie was busy fucking Ed behind the cabin.

China obviously noticed, because she said, "Gotcha."

Vanessa crossed the dirt road, holding China's hand as they descended an incline. "We can't always have what we want."

When they landed lakeside, they stood together. Hand in hand, they stared across the starry lake. The dark water reflected a pock-marked moon that glowed ghostly white. It was hauntingly beautiful.

"I've got no right to be jealous," Vanessa went on. "I mean, I'm the one who's always saying girls are too sensitive, you know, like when I go and sleep with someone else. They get so agitated about it, take it so personally. And look at me! I'm doing the same thing."

"That's love, I guess." China puffed her cigarette. "What do I know? I've got no heart, according to my ex."

Vanessa didn't know what to say, so she continued on the lakeside walk, her dapper shoes sinking in the sand with every step. "Whose bright idea was this?"

"Sorry."

"I'm kidding," she said, lest China take her derision of beach sand to heart.

"Have you ever gone skinny dipping?" China asked.

"Yeah. With Maggie, when we were younger."

"Yikes." Another long drag on that never-ending cigarette. "You're really hung up on that chick, eh?"

What was the point in answering a question like that? What was the point in talking at all? They'd reached a tree lined region of the beach and there was no one around, so Vanessa swept her suspenders down her arms and let them hang at her sides.

China laughed, tossing her extinguished cigarette in somebody's burnt-out fire pit. "Hold up! I want to get this on film." She pulled her phone from a pocket in her black dress and focused on Vanessa tearing off her unbuttoned shirt. "Damn. It's too dark out. I thought we could make you an audition tape."

Vanessa pushed down her pants. "Maybe another day, when you're in the city."

"I live in the city!" China hollered as she tucked her phone back in her pocket.

"Me too." It was like kismet. She stared into China's deep, dark eyes for a moment before kicking off her shoes and socks.

After Vanessa had folded her shirt, folded her pants, and arranged everything on a rock, China said, "You are quite the dapper dandy, aren't you?"

"I'd like to think so." Wearing only a sleeveless white undershirt and a pair of men's shorts, she swaggered across the beach and wrapped an eager arm around China's waist. "And what about you, sweet thing? You want to be my girl for one night?"

China's smoky breath escaped in a gasp. "Just one?"

Vanessa's heart raced as she found the zipper on China's dress. "How are your shoulders feeling?"

"Oh, fine." But when Vanessa slid the dress from her body, she winced.

"Doesn't sound fine to me."

"Maybe not a hundred percent," China admitted. "But they're better than they were."

Taking China's hand, Vanessa led her to the water. "No swimming for you."

They dipped their toes in the lake. The summer's warmth hadn't heated the water to quite the air's fine temperature, but it wasn't too bad.

In her silky purple camisole and shorts, China waded in. Vanessa felt like a bit of an old man as she tiptoed out, letting the water disrupt her leg hairs.

"This feels good," China said.

"Uh-huh..."

"Don't you think so?"

Vanessa latched on to China's swinging hips and swept her into a kiss that would defrost the Arctic. China's smoky tongue whipped across hers as Vanessa's jagged edges joined with China's luscious mounds. When lust finally weakened their knees, they collapsed into the lake, splashing warmish water though their underclothes.

When they rolled together in the shallows, Vanessa felt like a movie star. Maybe she *should* make queer porn with China—then she would feel this heroic all the time.

The lake soaked her undershirt, exposing her sharp, tight nipples through white cotton. Sopping fabric clung to her skin, but China's satin chemise bunched and bled. As China rolled in the water, her full, gorgeous breasts escaped and Vanessa bowed to consume them.

China gasped, then giggled. "There's sand in my crack."

"Oh yeah?" Vanessa rolled the girl over. If China wanted kink, she'd be as kinky as she dared. "Pull those knees up. I want your ass in the air."

Her dark hair stuck wetly to her back as she lifted her face out of the water. "What are you doing?"

"You'll see." With China on all fours, Vanessa shifted the wet silk of her shorts across one cheek, exposing her crack. The purple fabric was so waterlogged it hung heavily and rested where it was laid. "Wow. You've got one hell of an ass."

"Umm... thanks?"

"I'm serious. It's gorgeous." It really was. No hair, well taken care of, the prettiest asshole Vanessa had ever seen. "I don't think I can resist."

Splashing water down that sandy crack, she made China giggle and squeal. But that wasn't the whole of her plan. Oh no. She was only getting started.

In her see-through cotton underclothes, Vanessa knelt between China's legs. She placed a hand on either cheek and took in the invigorating scent. China's ass didn't smell like ass at all. It smelled clean and natural, just like the lake.

"I can't wait to run my tongue between these cheeks."

China gasped. "You're gonna lick my ass?"

"You've never had your butthole licked before?"

"Only on camera," she said. "And never in a lake."

"Well, there's a first time for everything." Vanessa imagined the thrill of playing to a camera as she bowed between China's sweet cheeks.

With the tip of her tongue, she found the base of China's slit and started licking from there. Slowly, she drew pussy juice up that glistening crack, tasting nature, tasting lake. When she arrived at the girl's purple pucker, she traced circles around it.

China's long moan echoed across the lake. "Oh wow, that's good." She arched like a cat, offering more of herself to Vanessa. "Do whatever you want to me."

If she didn't have her tongue stuck out of her mouth, Vanessa would have grinned eagerly. Instead, she found China's pussy with her fingers and entered. She slowly fucked that swollen, saucy slit while she licked up and down the girl's perfect asshole. She could never get enough sex.

How could any *one* woman keep up?

"Feels so good," China purred as Vanessa licked her hole. "Keep going. Don't stop."

How could she possibly stop when China's asshole tasted so good, so earthy? A bit of grit from the lake bed, but that's life. That's sex. If it's clean and perfect, who needs it? Gritty and dark—that's what Vanessa wanted.

She kneaded China's cheek against her face as she ate the girl's ass. *So good.* So good she couldn't stop fucking that sopping wet pussy while the waves lapped their nearly naked bodies.

"Fuck it," China grunted. "With your fingers. Fuck my asshole, baby."

218

Vanessa didn't hesitate for even a moment before withdrawing her fingers from China's snatch. Getting her face out of the woman's ass crack? That was a little harder. She moved her head to the side. Her fingers glistened. When she slathered pussy juice across the purple pucker, it opened like a mouth.

China turned her head. Her eyes pleaded, "Fuck my ass."

Who could say no to a request like that? Not Vanessa. She pressed one finger into the centre of the pucker, feeling its thick elastic muscle stretch and give. She pushed another one in, letting the lube from China's pussy do the work.

Making a sound like a lamb, China arched her back, driving her front into the sand. Vanessa made a V of her fingers, opening that hole, peering inside, spitting.

"Oh!" China's asshole clenched around her fingers, but she wasn't dissuaded. "You are one dirty chick, Vanessa... Vanessa... I don't know your last name."

"I don't know yours," Vanessa replied. "I probably don't even know your first name. I doubt it's *China*."

China went *heh heh heh*, but she must have swallowed water partway through, because she sputtered and gagged hard enough she had to roll over and sit up.

"Are you okay?" Vanessa asked.

She patted her chest, then held up one finger as if to say, "Give me a second." She coughed again, then shook her head. "I'm fine. Just swallowed some lake."

"I wasn't finished punishing your ass."

"Maybe it was a sign," China said.

"A sign of what?"

Reaching for Vanessa's crotch, China cupped her mound and squeezed. "A sign that it's time for me to give you a blow job."

"A blow job, eh?" Vanessa felt that word in her crotch, throbbing against China's warm hand. "How you gonna do that?"

Inching Vanessa's shorts down her thighs, China said, "Easy as pie. I just take your dick in my mouth and I suck."

"Oh yeah?" Vanessa rose to her feet, brushing wet sand from her knees. "I guess you'd better show me how it's done."

Vanessa's clit bulged rudely from between her pussy lips, and China capitalized on that. Wrapping one hand around Vanessa's hairy lips, she pulled down on them like a pair of balls. Getting on her knees, she put one arm around Vanessa's trim waist and planted her hot mouth around that naughty little clit. It perked up even more when she started to suck. In fact, it perked up so much her clit felt like an erection. It felt like an erection growing huge, hard, launching itself down China's throat.

"How are you doing that?" Vanessa gasped for breath as she held China's shoulders for balance. "I've never felt anything like it."

China didn't stop sucking to answer. She went at Vanessa's clit hot and fast, tugging her labia. God, what a fantasy. What she wouldn't give to grow a cock and try it out on some unsuspecting femme, or go at China all night. Oh, if only she could sprout a real cock and fuck that girl's snatch. The closest she'd come would be to fuck the hell out of China's throat right now, while her clit felt gigantic and her lips felt like balls.

"I'm gonna come," she warned the girl. "I'm gonna come in your mouth, baby."

"Mmm-hmm!" China sucked harder, yanking Vanessa's balls. "Mmm! Mmm!"

Every sound that came out of China's mouth was so urgent Vanessa wondered if they might come together. Maybe China was the sort of girl who could achieve orgasm through nothing but her partner's pleasure.

But Vanessa obviously thought too highly of herself, because when she looked down, she realized China's free hand had pulled aside those sopping silk shorts and was busy stroking off.

"Mmm! Mmm!" China was coming, not because Vanessa was close, but because of the four fingers scouring her pulpy clit. "Mmm-hmm!"

Slamming China's face against her crotch, Vanessa mashed her makeshift cock down the girl's throat. "You love it, don't you?"

"Mmm-hmm!"

"You love sucking cock."

"Mmm-hmm!"

"You love cock."

"Mmm!" China pulled harder on her balls, sucked faster on her dyke dick, and brought her hurdling down from space, down into the water and the sand, where they writhed in orgasmic ecstasy and kissed and kissed and kissed.

"I must admit," Vanessa said, panting and laughing as she lay beside China in the sand. "That was my first blow job."

"I'll have to train you to give one," China said.

"To you?"

She laughed. "To Brad, maybe. Or someone like him."

"I don't know." Vanessa wrinkled her nose as they crawled like rats from the shallows. "I'm not big on dudes."

"Well, what about a girl with a dick?" China fished her lighter out of her dress pocket and lit some kindling that had been left on someone's extinguished fire pit. "There are some great girls at the queer porn site I work for, and a few of them have cocks. Would that be easier for you?"

Vanessa's heart raced as she tossed a split log on the burgeoning fire. "Yeah, I can see myself hooking up with a girl who's trans. My aunt is, you know."

"Trans?"

Vanessa nodded, and stood beside China as they let their underclothes drip dry in front of the flames. "I'm not one of those dykes who thinks you have to have a pussy to be a girl."

"Good," China said. "Because you wouldn't fit in at our queer collective if you did."

Staring into the sizzling orange flames, Vanessa asked, "You really think I could do porn? Because I've always wanted to try."

"You're a natural." China squeezed her hand. "If you've got a girl at home, I hope she's more understanding than mine was."

"Don't worry about that. Nobody's waiting for me in the city."

"I will be." Another squeeze. "Brad and I are heading out in the morning."

"Maggie's wedding is at noon, then there's tea and whatever."

China let go of Vanessa's hand and sat on the barkless log by the fire pit. "I'm sorry the girl you love is in love with a dude."

Vanessa laughed, wryly. "I'm sorry the girl I love is getting married in the morning."

"Yeah, there's that too, I guess."

For a moment, they were quiet. When Vanessa broke the silence, it was with laughter. China joined in giggling as Vanessa sat on the log and put an arm around her. She kissed the girl's shoulder, and China kissed her cheek, and they kissed each other's faces and noses and lips.

Vanessa had never envisioned herself dating a porn model. Maybe she'd never thought of them as real people with real lives, but China was certainly for real. A girl who liked sleeping around needed to share her life with another girl who liked sleeping around.

And if they got paid for it, so much the better.

Wasn't life wonderful?

ABOUT THE AUTHOR

G iselle Renarde is an award-winning queer Canadian writer. Nominated Toronto's Best Author in NOW Magazine's 2015 Readers' Choice Awards, her fiction has appeared in well over 100 short story anthologies, including prestigious collections like Best Lesbian Romance, Best Women's Erotica, and the Lambda Award-winning collection Take Me There, edited by Tristan Taormino. Giselle's juicy novels include Anonymous, Cherry, Seven Kisses, and The Other Side of Ruth.

Giselle Renarde
Canada just got hotter!
Want to stay up to date? Visit http://donutsdesires.blogspot.com[1]!
Sign up for Giselle's newsletter: http://eepurl.com/R4b11
Weekly Audio Erotica at http://Patreon.com/AudioErotica

---

1. http://donutsdesires.blogspot.com/

2. http://patreon.com/AudioErotica